THE LONG WAIT

By Mickey Spillane

Born Frank Morrison Spillane in Brooklyn, New York City, in 1918, Mickey Spillane started writing while at high school. During the Second World War, he enlisted in the Army Air Corps and became a fighter pilot and instructor. After the war, he moved to South Carolina, having liked the look of it while flying over. He was married three times, the third time to Jane Rogers Johnson, and had four children and two stepchildren. He wrote his first novel, *I, the Jury* (1947), in order to raise the money to buy a house for himself and his first wife, Mary Ann Pearce. The novel sold six and a half million copies in the United States, and introduced Spillane's most famous character, the hard-boiled PI Mike Hammer. The many novels that followed became instant bestsellers, until in 1980 the US all-time fiction bestseller list of fifteen titles boasted seven by Mickey Spillane. More than 225 million copies of his books have sold internationally. He was uniformly disliked by critics, owing to the high content of sex and violence in his books. However, he was later praised by American mystery writers Max Alan Collins and William L. DeAndrea, as well as artist Markus Lüpertz. The novelist Ayn Rand, a friend of Spillane's, appreciated the black-and-white morality of his books. Spillane was an active Jehovah's Witness. He died in 2006 from pancreatic cancer.

The Long Wait

MICKEY SPILLANE

An Orion paperback

First published in the United States of America in 1951
by E. P. Dutton & Co. Inc.
This paperback edition published in 2015
by Orion Books,
an imprint of The Orion Publishing Group Ltd,
Carmelite House, 50 Victoria Embankment
London EC4Y 0DZ

An Hachette UK company

1 3 5 7 9 10 8 6 4 2

A CIP catalogue record for this book
is available from the British Library.

ISBN 978-1-4091-5870-7

Typeset by Born Group within Book Cloud

Printed and bound by CPI Group (UK) Ltd, Croydon, CR0 4YY

The Orion Publishing Group's policy is to use papers that
are natural, renewable and recyclable products and made
from wood grown in sustainable forests. The logging and
manufacturing processes are expected to conform to the
environmental regulations of the country of origin.

www.orionbooks.co.uk

To

WARD

Who hasn't changed
a bit after all.

CHAPTER ONE

The bus came up over the rise and there was Lyncastle nestling in the dark palm of the mountains like a jewel box with the moon shining on it. From a distance the avenues and streets were like burlap woven of lights and neon tubes, a crosshatch pattern that went on long after midnight, moving and screaming with a false, drunken gaiety.

I took the envelope out of my pocket and tore it until my lap was filled with the remains, then slid the window open and let the fragments whip out into the night.

The fat lady behind me poked a chubby finger into my shoulder and said, 'If you don't mind, I'd like that window shut.' The way she said it you'd think I was a damn kid.

I said, 'I'd like your mouth shut too.' She shut it. All day it had been flapping about everything from the way the driver handled the crate to the noise the baby up front made, but this time it was shut so tight even her lips didn't show.

The last of the shreds streamed by the window and I thought that there goes a big fat reason for killing somebody, scattered over a mile of concrete, and no matter how hard he tried, nobody could go back and pick up the pieces fast enough to find out why.

I left the window open and hoped it would blow the wig off the fat lady and I didn't close it until the bus angled into a port that was the other half of the railroad station.

The driver killed the engine and half turned his head while he said, 'This is Lyncastle. Change here for railroad and bus connections to Chicago and all points east. There will be a twenty-minute rest stop for anyone going south.'

For me it was the end of the line.

I waited until the fat woman puffed by and traded her a nasty grin for something she said too low to hear, then hauled

1

my metal overnight case out of the rack and followed her off the bus.

A mile off a train hooted twice and its eye swivelled around a curve and led it down the stretch to the station. A redcap inside the station was warning the group headed for the rest rooms that there was no time to waste and those who were making the connection ran for the platform.

I put the overnight case down and pulled the last cigarette out of my jacket pocket, lit it, and went into the waiting-room. A flimsy lunch counter ran along one side of the wall with a news-stand opposite it by the ticket booth. All the seats were filled so I went back to the men's room and did what I had to do.

For a minute I thought of washing up, but it was going to take more than a bowl and a jar of liquid soap to take the grime of a thousand miles out of my skin. I needed a haircut and shave more than I needed a change from the greasy pants and leather jacket. So I washed my hands and let it go at that.

This time there was an empty stool at the lunch counter and I could see why it was empty. The fat woman had the next one and was shooting her mouth off again. Something to do with the grease in the doughnuts. The tired-looking waitress was next to tears and if I hadn't climbed onto the stool fatty would have gotten her second cup of coffee thrown in her face. She shut up when she saw me and wrinkled her nose like I smelled bad or something.

The waitress came down and I said, 'Coffee. A ham and Swiss on rye, too.' She made up my order and rang up the change on the register. I had a second coffee to put a lid on the meal and turned around on the stool.

For the first time I noticed the old man in the ticket booth. But it wasn't the first time he had noticed me. I could tell that much. There were four people lined up in front of his window waiting to get tickets and he wasn't paying much attention to what he was doing. He kept looking past them, squinting alternately through and above his steel-rimmed glasses with his face drawn into a puzzled frown that held something of a father's worried look when his kid is sick.

For a thousand miles I had been wondering when the first time would be. For a thousand miles I thought and speculated and now it was here. Just a grizzled old man with a handlebar moustache that looked like a yellow-tipped broom from straining so much tobacco juice.

It wasn't like I thought it would be at all.

The last man in line picked up his ticket and walked back to the bus port and I took his place. The old man started to smile and I said, 'Hello, Pop.' Just like that.

It looked like somebody pulled his moustache up with a string. Forty-eight false teeth showed a great big grin that was hesitant going up but solid once it was there. 'Gawd! Johnny McBride. Johnny boy! . . .'

'It's been a long time, hasn't it, Pop?'

I couldn't figure the look on his face. But at least I was sure of one thing . . . he recognized me. 'Gawd, yes!' he said.

'How's things in town?'

He made a funny hollow noise with his teeth to keep the smile in place. 'Same as ever. You . . . planning to stay around?'

'For a while.'

'Johnny! . . .'

I picked up my bag. 'See you, Pop. I'm tired and dirty and I want to get sacked in for the night.' I didn't want to stay there too long. From now on I had to go slow and easy. Sort of feel my way around the details I didn't know. Too much at once could ruin a lifetime.

Over at the news-stand I picked up a pack of Luckies and a package of gum and had one of each while the attendant made change of my buck. When I got back to the platform I stood there in the shadows watching the bus that brought me pull out and I knew that it was too late now to do anything except go through with it even if I didn't want to.

But I did want to. I wanted to more than I ever wanted anything else and just thinking about it was nice, like eating a thick juicy steak when you were hungry. For somebody else it wasn't going to be so nice.

For three people. One was going to die. One was going to get both arms broken so he could never use them again. One was going to get a beating that would leave the marks of the lash striped across the skin for all the years left to live.

That last one was a woman.

Something in the deeper shadows that formed the corner of the building moved and evolved into the bulk of a man. He stood there a minute, broad and tall, then took a step into the light. He was ponderous, the way a heavyweight is when he goes to fat, but without losing too much of his speed and strength. The light from the window hit his face, highlighting the coarse features that seemed built around the stub of the cigar in his mouth. He had on a new broad-brimmed hat with a narrow rancher's band, but his suit was strictly working clothes and would have fitted if there hadn't been the bulge of a gun in his hip pocket.

I didn't look at him, but I felt it when he was by my shoulder. 'Got a light, buddy?'

I flicked a match with my thumbnail and held it out. The face I thought was only coarse took on a brutal appearance. He nodded and I blew it out, squeezing the head out of habit to make sure there was no warmth left before I chucked it down. 'Staying in town long? 'He blew the cigar smoke right in my face.

'Could be,' I said.

'Where you from?'

'Oklahoma.' I gave him a faceful of cigarette smoke and he coughed. 'The oil fields,' I added.

'No work like that here.'

'Who says?'

I wondered if he was going to swing on me. He did something with his hand, but all it was was to show the silver glint of a badge against a black leather folder. 'I says.'

'So?'

'We don't like migrants. Especially Oakies out of work. There's a bus leaving in twenty minutes. You better be on it.'

'What happens if I'm not?'

'If you're real interested I could show you.'

My cigarette hit and splashed sparks in the road. Just for the hell of it I leaned into the shadows where there was nothing but dark, nothing at all, and he was there in the light squinting a little to see where I was. 'I'm real interested,' I said.

There's one thing nice about the guys who play rough. They can always tell when they got a sucker or somebody who's not such a sucker. 'Twenty minutes,' he said. His cigar glowed to a cherry red as he pulled on it. 'They turn the lights back on out here then.'

A cab cruised in and slowed down. I picked up my case and walked over. The driver was a young kid with his hair slicked back and he gave me the eyes up and down while I opened the door. I said, 'Town.'

The cop moved out of the shadows and stepped off the kerb. The kid leered, 'What do I get paid with?'

So I took out the roll in my pocket and riffled through the twenties and fifties until I found a pair of singles and threw them on the seat beside him. He tucked them in his pocket fast and got polite all of a sudden. 'Town it is, friend,' he told me.

I shut the door and looked back out the window. The cop was still there, but his face was all screwed up in a scowl and he was trying to figure out how he had made such a big mistake twice in figuring me for a sucker and for a poor sucker at that.

The cab spun on to the main drag and I settled back against the cushions after telling the kid to take me to the Hathaway House. I watched the pattern of the lights shriek into a blaze of colour and thought that so far it had been a hell of a homecoming.

But it was about what I had expected.

CHAPTER TWO

The cab driver and the bellhop had a signal system rigged up. If I had gone in cold I would have gotten the treatment. The Hathaway House was the best hotel in town and it didn't take to anybody who wasn't lined with dough. The bellhop and the desk clerk had a signal system too, because I got a lot of smiles and nobody asked me to pay in advance. The hop did everything he was supposed to do and collected a five for it.

He laid the key on the table and said, 'Would you like anything brought up, sir?'

I said, 'What have you got?'

'The best of everything. Whisky if you want it. Women too.'

'What kind of women?'

'You won't be disappointed.'

'The woman might be though. Maybe some other time.'

'Sure, anything you say. Just ask for Jack. That's me.' He grinned on one side of his face. 'I can get you anything you want in town.'

He had wise little eyes like he knew everything there was to know. 'I might do that,' I said. He nodded and pulled the door shut. When he was gone I turned the lock and threw the bolt into the hasp and stripped off my clothes. I took out some clean underwear and socks from the case, tossed them on the bed with my shaving kit and stuffed everything else back in the case. Tomorrow I'd throw the works in some trash can and start over fresh.

Tonight I was going to clean up if I had to ream out each pore individually, then crawl in between fresh sheets and stay there until I felt damn good and ready to get up.

It was the sun that awakened me. It started at my feet and warmed its way up to my face until I had it full in the eyes. It was a bright, beautiful day that had gotten off to a good start. I stretched, got up and took a look out the window. It was a very beautiful day. It even made the town look good. And from up where I was looking down you'd never know that the place was called Little Reno because the saloons and gambling joints were still closed and aside from the black dots that were women in the shopping district, the streets were peacefully calm and deserted.

No, not quite deserted. There was a drunk lying in the gutter down there. A dog came over, smelled him and backed away.

I took another shower to wash the sleep off me, shaved fresh and called up room service for a breakfast. When they took my order I had the switchboard girl put me on an outside line to a fancy men's shop and reeled off a list of things I needed. I had just finished breakfast when a beaming clerk from the men's shop came in with a tailor to finish me off in party clothes. Luckily for me I'm one of those guys who walk right into a ready-made outfit, so there wasn't much to be done except let out a few things. I'm not a small guy, either.

The clerk walked off happy with a couple hundred bucks, a fat tip and all I needed was a haircut. I got that downstairs.

Barber shops are funny places. Like the three monkeys, only in reverse. For some reason, barbers seem to be frustrated reporters, orators and G-Men all wrapped up together. While they have you strapped down to a chair they make you listen to a summary of events that would make a news commentator blush. I told the guy working on me to cut it as short as he could get it and that's all I ever did get to say to him. He took it from there, started jawing about the people and the town and how he'd run it if he was mayor, got sidetracked into national politics then branched off into the first war, the second war and was well into his third.

If I had been listening I would have noticed the way he lost track of things and concentrated on shaving around my ears, but I was paying too much attention to the rhythm the old coloured boy was putting into the shine on my new shoes and missed it all. He whipped off the towel and nodded to me in the mirror. His face looked funny. His smile was all porcelain when he took the buck and something in his throat made his tie bob up and down.

I was climbing into my coat when the bellhop who could get me anything in town poked his head in the door and grinned at me. 'Thought I saw you come in here. There's a call for you at the desk. Guy says it's important and I told him to hang on while I rounded you up.'

'Thanks.' His fingers picked the quarter out of the air that went with it. I went back into the lobby of the hotel and he pointed to a row of booths.

'Number four. You can take it in there.'

I closed the door, picked up the phone and said hello.

I was thinking that I sure was a popular guy for somebody who had never been in the town of Lyncastle in his life. Maybe it was going to be fun after all. A nice, nasty kind of fun a lot of people wouldn't forget in a hurry.

The voice cracked in the middle when it said, 'Hello . . . hello, Johnny?'

I said, 'That's right,' and waited to hear the rest of it.

'Well speak up, boy. Good Lord, you had a nerve running off like that last night. Took me right until now to find the cabbie that brought you to town.'

He spoke like I was supposed to know him and I did. It was the old boy from the railroad station and he sounded like he was calling off trains. Everything all at once and jumbled. Like three trains on the same track at the same time. You know.

'Sorry, Pop,' I said. 'Had a long trip and I needed some sleep.'

He exploded into a barrage of words. 'Johnny, boy, are you out of your head? What's the idea coming back! You git yourself outa that hotel right now and get down here. I haven't been able to sleep a wink all night just thinking. That's all, just thinking. You git caught up with and you know what'll happen. I don't have to tell you about this town. You know what's gonna happen soon as you step outside the door. Now

8

you call a cab and get down here, understand? There's a bus going west in thirty minutes and I got your ticket all made out.'

I had been looking out the window of the booth and saw them come in. Two of them. One was the bruiser who guarded the railroad station after dark. The other was a little smaller, not quite as chunky. His face was all happy-looking like he'd just stepped on a snake and there weren't any fingers on his hands because they were all rolled up into fists. He had a bulge on his hip too. A pair of bulges. One on each side.

I said, 'Too late, Pop. They're here now.'

'Oh, my God, Johnny!'

'See you later, Pop.' I hung up and opened the door. The bruiser was watching the elevator and didn't see me come out. The other guy was just getting the clerk's attention and had the guy reaching for the registry cards when I walked up and stood beside him.

Maybe he didn't expect anything like that at all. He was looking at the card with 'John McBride 'scrawled across the top line, cursing silently to himself, when I said, 'I'm not hard to find, friend.'

Fingers seemed to crawl up his neck under the skin and peel the flesh back from his face. He dropped the card and I saw his hands start to come out slow and deliberately to take me apart right there and I looked down at him some and said, 'You put your hands on me and I'll knock you right on your goddamn ass.'

His hands stopped halfway to my neck and his eyes got wider and wider until there wasn't any place else for the lids to go. The bruiser came up on the double with a billy out and ready, looked at me, then his partner while he said, 'This the guy?' caught the faint nod and came back to me again.

'Well, well,' he said.

I grinned at the both of them. 'Don't let your positions go to your heads, pallies. Take me rough and I bet they carry three people out of here.' I grinned some more and kept my eyes on the billy.

The guy with the billy worked up a passable smile. 'You sure sound tough. You sure do.' He made like it was all a surprise to him, but he put the billy away. The other guy was staring at me in utter fascination. His hands had dropped, but his eyes hadn't. They were gone, completely gone. They were lifeless without being dead, yet there was death and hatred in them like I had never seen before.

Then they squinted a little bit shut and his face twisted wryly back into shape. 'Move, Johnny. Stay in front of me and I hope to hell you try to run for it. I hope to hell you try so I can break your spine in half with a bullet.'

I don't scare easy. In fact, I don't scare worth a damn. Anything that could ever scare me had already done it and now there wasn't anything left I'd let push me. I looked at each one of them so they'd know it and they knew it. Then I walked out front and got into the police car and let the bruiser and the other guy squeeze me in. The bruiser grunted to himself a couple of times, a sound that meant he was enjoying himself. The other one just sat and when he wasn't staring at me, stared straight ahead.

His name was Captain Lindsey. The sign on his desk said so. The other was either Tucker somebody or somebody Tucker because that's what the captain called him. Being in the room didn't happen just like that. There was more to it, a kind of open-mouthed wonder about the whole thing like the janitor who let his broom drop and the desk sergeant who stopped talking in the middle of a sentence to a guy he was bawling out and the news reporter who yelled, 'Gawd!' and dashed into the press room for his camera.

He didn't get any pictures or any story because Lindsey took me into his room where there was a desk, two chairs and a filing cabinet. The two of them took the chairs and let me stand there.

When I stood there long enough Lindsey said, 'You're a nervy bastard, Johnny. I never thought I'd see it happen like that.'

I pulled out a smoke and took my time lighting it. Now it was my turn. I said, 'You sure you're not making a mistake?'

The two cops exchanged glances. Lindsey smiled and shook his head. 'How could I ever forget you, Johnny?'

'Oh, lots of people make mistakes, you know.' I let the smoke stream out through my nose and decided to make it short and sweet. 'If you're holding me on a charge, name it or shut your face. I don't like being hauled into a crummy police station and talked to.'

Lindsey must have been saving that one sneer up for a long time. 'I don't know what kind of an angle you think you're playing, McBride, and I don't give a damn. The charge is murder. It's murder five years old and it's the murder of the best friend a guy ever had. It's a murder you'll swing for and when you come down through the trap I'm going to be right there in the front row so I can see every goddamn twitch you make and there in the autopsy room when they carve the guts out of you and if nobody claims the body I'll do it myself and feed you to the pigs at the county farm. That's what the charge is. Now do you understand it?'

Now I was understanding a lot of things including the way Pop's voice cracked over the phone. They weren't so pretty. This game was dirtier than I thought and I didn't know whether I was going to like it so much.

Murder. I was expected to shake in my shoes.

Like I said, I didn't scare easy. They saw it on my face again and were wondering why. This time I leaned on Lindsey's desk and gave him a mouthful of smoke to let him know how I felt about it. 'Prove it,' I said.

His face was cold as ice. 'That's a crappy angle. That's real crappy, McBride. The last time you didn't stay around long enough to know what we had, did you? Don't mind my laugh. I'm getting a charge out of this. I love every bit of it. I want to see you go right through all the stages until there's nothing left but jelly. You didn't know we found the gun and got the best sets of prints you ever saw, did you? Sure, Johnny, I'll prove it. Right now. I want to watch your face change.'

He pushed himself away from the desk and nodded for Tucker to get behind me. We went down the hall where the reporter was screaming to be let in on the deal and into another room with a lot of tricky gadgets and a sign over the door that said LABORATORY. Lindsey must have looked at the card so often that he knew exactly where it was. He pulled it out of the file, stuck it in the slide of a projector and switched on the light.

They were the prettiest set of fingerprints I'd ever seen in my life. Nice and clear with some real tricky swirls in the middle. Tucker tapped me on the shoulder. 'Over here, tough boy.'

Lindsey was waiting at the desk with a brand-new index card in front of him. He squeezed a quarter-inch of printer's ink out of a tube onto a glass plate and began spreading it out with a rubber roller. When it covered the plate the way he wanted it he picked up my hand and pushed the tip of my forefinger in the mess.

Maybe he thought I messed up the card purposely. He grabbed my finger and did it carefully this time.

The same thing happened again like I knew it would and he said something foul.

Instead of a print there was a solid black smudge because I didn't have any fingerprints.

I shouldn't have laughed, but I couldn't help it. The back of his hand smashed into my mouth and before he could do it again I hooked him under the chin and he and the desk and the junk slammed the floor. Tucker had time to get the billy unlimbered but not enough time to place it right. The thing ripped my coat open all the way up my sleeve and went back for another try. I had him then. I had him so goddamn good I nearly took his gut off. He folded up and never felt his face get turned into a squashed ripe tomato. I had time to see him vomit all over himself before my own head burst open in a blaze of fiery streaks that sent a curse of ungodly pain down into every single little nerve fibre throughout my body and I knew that this was what it was like to die. There was a crazy, violent screaming behind me that came from Lindsey's contorted mouth and it was the last thing I thought I'd ever hear again.

It was, for a long, long time.

Sound came back first. It was a voice that said, 'You're a fool for doing that, Lindsey.'

Then another voice that quavered slightly. 'I should have killed him. Honest to God, I tried. I hope the bastard dies.'

Somebody else was there too. 'Not me. I hope he lives. I'll work him over like he's never been worked over before, so help me!'

I wanted to answer that and couldn't. My head was shrieking with the pain in it and I felt my legs pulling up in a tight knot. I waited until it passed and made my eyes open. I was on a metal bed in a room that was filled with people. Everything else was white and the air had a sharp, pungent odour.

There was Lindsey with a lump on his jaw and Tucker still faintly recognizable through a maze of bandages and two other men in dark suits, a flat-faced girl in a white uniform talking to two more white uniforms with stethoscopes around their necks. The last two were looking at a set of films and they were nodding.

When they reached a decision one said, 'Concussion. Should have been a fracture. I don't know how he got away with it.'

'That's nice,' I said, and everybody looked at me. I was popular again.

Things were quiet too long. Lindsey smiled when he shouldn't have smiled. He came over and sat on the edge of the bed like an old friend and smiled some more. 'Ever hear of Dillinger, Johnny? He went to a lot of trouble getting his fingertips cut off too. It didn't work. You're a little smarter than Dillinger . . . or you had a better job done. We can't make them out yet, but they'll come through. Up in Washington they have ways of doing those things, and if there's so much as an eighth of an inch of ridging left they can prove it if it matches up. You got a little more time yet, kid. With Dillinger they had Bertillion measurements and photographs and we don't have anything like that on you. It's a cute set-up if ever I saw one . . . everyone and his brother knows you and we can't prove it.'

Tucker made a loud noise behind his bandages. 'Hell, you ain't letting him get away with it, are you?'

There was no mirth in Lindsey's laugh. 'He's not getting away with anything. Not one goddamn thing. The only way he can get out of this town is dead. Walk around, Johnny. Go see all your friends. Have yourself some fun because you don't have much time to do it in.'

I thought Tucker was going to make a try for me right then. He would have if Lindsey hadn't put his arm up to stop him. His eyes under the gauze were red little marbles that tried to do what his hands couldn't do. 'Damn it, we gotta hold him! Lindsey, if you let him . . .'

'Shut up. We can't do a thing right now. If I try to book him a lawyer'll have him out in five minutes.' He turned back to me. 'Just stay in town. Remember that. I'll be one step behind you all the way.'

Hell, I had to get in my two cents' worth. It wouldn't be any fun if I couldn't sound off when I felt like it. 'You remember something too. Every time you put your hands on me I'll knock you on your goddamn ass like I did before and that goes for your stooge as well.'

Somebody choked a little.

Somebody swore.

The doctor told them to go and the nurse closed the door. He pointed to the closet. 'You can get dressed and go if you want to. My advice is to stay here awhile. There's nothing wrong with you some rest won't cure, though I don't know how you got away with it.'

'I'll go,' I told him.

'O.K. with me. Be sure to take it easy.'

'Yeah, I'll do that.' I reached up and felt the back of my head. 'What about the bandage?'

'Four stitches in your scalp. Come back in a week and I'll take 'em out for you.'

'You're giving me a long time to live,' I said.

The doctor grinned at me.

I got dressed and went downstairs to the window where they took a twenty and gave me back five. My legs were wobbly and my head throbbed, but a good sniff of the night air put me back together a little.

It was pitch black and the stars were under cover. A worried guy sweating out a maternity call was pacing back and forth the ramp outside the door. He looked up hopefully when I opened it, saw me and went back to pacing. I walked down the ramp, turned onto the sidewalk and headed for the lights that marked the centre of town.

Behind me the glowing tip of a cigarette traced an arc through the air, splattered out in the grass that bordered the gutter and a pair of heavy feet began to match my stride.

The vigil had begun. Lindsey was behind me all the way.

Metaphorically speaking, that is. The guy wasn't Lindsey, but he was all cop. I was beginning to think that they didn't have any little cops in this town. The one behind me was a barrel on legs weaving from side to side. He was such a good cop that it took me nearly two blocks to shake him.

When I got to town I stopped at a drugstore and climbed into the phone booth. I dialled the hotel and asked for Jack. When I had him I said, 'This is McBride. You remember that barber who worked on me today?'

'Sure. Name's Looth. We call him Looth Tooth. Why?'

'Just curious. Thanks.'

'Don't mention it. By the way, where you calling from, Mr McBride?'

'A phone booth.'

'Oh?' He sounded surprised.

'Why?'

'You see the papers tonight?'

'Hell, no! I just got out of the hospital. I had my head examined.'

'Well, you oughta see 'em.'

He hung up before I could ask any more questions. I picked up a paper at the front of the store and I saw what he meant. It was quite an item. In fact, the whole front page was scrambled because the story that was supposed to go in had been yanked at the last minute. All that was left was a one-column squib squeezed in by an irate compositor who had to work overtime. The heading was: Police Hold Murder Suspect. Under it the item read, 'Held in the five-year-old slaying of former District Attorney Robert Minnow was John McBride, tentatively identified by police as a former resident of Lyncastle who fled following the shooting of the District Attorney during the sensational gambling probe of his era. McBride was released after questioning and Captain Lindsey of the Lyncastle Police refused to comment. Since the grand jury returned a murder-guilt verdict against the original McBride, this was the first suspect held in the affair.'

And that, dear children, is all. Nobody knew from nothing. I was a story that didn't happen . . . yet. Somebody had done a lot of pretty string-pulling in the police lab. I grinned until my mouth ached, remembered what I came after and went back to the phone directory and rummaged through it until I found what I wanted.

Looth Tooth was listed, but he wasn't home. Somebody told me the name of a bar where I could find him. I paid a hackie a buck to take me there and when I walked in Looth Tooth had himself an audience of eager listeners and he was telling them in details that never happened how he practically caught McBride all by himself.

He was doing great until I got into the crowd. I stood there and looked at him until something got stuck in his throat and he couldn't breathe. He believed everything I told him with my eyes, then Looth Tooth was something with pale blue lips and eyes that rolled up in his head, dropping to the floor in a dead faint.

I had one beer and left just as they were carrying Looth Tooth out the door. Everybody agreed that it was a pity he didn't get to finish his story.

Tomorrow I'd go down for a shave and ask him to finish it for me personally. He was going to be one barber who'd never go peddling his lip to the police again.

But it was still tonight and I had things to do. The hackie who brought me was still outside and I told him to take me to the railroad station. From where we were we had to go straight up the main drag of town so I had a chance to see what it looked like during business hours.

It looked pretty good. It looked like everything the newspapers, radio and magazine articles said it would look like. Maybe you've heard of the place. A long time ago it started out as a pretty nice town. A smelter turned ore into copper bars over under the mountains and everybody was happy. They were rough-and-tumble boys who built their houses and minded their own business.

That's the way it would have stayed if Prohibition didn't come and go like it did. Lyncastle took the switch in stride, but the three big cities on each side of it voted an option and kept themselves dry, so anybody who wanted a drink simply crossed the river into Lyncastle and got themselves a package. It wasn't long after that you could get anything else you wanted too. Lyncastle became what is known as a wide-open town. Little Reno. Ten feet off the sidewalk you had crap tables, slots, faro layouts, roulette . . . hell, everything. Nobody bothered to work in the smelter any more. The gambling rooms were paying high for bouncers, croupiers, dealers, shills and whatnot.

I wondered what they'd pay a killer to knock off a D.A. who didn't like what they were doing.

The hackie was holding the door open for me. 'Here y'are, buster. Buck and a half.'

'Take two. They're little.' I slammed the door shut and stepped up on the platform.

The station was practically deserted. A young coloured boy was curled up in a handcart, his head nestling on a pillow of mail sacks, and inside a woman with a baby in her arms was dozing off on a bench. Across the platform a bus, dark and dead-looking, was hiding in the end port. Over there was where the bruiser hung out and I looked for something moving in the shadows.

I waited a long time, but nothing moved. Evidently he only checked incoming schedules. I crossed the platform and stood in the doorway, looked around quickly and stepped inside.

The old boy was just closing his ticket window when he saw me. His voice was lost in the slamming of the grillwork and the rattle of the shade being drawn over it. A door opened in the side of the booth and he was waving me inside furiously. He was so worked up he hopped around like a toad, making sure the door was locked tight before he pulled a couple of benches together.

'Damn, Johnny,' he said with his head wagging from side to side, 'you sure beat all. Sit down, boy, sit down.'

I sat down.

'Anybody see you come up here?'

'Nope. Didn't matter if they did, Pop.'

I got the puzzled squint again while he fingered his moustache. 'I heard talk an' I read the papers. How come you're here and what's the bandage on your head for? They do that to you?'

'Yeah, they did it,' I told him easily.

'Damn it all, finish it!'

'Not much to finish. Guy named Lindsey wanted to talk to me. We talked. It got a little bit rough and we finished talking in the hospital. Nobody got around to saying much. Lindsey seems to think we'll be having another talk soon.'

'Never took you to be a fool, Johnny. Took you to be a lot of things, but never a fool.'

'What else did you take me for?'

I put it to him too fast and he shifted uncomfortably. 'I'm . . . sorry, son. Didn't mean to bring that up again.' Then his face pinched together. 'Maybe I was wrong.'

You can cover a situation nicely by sticking a butt in your mouth. That's what I did. I still didn't know what he was driving at and I wasn't tipping my hand asking questions about something I should have known.

'Maybe,' I said through the smoke.

'There's a bus going out tonight.' He checked with his watch. 'Better'n two hours yet so you can wait here. If nobody saw you come in they won't know you're here.'

'Forget it, forget it. I like it here.' I grinned at him slowly. 'Pop, what do you know about Lindsey?'

'Johnny, you . . .'

'I asked you something.'

'You ought to know what he's like. After Bob Minnow died he swore he'd get the guy who done it and he's never stopped trying. He'll never give up, Johnny. He ain't like the rest. Lindsey's straight as they come. He's the only decent guy left and he stays that way because that's the way he's made. I'm telling you, Johnny, nothing'll pull him off your neck. Not money or nobody or nothing. God knows they tried. He woulda been ousted long ago for not playing ball the way everybody else does, only he knows too much. He don't talk, but if he did it would be pretty tough.'

He stopped and took a breath. I said, 'Spell it out. A lot of things happen in five years. What's the pitch?'

'Yeah,' he nodded, 'I guess you might not know about it at that. Things ain't peaceful any more like they was. You saw the town, didn't you? Sure. Gin mills on every corner and nothing but gambling joints in between. Drunks and lushes all over the place. Prostitution in the North End and who cares? Nobody cares so long as the money rolls in. There's more of it in this town than the state capital and just like the boys want it. You'd think that the people would say something.

'O.K., they vote and so what? The election always winds up to keep the town laws the way they are now. The city council moves the way the merchants want 'em to move and no other way. That's what's so screwy about it. There's better'n fifty thousand people in this town and every year it looks like practically all of 'em are in favour of a good cleanup. They swamp the polls and still the opposition makes 'em look sick.'

'Who runs it all?'

'Runs it? Hell, you got the mayor, the council, this association, that association, the Republicans, the Democrats. Hell . . .'

'I mean who runs it, Pop. Who runs all the works together?'

'Come again?'

'Somebody's behind the works.'

'Oh . . . sure, sure! You take the joints in town now, they belong to the Lyncastle Business Group. That's Lenny Servo's bunch. He heads up the saloons and the game rooms.'

'What does he own?'

'Own? Hell, he don't own nothing. He got the cigarettes and hat-check concession in all them places and makes more'n they do. Nope, he don't own a thing, but he's got enough cash to stake a guy who wants to open up a joint. Lenny, he don't take any chances. He sits back and takes it easy while he runs his organization.'

I took a deep pull on the cigarette and let it settle in my mind. 'He sounds like a nice guy,' I said.

'Great guy. Everybody wants to be palsy with him. He's free with his dough if it means he gets something back. Like the recreation park he "donated" to the city . . . if they'd give him some swamp land on the river. So now the swamp's gone and he's got a layout there that pulls in all the river traffic during the summer. Real fancy place it is.'

'Where's he from?'

The old guy shrugged. 'Who knows? He moved in about six years ago. Ran a saloon for a while before he branched out.' He stopped speaking at the floor and let his eyes come up to mine. 'You got a lot of curiosity about a town you gotta get out of, Johnny.'

'I'm not getting out of anything.'

'Can I ask you something?'

'Go ahead.'

'You kill Bob Minnow?'

I said it like it was the answer without saying a thing at all. 'Guess.'

The clock made a whirring noise on the wall. Outside the baby whined then was still. 'I didn't figure you did, Johnny.' He smiled at me and his shoulders went up and down in a sigh. He looked at me again and shook his head. 'Never figured you did, boy, but now I'm not so sure.'

I could feel the nasty sneer trying to crawl across my mouth. 'Why?'

'Didn't think you had the guts, that's why.' He set himself for something he thought would happen.

'What changed your mind?'

I got that look again, the one with the puzzle behind it. He took a long time saying, 'It took more guts to come back than to kill old Bob.'

I mashed the last of the butt under my heel. 'Never try to figure a guy, Pop. It doesn't always work out.'

'No . . . no, it sure don't at that. Mind telling me what Lindsey had to say about all this?'

'Lindsey's a pretty sore cop. He was all set to line me up for a murder rap, I guess. He had the gun that killed this Bob Minnow and it had my prints on it. He said.'

Pop's eyes went wide. 'Then you didn't . . .'

I held up my hands so he could see where the tips of my fingers used to be. 'He couldn't prove it, Pop. He wanted to, but even though he knew every inch of my body by heart he couldn't prove that I was me. Silly, isn't it?'

'Johnny,' he gasped, 'it'll never work!'

I laughed at him. 'What do you bet?'

He climbed off his stool, his face a mixture of confusion and bewilderment. 'Look, I need a drink. Got a couple hours before I open the window again so let's get a drink.'

'Now you're talking.' I opened the door and walked out while he locked up his money drawers. The woman with the baby was walking up and down the platform outside and the waiting-room was deserted. Even the shadows outside were deserted. The old man came out, snapped the lock on the door and checked it, then pulled on his coat.

A penny post card was sticking out of the side pocket and when he came alongside me I picked it out, dropped it on the floor and made a play of picking it up. 'Dropped something.'

He said thanks and stuck it back in his pocket. But I had time to catch the *Nicholas Henderson*, 391 *Sutter Place* on the address side.

He had a battered '36 Ford out back and got in under the wheel while I wedged in beside him. 'Where we going?'

'Up here a piece. Only place where you can get a decent steak any more. Got girlies too, if you're interested.'

'I'm always interested in girlies,' I laughed.

His head turned so sharply it almost threw him off balance. 'You're changed.'

'Five years is a long time, Pop. Enough to change a guy,' I said easily.

He backed out of the space with a jerk and swung around in the bus port. 'Yeah, guess you're right there,' he agreed.

CHAPTER THREE

The place was a roadhouse on the north-south highway. There was nothing fancy about it except the sign that said LOUIE DINERO'S STEAKS AND CHOPS. It was a real log-cabin job with a big fieldstone fireplace on the bar side and from the number of cars parked in the drive, business was booming.

'Kind of far out for such a trade, isn't it?'

'Don't make no difference. It's the only good place left to eat. Catches all the trade going home.'

Inside a rumba band picked up the beat and a lot of people started whistling at something happening on the dance floor. Pop said hello to a few people, got a big hello in Italian dialect from Louie himself and introduced me with a half-hearted wave. I think I said hello. It was hard to talk and watch the blonde wrapped around the microphone at the same time. She was a real bottle-yellow blonde in a green dress that went on like a bathrobe and was held together by only one button in the middle. No matter which way she stepped you'd see almost all the inside of a lovely tanned leg that was a tantalizing flash in the amber spotlight. She started off the song with little steps that got larger and more critical and had everybody forgetting their chow waiting for the inevitable.

The song was about three bars too short and the inevitable stayed hidden. Instead of giving the patrons a breather she started a new routine with the top of the dress and for a minute I thought she would come out of it altogether. That song ended too fast too. She got one hell of a round of applause and disappeared behind the curtains beside the band. Louie said, 'You like?'

I said, 'I love.'

He gave me a big smile and patted his belly contentedly. 'Wendy, she was good tonight. Very good. Sometime soon she make the big time.'

I grunted, 'She had it made a long time ago.'

'So true. But she like it here and won't leave. I pay tops. Very nice girl. Now, Nick, you and your young friend like to eat?'

Pop said, 'Sure, I need something. Get us a coupla steaks, but bring a drink first. We'll be over at the corner table.'

By the corner table he meant the one that was wedged so far in the corner behind a palm and some draperies that it was empty because nobody knew it was there. The drinks reached the table the same time we did and went down in time for the waiter to bring back the empties for a refill.

'This a regular hang-out of yours, Pop?'

'Guy gets tired of boarding-house cooking sometimes.'

'Nice job you got. Maybe you own the bus line.'

'Hell, Johnny, it ain't expensive here for me. Friend of mine supplies Louie at a cut rate, so Louie makes up the favour on the bill. The steaks are something special.'

He wasn't kidding there. They were very special. I didn't know how hungry I was until I worked mine over until there was a big shiny T in the middle of the plate. I pulled out a smoke and sat back to enjoy it when the blonde came in around the palm and I sat there with the match burning down to my fingers.

She didn't have on the green dress, but the one she wore was just as good. When I studied her a little closer I decided that it wasn't the dress at all but what was underneath it. She said, 'Hello, Nick,' in a rich, husky voice and wrinkled her nose at me.

'Hi, Wendy. Meet Johnny.'

I like women who stick out their hand and shake like a man. It gives you a chance to feel what they're made of. This one was O.K. 'Hello, Wendy. I liked your number.'

She laughed deep down in her throat. 'Not disappointed?'

'Well, a little bit. I had hopes there for a while. Someday the threads holding on that button will wear out.'

'I'd get awfully cold,' she said.

I grinned at her. 'Uh-uh. I'd keep you warm.'

'You'd have to beat off the mob with a club,' Pop grunted. 'Sit down, Wendy. You through for the night?'

24

'All done and ready to go home. You going to drive me back?'

'Sure. Take you as far as the station and Johnny can go the rest.'

That was nice of him.

Wendy said, 'Swell. Or will I have to fight you off?'

'Don't be so damn anxious,' I told her. 'When I have to fight a dame for what I want I'll hang up.'

She propped her chin in her hand and smiled all over her face. It was a beautiful face with eyes that were all sex and a mouth to match. She even looked good with the bleach job and that's not easy. 'I was just asking,' she said. 'It's hard to tell what a guy's like these days and you look like you already had one hung on you.'

'You mean the head?'

'That and your jacket.'

Pop shoved his plate back and picked up the last of his drink. 'He got that from the cops, honey.'

The smile waned away. 'Cops?'

'His name is Johnny McBride.'

That beautiful mouth made a curve that said a silent 'Oh!' that became part of a frightened scowl. 'You mean . . .'

I took it up from there. 'The police would like to prove that I killed somebody.'

'But . . . they did!'

'You ought to speak to them and find out.'

Her eyes went between me and Pop. He jerked his thumb at me. 'Look at his fingers, Wendy.'

I turned my hands over and let her have a peek at the smooth surfaces of my fingers. There was nothing ugly about them. A lot of hard work rigging oil derricks had taken away most of the discoloration and they would have looked just like fingers if they weren't so slick.

She was going to say something, but Pop beat her to it. 'He's crazy.'

I pulled my hands back and picked up the butt. 'You'd be surprised how sane I am.' My voice had a hard edge to it.

Pop caught it the first time. 'What do ya mean?'

25

'Why'd you bring me here, Pop? There were plenty of places to eat in town.'

He didn't answer.

'Before you left you made a phone call. It was to blondie here. Why?'

It caught him with his mouth open. He let it hang that way for a second before closing it sheepishly. 'You was listening,' he accused me.

'Listening nuts! I'm guessing and I'm guessing right.'

'You're right, Johnny. He called me.' I grinned at the blonde and let her throw the ball to the old duffer.

'O.K., Johnny,' he said, 'I called her. Now I'll tell you why. I think you're a plain damn fool for sticking around, but that's your business and I'm not butting in there. Just the same, you park right out where everybody can see you and you're asking for trouble. Wendy here owns a pretty big house and she's going to take you in.'

'That all?' I asked.

'That's all, Johnny.' He stopped and stared at his plate. 'Can't you tell me what's biting you?'

'No. Nothing's biting me.'

'Ah, I don't know. A guy's not much help when he's old, I guess. When you was a little kid and used to hang around the station I was the guy who fixed your kites and took the knots outa your fishing line. Ever since you got into trouble I've worried myself sick over you. Come on, let's get outa here.'

And there it was, another piece of history that went back twenty years. Like most kids, I was supposed to have made the station a regular hang-out. I bet I even used to know the schedules by heart. Now I could quit worrying about why the old guy was so damn friendly. It was nice to know those things, especially when I had never seen him before in my life.

Wendy picked up her hat and purse, said so-long to Louie and the bar crowd, then joined us outside. There was only room for two in the front of the Ford, so I got in back and took it easy awhile. Nobody said anything until the car rolled

26

in against the platform, then the old boy got out and told me to get up front.

I said, 'Sure, Pop.'

He gave a tug at his moustache and glared at me. 'And, damn it, stop calling me "Pop"! You know my name as well as I do!'

'O.K., Mr Henderson.'

'You sure got fresh in five years, Johnny.' He stamped away, but got over his mad soon enough to turn around and wave.

We waved back and he disappeared inside.

The station was still empty.

'Where you staying, Johnny?'

'Hathaway House.'

The blonde nodded, made a turn and cut down to the main drag. 'We'll go right to my place and you can send for your baggage in the morning.'

'I don't have any baggage. I'm not going to your place yet either. Maybe tomorrow, but not tonight.'

She didn't argue about it. 'That's your affair. I'm only doing it as a favour for Nick.'

I waited until she was stopped for a red light and grinned so she could see it. 'Look, Wendy, you're a nice little mouse and all that, but you're strictly the kind of sex I can't afford to have around right now. I got things to do.'

Her eyebrows slid up disdainfully. 'Don't worry, you won't get raped.'

'It's been known to happen,' I said.

'God, what an ego!' The light changed and the car shot forward with the gears mashing noisily.

'Don't fool yourself, baby. I'm as much man as you are woman and like Freud says, it's sex that motivates everything.'

'You're an educated bastard.'

'Yeah.'

A smile played around in the corner of her mouth. 'Perhaps I should change that song routine of mine.'

'Do that. Either let 'em see it or keep it hidden altogether. I hate to be teased.'

She threw back her head, laughed and I laughed with her. Then we both shut up until we were a block from the hotel. I saw the sign up ahead and told her to stop. I got out, shut the door and leaned on the window. 'If the invitation is still good, where do I find your place?'

Her face was a pale oval in the gloom of the car. '4014 Pontiel Road, Johnny. It's a white house on the crest of a hill. I'll leave a key in the big flowerpot on the porch.'

There was something in her voice that was all honey and butter like when she sang that song and I could see her in the green dress with all the light tan skin showing. I reached out and pulled her halfway across the seat until her mouth was there, full and ripe, and I tasted it hungrily, feeling the hot lance of her tongue before she stiffened and jerked away.

'Damn you! That was a nice line about not fighting for it!'

'Hell, that was just sparring around,' I said. Then I laughed and she let the clutch out so fast I almost went on my neck. I couldn't wipe the grin off my face because she was a hot little mouse who liked to tease and couldn't take any teasing back. She didn't know it, but she was due for some lessons in Freud at that Pontiel Road address.

Instead of going in the main entrance of the Hathaway House, I used the side door and saw the big cop before he saw me. He was slouched in a chair trying to read and watch the exit at the same time without doing a good job of either.

I tapped him on the shoulder and if he wasn't so big he wouldn't have gotten stuck in the chair trying to get up. I said, 'Oh, sit there, junior. I've already been so I'm not going any place. If you should want me, just ring my room.'

He sat back and gave me a dirty look and made sure I got on the elevator. Then he picked up the paper again and started reading. I stepped out on my floor, walked down the corridor and poked the key in the lock.

Before I had my clothes off I knew somebody had been through the room. There was a smell that shouldn't have been there and it was a newly familiar smell I couldn't miss. It took a while but I got it. The stuff was an antiseptic. Like hospitals. Like Tucker's beat-up face under a bandage.

Whatever he was looking for he didn't find because there wasn't anything there to find in the first place. I tossed my new jacket in the handbag with the other junk and took a shower. The shock of cold water started my head aching again, so I warmed it up until I turned pink in spots and the ache went away.

I was drying off when knuckles rapped the door. I yelled to come in and wrapped the towel around my middle. Jack, the bellhop, stood there in a listening attitude, one ear cocked towards the door. Apparently he was satisfied with what he heard. 'You know there's a bull downstairs?'

'Uh-huh. He tried following me awhile.'

'Slip 'im, huh?'

'Ran away from him. He's not very fast.'

'That true stuff about you being the guy who knocked off the D.A.?'

'A lot of people seem to think so.'

'What do *you* think?'

I gave him a hurt look and climbed into my shorts. 'Now what would I want to knock off a D.A. for?'

He grinned at me slyly as if I had spilled the whole thing. 'You had a visitor before. A mummy.'

'Yeah, I know. I could smell him.'

'That was Tucker. He's a son of a bitch. You and him tangled, hah?'

'In a minor sort of a way I belted the crap out of him. Why you handing out all that nice information?'

The grin came back. 'You give me a fin. He didn't. Besides, he's been on my neck a long time. The bastard wants his cut of everything that goes on and he gets it. Not from me though,' he added. 'Anybody who takes him is a pal of mine.'

'Hi, pal. What's your racket? Everybody else in town seems to have one, so what's yours?'

'Women.'

'Good, send me two. A redhead and a brunette.'

29

'O.K., and you know what I said before. Anything you want, you holler. I like the way you messed up that bastard Tucker. Any more come busting in I'll give you a ring. There's an emergency exit and a service elevator down the hall. I'll leave the car on this floor so's you can use it if you hafta.'

He listened again and ducked out. I crawled into bed and shut my eyes. It was late as hell, but from the street noises you'd think it was the middle of the day.

If I did sleep it was only for about five minutes. The door opened again and the lights came on.

There was a redhead and a brunette standing there.

The redhead said, 'Jack sent us.'

I let out a tired groan. 'Tell Jack hello and to go to hell, will you.'

'But he said . . .'

'I was only kidding. Honest, I'm too tired.'

'Not *that* tired,' the brunette smiled. She walked over and whipped the cover off me. 'I guess he is at that,' she told the redhead.

So they laughed and went out and I tried to get some sleep.

CHAPTER FOUR

At half-past eight I went downstairs and woke up the cop in the chair. I said, 'I'm going out and eat. You want to come along or wait here?'

'Don't be a wise guy, Mac.' He squirmed out of the chair and shuffled off behind me.

I got on the street, looked over a place that seemed to suit my purpose, and went in and had breakfast. The cop took a table near the door and ordered coffee. I put some ham and eggs away, called for another round of toast and coffee and laid a buck on the table. The cop looked over, saw I was staying and ordered more coffee for himself.

The first time he stopped looking at me and glanced out the door I made my move. I got up, half ran for the kitchen door, shoved it open and stepped behind it. The chef looked at me coldly. 'You want something?'

'Just wanted to say what a swell cook you are.'

He scowled and I went back where I came from.

The cop was gone.

I told the waiter the dough was on the table and went outside. Across the street was a drugstore with a grub counter and I hopped on the end stool. Thirty seconds later the cop came pounding back down the street with a police car screaming along behind. They all stopped in front of the restaurant and ran inside.

They came back right away, looked up and down the street and started arguing among themselves. Then Lindsey got out of the car and gave them hell.

He shouldn't have used such an old dodge. The fat cop was just a decoy I was supposed to duck and forget about, then the one they had planted behind the building waiting for me to come out would have picked me up as easy as eating pie.

Tucker found out right away that I wasn't such a goddamn sucker as he thought. With Lindsey it was going to take a while. I ordered some more coffee and waited for them to scram.

When the counterman came back I asked him where the public library was and he drew me a diagram on the back of a menu. I paid him, stuck the menu in my pocket and took off down the street.

The library was a new building three storeys high on the block backing up the main drag. It was set in the middle of a half-acre lot that had a playground on one side and a parking space on the other. Right next to the door a bronze plaque was inscribed 'Lyncastle Public Library. Donated by the Lyncastle Business Group'. It made a nice chunk of bribery, a monument to the effectiveness of having a town wide open. That Servo lad knew what he was doing.

A girl in her early twenties was sitting at a desk inside the door trying to make like she wasn't chewing gum. I said, 'I'd like to take a look at some newspapers. Where are they?'

'Current ones?'

'No. These go back six or seven years or so.'

'Oh, well, they'll be downstairs.' She pointed over her shoulder to an arch. 'Take those stairs right there. Everything is arranged by the date and you won't have any trouble finding them. Please put them back the same way.'

I said I would, thanked her and went back through the arch.

It took about twenty minutes to get what I wanted. It was a copy of the *Lyncastle News* six years, two months and nine days old. There were banner headlines in big, black type that said, 'District Attorney Killed'. I scanned the copy and picked out the facts. He had been shot in his office with a .38 revolver stolen a year before from a pawnshop. The police were making no comment on the shooting except to hint that the killer was known to them.

The rest of it was a flashback over the past year and I went back to where it seemed to have started and picked it up from there.

The beginning came not long after the cities on the perimeter of Lyncastle voted an option and kicked out liquor. A business survey noted that the gin mills in town were booming with new trade and Lyncastle was enjoying the mild prosperity that went with it. The original residents were the kind of people who believed in as few laws as possible, so nothing was ever done about gambling. The police were having some trouble with minor infractions of the law because of the wide-open situation, but since it was all confined to a small area it was a matter passed over lightly.

Someone introduced a resolution in the city council to outlaw gambling, but it got beaten down because nobody wanted to give up the sudden influx of new dough. The argument was that the *status quo* would remain as it was and not increase and since the situation wasn't out of hand why worry about it?

That was real nice. It was perfect.

The *status quo* got un-statused in a hurry. Almost overnight the town blossomed out in some of the fanciest gambling houses ever seen and the good citizens were caught with their pants down. When a half-dozen people got themselves killed one way or another the D.A. launched a probe to get to the bottom of things.

The next paper to throw any light on the matter was a Sunday sheet. A nosy reporter had dug up some dope on one Lenny Servo who had established residence in town a year before. He was red hot out of the East with some nice charges against him, but had enough dough stashed away to reach the right people and had extradition proceedings squashed in court. Evidently he had spent so much he was flat broke, but Lenny was a real promoter and in no time at all he had himself a bank roll and was in the real-estate business. It later developed that the properties he picked up were strategically located for gambling purposes and he was having a rapid turnover in buildings and lots.

Robert Minnow had him in court twice without finding out where his money had come from and for a couple of months nothing more was said. Then the D.A. pulled out the stops and at an annual Town Hall dinner affair gave out the news that Lyncastle was in the hands of a criminal element whose hands were in the city's pockets and around the necks of every citizen in town. He was after certain conclusive evidence that would lay several murders at the feet of the right people and promised to expose one of the biggest scandals of all time.

He never got around to doing it because a week later he was dead.

That's where John McBride came into it.

Me.

Upon complaint of the State Auditor, the District Attorney's office was conducting an investigation of the National Bank of Lyncastle's books. A check revealed that the bank was short two hundred thousand smackeroos and one John McBride, a teller on vacation, had juggled the books in a neat, but not neat enough manner. The D.A. had a warrant out for his arrest.

During that time somebody knocked off Minnow. He was found dead in his office at ten o'clock at night by a cleaning woman. The gun was on the floor, the corpse behind the desk and whoever had let him have it had stepped inside, pulled the trigger and blown without anybody being the wiser. The coroner stated that he had been killed about an hour before his body was found and a later police report said nobody had seen the killer enter or leave. For a week the police made vague hints, then Captain Lindsey came out with the statement that the killer was John McBride, the motive revenge, and before the month was out the guy would be standing trial.

It must have been a long month for Lindsey.

Well, there it was in a nice little package. Robert Minnow's rising star had been nipped just short of its peak by a dirty bank absconder. I even made some of the out-of-state papers.

I folded them up carefully and slid them back into the racks. Then I stood there looking at them. Inside, I had a vaguely unpleasant feeling, a gnawing doubt that told me I could be

34

wrong and if I was I would hang for the mistake. The basement got cold and damp suddenly.

But it wasn't the basement. It was me. It was that damn doubt telling me it could have happened that way after all and my lovely crusade was nothing but a fool's errand.

I could feel the sweat start over my eyes and run down my cheeks. I got so goddamn mad at myself for thinking that I could be wrong that I balled up my fist and slammed it against the side of the metal bin until the place echoed with a dull booming and my knuckles were a mess of torn skin.

I sat down until the mad passed and only the doubt was left. Then I cursed that and everything about Lyncastle I could think of. When I got done swearing to myself I yanked out a couple of the sheets again and opened them to a feature section that sported a two-column spread by a writer named Alan Logan. I jotted his name down in my memory and tucked the papers back.

Of all the people who had anything to say about Robert Minnow or me, he was the only one who didn't convict me before the trial. The rest had me drawn and quartered *in absentium*. I went back upstairs and outside where I could smoke, standing on the steps trying to think. I was so damn deep in thought that the *chunk* I heard didn't make an impression until I noticed the two kids looking at the wall behind me. I turned around to see what they were looking at, saw it and went flat on my face on the concrete just as there was another *chunk*.

On the wall right behind my back was a quarter-sized dimple plated with the remains of a soft-nosed lead bullet and if I had been standing up the last one would have gone right through my intestines.

If I had rolled the kids probably would have followed me, so I got up on my feet and ran like hell. I tore around the back of the building, shoved the gate open and angled off into an alley that led to the street.

Now the fun was beginning. This was more like it. Guys who were better at tailing somebody than the cops. Guys with silenced rifles who didn't give a damn about kids standing around their target. Now I didn't have any doubt any more.

I made a quick circuit of the block until I reached the corner where I could see the library. Opposite the building the street was lined with private residences and it was a sure bet that I wasn't being potted at from there. They wouldn't have missed if they were that close.

But behind the private homes on the other side of the block was a solid string of apartment houses with nice flat roofs that were perfect gun platforms and anybody at all could get to the top if they wanted to badly enough. There wasn't a bit of sense looking for them. They had plenty of time to get away, and a gun could be broken in half and carried on the street wrapped up in a mighty innocent-looking package.

Out of plain curiosity I crossed the street, walked the one block and turned in at the first apartment. It was a five-storey affair like the rest with a self-service elevator. I took it to the top, got out and walked up the short flight of stairs to the roof. That's how easy it was.

A guy was bending over fastening a television antenna to the chimney and gave me a 'howdy' and a nod when he saw me coming. I said, 'Anybody been up here the last few minutes, Mac?'

He dropped his wrench and stretched his legs. 'Umm, no, not that I know of. Think there might've been somebody down a couple places or so. Heard a door slam.'

'O.K. Thanks.' He went back to work and I stepped over the barrier between the buildings.

You could see the library from nearly every roof top, but you could command it properly from only two if you wanted a good background for a target standing on the steps.

The first one I looked at was where the guy had been.

He was smart, too. There weren't any empty shell cases around, no scratches on the parapet where a careless guy would have propped a gun, no trinkets that might have fallen from the pockets of a gunman shooting prone, no nothing. I'd even bet the bastard threw his clothes away to get rid of any dust traces he could have picked up.

Yeah, he was smart, all right, but not smart enough to rub out the marks his toes and elbows had left. They made four cute little hollows in the gravel of the roof and when I stretched out on top of them with my own toes in the impressions he made my elbows came out about eight inches above his.

Junior was a shortie. A guy about five-six. And he was going to be a hell of a lot shorter when I caught up with him.

I used the same entrance he had used and didn't meet a soul going out. I walked to the corner and back up to the main drag without getting shot at either.

It was ten after ten and I used up another half-hour buying myself a second jacket. Next to the store where I got the jacket was a pawnshop that had a nice selection of guns displayed in the window and I would have picked one up right there if it weren't for the sign that said a certificate was required for purchase of any hand gun.

If you wanted to shoot at anybody you had to have a certificate.

Two doors down was a cigar store with a telephone plaque on the front. The old lady behind the counter changed a buck into silver for me and I picked up the *Lyncastle News* number from the directory.

A voice said hello and I asked for Alan Logan. There was a rapid series of clicks, then, 'Hello, Logan speaking.'

I said, 'Logan, you tied up right now?'

'Who is this?'

'Never mind who it is. I want to speak to you.'

'What's on your mind, feller?'

'Something that might make a good story. An attempted murder.'

That was all the answer he needed. 'I'm not busy. Why?'

'Pick out a nice place where I can meet you. No people, understand?'

'You mean no cops, don't you?'

'They're included.'

'There's a bar on Riverside,' he said. 'It's called the Scioto Trail and it's probably just opening up. The owner's a friend of mine and we can talk in the back room.'

'O.K. Say in a half-hour?'

'Good enough.'

I stuck the receiver back in the cradle and went over to the counter. The old lady told me where Riverside was, but I wasn't about to walk any three miles to get there. I called a cab and had a soda until the cab beeped outside for me.

The guy said, 'Where to?'

'Know where the Scioto Trail is on Riverside?'

'Sure, but they ain't open yet, bud.'

'I'll wait for it to open.' The driver shrugged and crawled out into the traffic.

The Scioto Trail was a big white frame building that had started life as a private home, lived until the river made a bed in its back yard, then made a quick switch into a gin mill whose owner stuck a dock out from the back porch to pick up the yacht club trade. The parking lot was empty and except for the kid on the gasoline barge that was swinging at anchor near the dock, the place seemed deserted.

I paid off the cabbie and walked around the building to the veranda. A new Chevvy was crowding the back of the building behind a Buick sedan, so the place wasn't too deserted after all. I rapped on the door a few times, heard heavy feet pounding across the floor inside and a tall skinny guy with a crooked nose pulled the door open and said, 'Yeah?'

'Logan here?'

'He's here. You the guy he's waiting for?'

'Yeah.'

'Come on in. He's in the back.'

He slammed the door shut and pointed to a door at the end of the bar and went back to swabbing down the floor. The door took me through a narrow hall with the washrooms opening off it and led to a square hall with a bandstand and dance floor. Tables were scattered around liberally and for the people who wanted a little privacy there were booths in an alcove that jutted out from one wall.

That's where I found Logan.

He sure as hell didn't look like any reporter. One ear was cauliflowered, his nose was flat and scar tissue showed over both eyes. He was bunched over a paper doing the crossword puzzle and looked like his shoulders were going to pop right out of his coat.

I shoved my hands in my pockets and came along the wall without him hearing me until I crowded the booth where he was sitting. I wasn't even taking a little bit of a chance. The guy could be a pug, but if he was he wouldn't be making any passes from a sitting-down position.

'Logan?'

His face wrinkled up at the edges. It went flat in surprise and wrinkled up all over again showing short, squared-off teeth under lips that were a thin red line.

'I'll be damned! I'll be good and goddamned!'

'Maybe. You got a driver's licence or something?'

He didn't get it right away. He crinkled his eyes thinking about it then threw his wallet on the table. It opened to a flap that showed his licence and a card certifying that he was a member of the Newspaperman's Guild.

So I sat down.

He was another guy I fascinated. He couldn't take his eyes off me a second. He stared until words came to him and squeezed out in amazement. 'Johnny McBride! I'll be damned!'

'You already said that.'

'When I heard about it I couldn't believe it. I thought Lindsey was out of his head. I was sure of it when I found out what happened up there in Headquarters.' His fingers were hanging on to the edge of the table like he was trying to break off a piece.

'Nobody seems very glad to see me,' I said.

Those lips went back and I saw the teeth again. 'No, they wouldn't be.'

I could make faces too. I made him a good one. 'Somebody tried to knock me off a little while ago. Right in front of the library.'

'That the story you wanted to tell me?'

I shrugged. 'That was just a gimmick to get you here. First you're going to tell me something, then if I like it I'll tell you.'

You'd think I'd smacked him right between those narrow eyes of his. 'You son of a bitch, it's too bad they missed!' he rasped.

I grinned at him. 'You don't like me either, right?'

'Right.'

'For a guy who doesn't like me you did a nice job of going easy on me in that column of yours. Everybody else crucified me.'

'You know damn well why I went easy. I'd just as soon see you swing as look at you. The next time I'll take you apart piece by piece.' He half stood behind the table and sneered at me.

'Sit down and shut up,' I said. 'I'm getting tired of all the crap I've been handed since I got here. Nobody's taking me apart, especially you. Tucker tried it and Lindsey tried it. They didn't do so good.'

Logan started to smile, a loose nasty smile and he sat down. His hands weren't hanging onto the table any longer. They were there in front of him and everything in his eyes said he was getting ready to take me as soon as he found out what it was all about.

I said, 'Tell me about myself, Logan. Make like you didn't know me and was telling somebody all about it. Tell me about the bank job and how Bob Minnow was killed.'

'Then what will you tell me, Johnny?'

'Something you won't expect to hear.'

Logan was going to say something and changed his mind. He gave me a studied glance and shook his head slightly. 'It's going over my head, way over. I've heard some screwy things before, but this takes the cake.'

'Don't worry about it, just tell me.'

His hand went out absently for a cigarette and he stuck it in his mouth. 'O.K., you're Johnny McBride. You were born in Lyncastle, went to school here and started working in the bank after two years away at college. You went into the army, saw a lot of action and came home a big hero. At least all your medals said you were a big hero.'

I stopped him there. 'What's that supposed to mean?.'

'Don't play dumb. You're the only one who knows the answer to that. Maybe you were a big hero overseas. If you were then something happened that changed you plenty. So you came home and went to work in the bank.' His fingers curled around the cigarette and bent it. 'And you found yourself a girl. It didn't make any difference whose girl she was. You played up that hero stuff and she went for it.'

'Who?'

Logan's eyes were a pale, watery blue watching me steadily; eyes hazy with a venom that had never ceased being deadly. 'Vera West. A lovely, wonderful girl with hair like new honey. A girl too damn good for somebody like you.'

I laughed insolently, a laugh that cut him right in half. 'I took her right out of your arms, didn't I?'

'Goddamn you!' He was getting ready and I didn't move. His teeth came together in a crazy attempt to control himself and he had to hiss to speak. 'Yeah, Vera went for you. She went overboard like an idiot and let you ruin her life. She was so much in love that even after you used her like a dirty rag she stayed that way. That's why I went easy on you. I didn't want her hurt any worse!'

'I'm a bad boy. What else?'

'You're going to be a dead boy, Johnny.'

'What else? How'd I use her?'

He had to push himself back on the bench. 'You know, I figured that out before the cops did. Because Vera was Havis Gardiner's secretary she had access to a lot of private stuff you as a teller couldn't reach. You did real well making her hand over those books without arousing her suspicions. You did a beautiful job of juggling those accounts, too. It's too bad you were on vacation at the time the state auditor dropped in. They caught you up in a hurry then, didn't they? It went into

41

Minnow's lap and he started a search for you and never found you because you found him first. You were so jerky that you blamed it on him and put a bullet in him!'

'And Vera?' I asked him.

'That's something I want to hear from you, Johnny. I want to know why a girl as lovely as Vera went to the dogs with herself until she wound up slutting around with a heel like Lenny Servo. I want to know why she became nothing but a beautiful drunken bum who could make Servo look good even at her worst.'

'Where's she now, Logan?'

'That's what I'd like to know. She disappeared three years ago.' Logan's mouth twisted in a snarl. 'That's what you did to her, you stinking yellow bastard. That's what our hero, Johnny McBride, did to her.'

He started to reach for me across the table. Slow. His left out further than the other so I couldn't get away before he grabbed me.

I said, 'Johnny McBride's dead.'

Those hands came to a dead stop as though they ran into an invisible wall. He looked at me like I was crazy or something, trying hard not to believe me but having to because I sat there smoking without getting excited about an ex-pug who wanted to murder me with his hands. He barely whispered, 'What?'

'McBride's dead. He fell off a bridge scaffolding into the river and all that was ever found of him were a few pieces and some torn clothes. He was battered to bits in the rapids and what was left I saw buried not two weeks ago.'

You don't tell a guy that somebody's dead when he's looking at the corpse breathing and talking right in front of him. You don't tell him that in one breath and make him believe it. No, first it has to sink in and swirl around then it has to come out in little pieces that don't make any sense at all and show on your face like a blank mask a little too white and a little too strained.

Logan let his legs relax and he teetered on the edge of the bench. 'You're lying!'

42

'There's a death certificate filed if you want to look at it.' Nobody could have said it the way I did and not be telling the truth. He knew and I knew it yet his face went cynical as he said, 'Then who the hell are you?'

'That,' I told him, 'is something I'd like to know myself.'

'You're nuts! You're batty as hell!'

'Nope, I'm not a bit nuts, Logan. It may *seem* nuts, but it's the truth, and like I said, it won't take you more than one phone call to find out for yourself. There's an outfit called the Davitson Construction Company out in Colorado right now. They build bridges and rig oil wells. Ask anybody in charge about it.'

His hand covered his face until all I could see were his eyes. 'Keep talking.'

'Believe in coincidence?'

'Sometimes.'

'That's what I ran into. A coincidence that won't happen again for another thousand years. I'll tell you about me and Johnny as far back as I can go, and that's only two years. When I said I don't know who I am that was only partly true. I know *who*, but that's all. I know my name is George Wilson because I had that identification on me at the time of the accident, but there was no address and no history and no way of finding out who I was or where I came from. I don't know if I had a criminal record or ever served in the army because I don't have any fingerprints. See?'

I turned my hands over and he nodded through a frown. 'I heard about that.'

'That's only part of the story, Logan. I can fill in about twelve hours before the accident, but that's all.'

'Let's hear it.'

I pulled out another butt and lit it. 'Two years ago the Davitson Company sent out a bus to pick up some construction workers. Fifteen men signed on for the job, threw their luggage on the bus and had a last fling in town. At eleven that night the bus loaded up with fifteen drunks and started off to camp.

43

'Coming down a steep grade the bus ran off the road, went nose first over a cliff and wound up a burning wreck at the bottom of a gorge. I remember something smashing into my head and being thrown through the air.

'As far as I can figure out, I was knocked cold, lay there on the ground a few minutes, then came around. The bus was a mass of flames and you could smell the men cooking inside. It wasn't very nice. Somebody was screaming his head off and I could see a guy trapped under one of the fenders with the fire starting his way. I managed to crawl over to him and lift the wreckage that was pinning him down so he could get out. That's how I lost my fingerprints. The damn metal was red hot.

'Just as we had gotten back about fifteen feet or so the gas in the tanks exploded, knocked us flat and scattered what was left of the bus all over the place. I went out like a light again, only this time it was dark when I woke up.

'The other fellow had found a stream and washed me down. My hands looked like raw meat and the first thing that hit me was that I had lost my memory. I got so excited I went off my rocker a little bit and passed out. Two days later I came around in a company hospital. The other guy had managed to flag a passing car and called for help.

'Here's the funny part. When I came to in that hospital I thought I really was nuts. I was lying on the bed looking up at myself. Screwy, wasn't it? You should've seen how I felt about it. It took a doctor, a couple of nurses and Charlie Davitson himself to convince me I was sane. The guy I was looking at was me in every detail and if we had been born twins we couldn't have been more nearly identical.

'Oh, the doctors went into a big speil about it. I made a good case history for them; first because I was a true amnesia case and second because of that freakish resemblance to the other guy. His name was John McBride. I had my name written inside my shirt, but that was all I had. My luggage was one of the ones completely destroyed. All the company records and personal papers they carried on us were destroyed too. Some

44

of the bags had been thrown clear and Johnny's was one of them. He was luckier than me all around.

'Anyway, after that the two of us were inseparable. Whatever we did we did together. For two guys we got into enough trouble for ten and they started calling us the "Devil's Twins".'

I took a drag on the cigarette and let it hang there in my throat. I had gone over it a dozen times in my own mind, but when it came to speaking about it I couldn't get the words out.

'A few weeks ago we were working on a bridge. I slipped and was dangling by a safety rope. I was hanging over a fifty-foot drop and the wind was whipsawing the rope against a girder overhead and fraying it fast. There wasn't much time and it looked hopeless, but Johnny came down his own rope to tie onto me and just as he secured, his own rope broke and he went down into the river. I got hauled up.

'It took a couple of days to locate his remains and bury him. As far as was known, he didn't have any family. I sort of took over his personal effects and went through them. You see, Johnny never talked about himself. I found out why. I came across a letter he had started to write. It was tucked in some old junk where he had forgotten about it, but it gave me an idea of what his life had been like.

'I remember every word of that letter. Want to hear it?'

Logan's nod was scarcely perceptible.

I said, '"They ran me out of Lyncastle five years ago. They took my money, my honour and my girl. They took everything I had and she laughed while they did it. She laughed because she was part of it and I was in love with her. She laughed then she went with him while that sadistic bastard who works for him tried to kill me with a knife. I ran. I ran and I ran and I'll never stop running as long . . ." and that's how it ended.'

'I didn't hear any names,' Logan said.

'That's right. There weren't any names. I don't need any. I'll find out who they were without any names to go by and you know what's going to happen?'

He waited for me to tell him. I let him guess at it. I grinned like a damned fool while he was guessing and he guessed right. He said, 'What are you doing this for?'

'For? Because Johnny was the best friend I ever had. He was such a good friend that he died trying to save my life and by God, I'm going to get back everything they took away from him. Hear me?'

'That's big talk. You're taking a lot for granted, aren't you? Without knowing anything about it you're ready to say he wasn't guilty.'

I got up and stuck my cigarettes in my pocket. He was right behind me. 'You get to know a guy pretty well in a couple of years. When you eat, sleep and fight together you get so you know all about a guy. Johnny didn't kill anybody.'

We were right in the middle of the dance floor when Logan tapped me on the shoulder. There was something screwy about his face and the way he stood. He was on his toes with his hands hanging limp looking like the pug he might have been at one time.

'That was a nice story, Johnny. I'm going to find out how much of it was true.'

'I told you how you could find out,' I said.

His lips folded back over his teeth. 'I got a better way to find out if you're Johnny McBride or not.'

He swung that right hand so hard I barely had time to get under it before he nearly tore the top of my head off. I caught him with the side of my palm across the neck and dug my fist into his belly the same time I rammed him against the wall. I gave him another in the gut doubling him over my shoulder then I had him in my hands and threw him halfway across the floor.

Logan lay there staring at the floor with glassy eyes, his dinner trying hard to get past his clenched teeth. I gave him a good ten seconds to get up and he couldn't make it. He was nuts if he thought I was going to be a sportsman about it. I walked over to him and he was just about to get his goddamn teeth kicked down his throat when he turned his head and grinned at me.

That's right, grinned. Like something was funny. His mouth was all bloody and he managed a good, solid grin.

'You're O.K., Wilson,' he said.

I gave him a hand up, holding him until he could do it by himself. 'That was a crazy stunt. What'd it get you?'

'You,' he grinned again. 'The real McBride wouldn't't've done that. Johnny was as yellow as they come. He was scared to death of getting hurt. You're O.K., Wilson.'

'McBride. Johnny McBride, remember?'

'O.K., Johnny.'

'And never get the idea I'm yellow, Logan.'

'No, I won't. I know some others who might think so.'

'They're going to be awfully surprised.'

Logan said, 'Yeah,' looked puzzled a second then grinned again.

CHAPTER FIVE

I had to help Logan out to the Chevvy and feed him cigarettes until he was ready to go back to town. He kept shaking his head to clear it and there were raw patches on his elbows from where he skidded along the floor, but he wasn't holding it against me.

When he kicked the engine over he said, 'Where'd you pick up the rough stuff?'

'That went with the job, I guess.'

'Ever think that you might have been a pug before?'

I frowned at him, then shook my head. 'If I was I don't remember it.'

'You're no amateur at that business, kiddo. Suppose I do a little poking around and see what I can find. Maybe you have a history I can run down.'

'Go to it, pal. I tried and didn't get very far.'

'You might not like what I dig up.'

I tossed the cigarette out the window and watched it sizzle out in the water. 'Maybe not, but it's better than not knowing,' I told him finally. 'Sometimes I get to thinking things that give me the willies. I can do things I didn't know I could do . . . or at least my hands do them without thinking. I can handle a rod like a knife and fork and I know how to kill a guy the easy way. One day I found out I could open a lock with a piece of wire as easy as with a key. Nobody ever taught me how to use nitro or a burning torch either. The boys used to kid me . . . said I'd make a good safe cracker.

'It was real funny at first, then it wasn't so funny. I picked up an old safe on a dump heap and tried to open it. You know how long it took? Four minutes working the dial. The boys caught me at it and I showed them how to blow the thing apart with a little soup. That door came off like it was sliced off.'

I looked at Logan and grinned. 'See what you can do with that angle. Maybe I'm wanted for burglary some place.'

'And if you are?'

I held out my hands where the fingerprints used to be.

He shrugged. 'Lindsey says they can still bring out impressions.'

'O.K., let 'em try. I'm willing.'

'You seem to be pretty cocky about it.'

'Why not? You think I didn't try to find out who I was? Hell, man, I went to the Army, Navy, Marines and Veterans' Bureau trying to see what they could do. I've had a half-dozen doctors and experts try to bring out even the faintest sign of a print. They didn't get anywhere.'

Logan nodded, the warning plain in his face. 'I'll look around then. If I dig anything up I'll let you know.'

'Before or after you give it to Lindsey?'

'That depends on how good it is,' he told me.

He swung the car around and headed back up the highway. Traffic was light in both directions and we just loped along taking it easy. I knew he was feeling around for words, then he came right out with it. 'What are you going to do about it?'

'Find this Vera you spoke of.'

His face got tight again. 'Why her?'

'Because she's the key, that's why. I told you what was in that letter Johnny wrote. They took everything he had and she laughed while they did it because she was part of it.'

'Goddamn it! 'His hand smacked the wheel violently. 'Don't push everything off on her. You're not sure, you know!'

'You still in love with her?'

'No.' He glanced at me and his face wrinkled up. 'No, I'm not. But I was and maybe that makes the difference.'

'How well did you know her?'

'Well enough and long enough to know she wasn't a tramp.'

'Logan,' I said, 'in the few years that I remember anything, I've found out that no man knows a damn thing about any woman and that goes double when he's in love with her.'

I handed him a cigarette and held up a light 'This newspaper of yours. Does it have any police photos?'

He looked at me over the light. 'Some. Why?'

'Maybe it has one of the murder room where Minnow was shot?'

'Maybe.'

'Let's go see, huh?'

He looked at me again without saying anything, took a drag on the cigarette and shoved the car in gear.

He drove through town to the *News* building and I waited downstairs while he was gone. Ten minutes later he walked over to the car with a brown folder between his fingers, got in and handed me four blown-up photos.

The first one showed Minnow dead, slumped forward on his desk, the blotter soaking up the blood that ran down his face. All around him were papers that he had been working on. In one hand was a pencil that had snapped in two when it dug into the desk with a convulsive movement. A stack of letters had been knocked to the floor by the same final twitch and showed spread out on the floor in the corner of the photo.

The other two pictures were angle shots of the body taking in part of the office background, showing one of the filing cabinets open, Minnow's coat and hat on a clothes tree, a bookcase that apparently contained his law books and an umbrella stand. The last picture showed the gun on the floor.

I turned them to odd angles, checking them again. They were pretty clear in detail and a lot of the papers on the desk were readable. Most of them were parts of briefs, one a copy of an indictment and the rest of a general legal nature. Some of the letters scattered around had cancelled stamps on them while a few were outgoing. One or two had something written across the face to identify the contents and nothing else.

When I finished I tucked them back in the folder. Logan said, 'Well! What do you make out of them?'

'Nice gun,' I said.

'Police positive. Fully loaded and one shot fired.' His mouth tightened. 'Your prints were all over it.'

'Not mine.'

'That's right. *His*. It didn't take long to check them, either. The bonding company the bank used had them on file right here in town. They checked with Army files in Washington.'

I could feel the frown start creasing my forehead. Something was wrong as hell. I pulled the photos out, looked them over carefully again and shoved them back in disgust. I said, 'How easy would it be for somebody to get in the building?'

'It wouldn't be hard to force a window. Not that it would have been necessary. A couple were open. One was in the hall off the back court that led directly up to Minnow's office.'

'I see.' I handed him the stuff back and sucked on my cigarette. I couldn't get it out of my mind that something stunk and my nose wasn't big enough to catch the smell. Without thinking I finally asked, 'What was Minnow working on that night?'

'The same thing he always worked on. He was after something that would incriminate Servo and get rid of the rottenness in this town.'

'Is it just Servo?'

'There's a lot of them. Servo's the boy with the brains. No, that's not the word. Let's say nerve. He's ruthless. It's a sort of gentlemanly ruthlessness that he's acquired. He owns everything and everybody. Hell, you got to face it, nobody in the city government wants to make a move against him.'

'Wonderful situation.'

'For Servo. Some day it'll change.'

I said, 'Well, thanks for the stuff. Having you around is a big help.'

His eyes squinted under the scarred lids. 'That's O.K. I'm still waiting for that big story. Maybe more.'

'Vera?'

'Yeah. I'd still take her back no matter what she was.'

'You mean as long as she wasn't a killer or an accessory before the fact,' I grinned at him.

He said something nasty.

'There's something I forgot to ask you,' I said. 'Vera and Johnny worked together until the monkey business in the bank came out. How long after it happened did she continue to work there?'

'Not very long. The two of them took their vacations together. It was during that time that the auditors checked the books and uncovered the theft. I never got to see Vera to talk to after that. She just left the bank and started hanging around the gambling houses in town. She was making quite a splash when Servo picked her up. After that she was with him constantly until the day she just dropped out of sight.'

'No trace of her since?'

'No trace,' he repeated dully.

'I want a picture of her, Logan. Got one?'

He reached his hand into his pocket and pulled out his wallet. 'There's one in the card-case,' he told me, 'on the bottom of the pile.'

I shuffled through the cards until I found it, a two-by-three-inch photo on heavy linen paper. And there she was, a lovely natural blonde with hair like new butter flowing down to her shoulders. The photographer had caught her in a coquettish pose, but there was a freshness about her that had to be real. Her mouth was full and soft, her nose tilted gently, ready to laugh. It was hard to tell much about her eyes. They might have been soft eyes or they might have been hard. I couldn't tell.

Logan said, 'What do you think?'

'Beautiful.'

'She was that all right. You can keep that picture if you want it.'

'Thanks.' I stuck it in my pocket and handed his wallet back.

'You still didn't tell me what you were going to do about it,' he said.

I watched the houses flash by the window a minute. 'Logan, Johnny was run out of town because he was involved in something big. Like two hundred thousand bucks is big. I don't think Johnny took that dough.'

'Frame?'

'Maybe. Vera was involved and when I find her I'll find the answers.'

There was a red light up ahead and Logan slowed down for it. When he came to a stop he stared at me meaningly. 'I'm pretty well convinced you're not McBride, but when you started telling me about those unnatural talents of yours I started thinking of something.'

I caught it fast. 'You mean did I discover I was a handy man with figures too?' I asked him.

'Yeah.'

'Chum, the only figures I'm good with walk on high heels. I still count on my fingers. I'd make a lousy bank teller.'

'And the Johnny McBride you knew?'

I bobbed my head. 'He was a mathematical whiz, that guy. He kept the company accounts.'

The light changed and the car rolled ahead. We were on the edge of town now and Logan took the time to point out some of the bigger hot spots. Most of the places were just starting to get a play and before the hour was out they'd be packed to the doors. Most of the cars in the parking lots were from out of town and about half from out of the state entirely. Lyncastle had the kind of reputation to draw the tourists.

I noticed little blue signs in a lot of the windows and mentioned it to Logan.

'Members of the Business Group,' he said, 'Servo's outfit.'

'What happens if you don't belong?'

'Oh, hell, there's no rough stuff involved. About a tenth of the places are independents, but they don't make out so well. If there is any trouble and you are a member of the group, there's a lot of money for the best lawyers. Besides that, Servo has a liquor monopoly in town and if you don't belong you don't get the kind of stuff the customers want.'

'Never any trouble from the public?'

Logan grunted mirthlessly. 'There would have been at one time. There would still be if the damn public would get the merchants out of politics and run the town themselves. What

53

the hell, you can't blame them too much. There's a lot of new money in town now if you can stand to live with the kind of people who have it.'

'You ought to have an opinion on it, Logan. What is it?'

I saw his lips come back in a sneer. 'I've covered murder cases, I've seen kids who were raped on the streets, I watched them pull young mangled bodies from the wrecks of cars that had a drunk at the wheel, I've had to live under laws set up by a pack of ignorant bastards who take all the cream and throw the rest to the people who vote for them. Now you know what my opinion is.'

'Who runs the town now?'

'Balls.'

'I mean it.'

'Who the hell knows?'

'You should know, you're a newspaperman,' I said.

'Yeah, I should know a lot of things. Look, feller, whoever is at the top pulling the strings does it under the nicest cover you ever saw. There's more money in this town than you can imagine, but it isn't going down into any books. We've had the Feds in here and boys from the Attorney General's office trying to get to the bottom of it and they all come up shaking their heads.

'A lot of people try to put it on Servo, but he's clean. He pays his taxes and stays out of trouble. They try it on the mayor and the city council and what happens? Nothing, absolutely nothing. Nobody knows from nothing.'

He stopped abruptly and looked at me sidewise. 'What are you getting at?'

'Nothing special.' We were in the centre of town by then and slowing down for another light. 'Let me out on the corner, Logan.'

He pulled in to the kerb and stopped. I swung out of the car and slammed the door shut. He said, 'If you stay alive long enough to find out anything, you can reach me at the office.'

'O.K.'

'And I'm going to backtrack over your story, you know.'

'I expected that.'

'Where can I find you?'

I laughed at him. 'You can't, pal. I'll find you. If I'm still alive, that is.'

I watched him pull away into traffic, then went into a joint and had a beer. The place was called Little Bohemia and had a blue sign in the window. There were slots all around the walls going full blast, an ornate juke box to drown out the sound of more money going into them than was coming out, a sheet-covered roulette wheel and two crap tables in the back and a chrome-and-plastic bar forming a huge oval in the centre of the place.

Beer was two-bits a throw.

A sign said something about not serving minors, but I'd like to have a buck for every overpainted chippy in the place who hadn't seen eighteen yet. Most of them were there for strictly one reason, sipping their drinks until they found a sucker to finance some faster drinking.

I had my beer and went next door where there was no blue sign in the window. Beer was a dime, but there weren't any customers, either. The bartender was feeding the relic of a slot machine until he saw me. I said, 'Where'd that come from?'

'Boss had it in his cellar ever since Prohibition. What'll you have?'

'Beer. Where's the crowd?'

'You new around here?'

'Yeah.'

'Oh! They come in later. They get squeezed outa the other joints or run out of dough. Then we get 'em here.'

'You ought to get in some slots.'

'Yeah, tell that to the boss. He's one of them rugged indi-vidualists, he is.'

'He won't play Servo's game, hey?'

'I thought you was new around here.'

'Hell, this town makes the news all over.'

'Yeah. Another beer?'

'One more.' He set it up for me, had one with me, then I asked, 'Look, maybe you can help me out. I'm looking for a girl named Vera West. She's a relative of mine, see? About five years ago she got in some kind of a jam at the bank here in town, then went to the dogs. She used to go around with Servo.'

The bartender sipped his beer and made circles with the glass on the bar. 'Servo has lots of women.'

'This one was a blonde, a real honey blonde.'

'Nice build?'

I couldn't say for sure, but women take care of those things if they haven't already got them so I just nodded.

'He had one tomato a long time ago who was a knockout. She was a blonde.'

'Remember her name?'

He made more circles with the glass. 'Mac, if I did know I don't think I'd tell you. I'm a family man. I work here and let it go at that.'

'Servo's trouble?' I tried to act surprised.

'Not personally . . . he's too much of a big shot to do his own knuckle-work. Let's quit asking questions.'

'Sure, sure,' I agreed, 'but you know how it is. I'd like to find her.'

He spoke more to the open door than to me. 'The babes Servo makes usually wind up in the cellar. Try the red light district once.'

I tossed the beer down and pushed the change out to him. 'I'll do that. Thanks.' He picked up the change with a nod and was feeding it in the slot when I went out the door.

It was hot as hell again. The sky was a hazy grey and over in the east I could see the outlines of an early thunderstorm building up. It didn't seem to bother any of the people on the street. Not with all those nice air-conditioned places with the blue signs in the window to wait out the weather. That was another monopoly Servo seemed to have.

I took it easy walking down the street, acting like I had

56

all the time in the world on my hands. I spent an hour at it, getting an idea of what made the city tick. There were a lot of things that helped, like the cops who poured the coal on the residents for parking overtime while anybody with a tag from outside the city got away with murder. Practically.

Like the candy store where I bought the paper and saw a guy in a flashy sports outfit stuff a roll of bills in a briefcase and hand it over to another guy who had a car waiting outside.

Like the women who had everything but 'for rent' signs hanging from their nipples cruising the streets for customers.

Like the expensive-looking guy who had an early load on being helped into a police car very gently with orders from the bar owner to see that he got to the train station safely.

Like the shoeshine boys who charged a half a buck for a polish and rub then griped when there wasn't any tip besides.

Oh, Lyncastle was a great town. Great.

Then I saw Lindsey. He was having a coke at the counter of a modern version of an old general store. The sign over the front read 'Philbert's' in neon script and a directory listed what was to be found inside. Food and drugs on the left. Sodas on the right and beer farther back. Hardware, paints and home supplies up the middle aisles. Printing, photostatting and office supplies in the back.

I walked in and sat down beside him. Like the spider and Miss Muffet. I said, 'Howdy, pardner,' and he didn't even look at me. His face seemed to puff up around his mouth and the straw flattened out from too much pressure at the top. I said, 'Cat got your tongue?'

He turned around slowly. 'Johnny, you're too goddamned wise for your own good.'

'So I've been told.'

'I'm telling you again.'

'Then get some smarter cops. That deal you pulled this morning stunk.'

'You seem to know a lot about cops.'

I ordered a coke and a sandwich for myself. 'I do . . . about the kind you have in this burg. You know about them?'

'I know all about them.' His voice was a flat snarl.

'Then keep them off my back, Lindsey. When you slap me with a murder charge you can do what you damn well please, but until then, lay off.'

'You bastard!' He almost whispered it.

I took a bite of my sandwich and grinned at him. 'You know, it's a wonder you don't at least ask me whether or not I killed your friend.'

He was so mad he could hardly speak. 'I don't have to!'

'Don't, then, but if you're the least bit interested, I didn't kill anybody.'

His teeth made a white pattern under his lips and in the mirror behind the counter I couldn't see his eyes at all. I went ahead and finished my sandwich, drowning it with my coke. When I was done I shoved a quarter across the counter and picked a cigarette out of Lindsey's pack.

'Some day . . . if you get around to it, try giving me a lie-detector test,' I said. 'I won't mind a bit.'

He stopped playing with the straw and his eyes came open enough so I could see the colour of them. They were blue. His mouth relaxed and that puffed-up business went away. He didn't get it. Not a bit. So I let him sit there until he did get it.

The National Bank of Lyncastle was a white stone building that occupied half a city block in the heart of town. I got in a few minutes before closing when the place was about empty and I wasn't there two seconds before I noticed the sudden silence. It was a dead kind of silence that comes when machines stop operating and people are momentarily stunned.

There was a uniformed guard standing behind one of those glass-topped tables trying to decide between pulling his gun out and saying hello. I said hello first, so he didn't pull his gun out. He swallowed hard, looked a little foolish and said tentatively, 'Johnny?'

'Who else, Pop?'

He gulped again, his eyes darting around for advice that didn't come.

'Where's Mr Gardiner, Pop?'

'In . . . his office.'

'Feel like telling him I'm out here?'

He didn't feel like it, but he picked up the wall phone anyway. He didn't have to. The gate down the end swung open and the guy standing there couldn't have been anything else but the president. I started the walk across the marble floor and heard the last closing of the bronze doors behind me.

'Hello, Mr Gardiner.'

Amazement. Nothing but pure amazement was there on his face. Havis Gardiner was one of those tall, spare guys with greying hair like you see in the ads, only now he resembled a kid seeing a circus for the first time. Too damn excited to do anything but stare.

I said, 'I want to speak to you alone.'

'Of all the colossal nerve . . .' The amazement made a quick change into fury.

'Yeah, I have that, Mr Gardiner. I still want to talk to you in private. In case you're worried, the police know I'm in town. Now, do we talk?'

His lips pressed together. 'I'm at a board meeting.' I grinned at him just once and his hands made tight fists. 'It can be postponed for this,' he added.

I went in through the gate and it made a mechanical clang when it closed. Outside everybody started talking at once, an awed murmur that disappeared when we were in the office marked 'President'. Gardiner made a quick call that ended the board meeting and swung around in his chair to face me.

It was some dump, plush and mahogany with all the trimmings. He didn't ask me to sit down, but I pulled up a chair anyway. If there was going to be any talking done, I was going to have to start it. Havis Gardiner was trying so hard to control his temper he was about to blow a blood vessel.

'I'm looking for Vera West, Mr Gardiner. Got any idea where she is?'

Instead of answering my question he picked up the phone and asked for the police. He told them I was there and wanted to know the reason why.

Somebody told him.

His face came apart at the seams and he hung up slowly. 'So you think you've gotten away with it!' he rasped.

'That's right, I did. Now let's talk about Vera West.'

Gardiner studied me for a full minute, his eyes going over me from head to toe. 'I certainly don't know where she is, McBride. And do you know what I'd do if I were you?'

'Yeah, cut my throat. Shut up and listen to me a second. I'm going to tell you right out and you can believe it or not, but you'll be better off if you do. I never stole a cent from this outfit. O.K., so I took a powder, but that's my business.'

The study he was making of me took on an intense concentration. Every emotion he was possible of having flitted across his face until he wound up leaning halfway across the desk towards me.

'What are you saying, McBride?'

'That I was trapped in a nice frame. Is that plain enough?'

'No, it isn't.'

'Let me put it this way then. Why was I accused of misappropriating that two hundred grand?'

Gardiner couldn't decide whether to be puzzled or worried. He opened his hands, stared at them, then looked back at me again. 'You know, McBride, if the law had caught up with you I wouldn't even consider arguing this matter. Your coming back voluntarily even with a possible escape like those missing fingerprints of yours, changes the matter somewhat.'

'It should,' I said. 'Nobody ever heard my side of it before.'

'What *is* your side?'

'Tell me how it happened first.'

His hands made a gesture of resignation. 'I . . . I don't know quite what to think now, McBride. Only Miss West had access to those unclaimed account books. She never had use of them either. I happened to notice her with them one day

60

and wondered why she was taking them out of the vault. She said you wanted to see them. I was curious enough to check and believed I found evidence of fraud.'

'How much was missing?'

His mouth pursed speculatively, as if I should know without asking. 'Two hundred one thousand and eighty-four dollars exactly,' he said.

'That's a screwy total.'

'The District Attorney thought the same thing. An indication that there was an intention of taking more and more. The eighty-four dollars was the remainder of one account that hadn't been entirely cleared out.'

'I see. What happened next?'

'When I sent you and Miss West on vacation at the same time I contacted the District Attorney who, in turn, brought in the State Auditor. They found the shortage and traced it directly to you.'

'That was nice of them,' I said.

'McBride . . . why did you run?'

I wished I could have answered that. If I could say why there wouldn't be a problem left to solve. I shrugged unconcernedly. 'I blew up, that's all. I got chicken about it and took a powder. I'm back now and that's what counts.'

'You came back . . . to clear yourself?'

'What else?'

He leaned back in the chair, folding his arms across his chest. 'This is incredible, simply incredible. I . . . don't know whether to believe you or not.'

'That part's up to you.'

'If . . . mind you, *if* you are telling the truth, I certainly want to see you cleared of this matter. Until now I've had no doubt about it.' He smiled at me sagely. 'But I've made mistakes before and I'm always thankful to be corrected in time. McBride, I'll reserve my judgment until this matter comes to a head one way or another. However, I'm going to put every means at my disposal to work to get the truth.

Every indication we have points to your guilt. Can you give us something to start on?'

'Find Vera West,' I said. 'She'll know.'

'Do you know what happened to her?'

'I've heard a few things. First Servo, then a disappearing act.'

'Then you know quite as much as I do.'

'You'll look for her?'

'I most certainly will. At least the insurance company will and they'll be notified immediately.'

'When she left here, did she leave anything behind? Letters or anything of that sort?'

'No, she cleaned out her desk completely. She's never corresponded with us since, either. If she's working somewhere else she never wrote here for a recommendation.'

I stared at him a second and nodded. I glanced around the room with elaborate casualness, smiling and bobbing my head as if I appreciated the homecoming. I said, 'You know, I miss the old place. How about letting me take a look at my old stall?'

He scowled an answer. 'I don't see . . .'

'Ah, you know how it is after five years. Old things look good.'

He didn't like the idea a bit. It wasn't a businesslike thing to do. But he decided to let a whim be a whim and stood up. If the whole thing hadn't been such a surprise he probably would have tried having me tossed out on my ear. I followed him out the door, down a corridor, through a couple of steel-ribbed gates and into the cashier's booth that was like any other cashier's booth in any other bank in any other city in the world.

There was a guy with a permanently curved back hunched on a stool. He glanced around, then went back to his work. Packets of currency were everywhere. Little individual files flanked the guy on the stool hemming him in. Three open ledgers lay on the side tables.

I saw the alarm button under his foot and another alongside his knee. The handle of a gun stuck out of a shelf under his table-top. While we watched the guy dropped a dime. He was off the stool in a hurry and went down on his knees until he found it. I guess we made him nervous.

I backed out of the booth grinning and shut the door. Gardiner said, 'I don't understand . . .'

'Sentiment,' I muttered.

Sentiment hell. I was feeling sorry for Johnny. Even if he had copped a wad it would have been a good enough excuse to get out of that cage. Now it was easy to see why he took to the outdoors. You got dirty, rained on, cursed at and worked to death, but at least you were free. There was plenty of air around you.

Gardiner took me to the door, unlocked it, passed me through the grillwork outside and walked across the hall to the front door beside me. The animals in their cages stopped talking and tried to make like they were very busy. The guard unlocked the front door and held it open. Gardiner said, 'You'll be staying around town, of course.'

I let the grin split my face in two. It was the kind of a grin that said somebody would die before I left if I left at all. 'I'll be around,' I told him.

Lyncastle Business Group, the plaque read. It was made of bronze set in a mahogany frame and recessed into the wall. The office took up the first floor of the building and none of the doors ever seemed to fully close before somebody shot through them again. I picked what looked to be the main entrance and stepped inside.

A guard in a blue uniform gave me what was supposed to be a polite smile and pointed to a row of benches along the side. There were a dozen men and an elderly woman already parked there waiting. Most were fingering briefcases and casting anxious glances at the clock over the receptionist's desk.

I cast anxious glances at the receptionist.

She was worth looking at. There was no top to the dress. It was cut low across her chest and hugged each breast separately like hands reaching around from behind her. She sat away from the desk so nothing would be in the way of anybody caring for a look at her legs. The dress was black. It had to be black to set off the platinum of her hair. It had to be jersey to stick to her the way it did. Her legs were crossed, but they had to be that way to give somebody in the benches a charge when she uncrossed them.

I walked over to the desk and said, 'You ought to move the clock.'

Her face came up from the cards she was filing still creased with the effort of trying to remember the alphabet. 'Pardon me?'

'Nobody's looking at you.'

'Me?'

'The legs. The bosom. They're the biggest and best in town. Nobody's looking. They're all watching the clock.'

Her eyes ran up the wall to the clock then checked with her wristwatch. 'The clock's right,' she said.

'Skip it. I want to see Lenny.' Such a body going to waste under a brain like that.

'Oh! I'm sorry, but you'll have to wait. You . . . said Lenny?'

'That's right.'

'A friend of his?'

'I could be.'

She scowled again, trying to concentrate on the next question. 'If it's business then you'll . . .'

'It isn't business, beautiful.'

'Oh! Then you're a friend. Well, I'll tell him you're here. Name?'

I told her. She picked up the phone, waited until the connection was made, then told somebody a Mr McBride was outside. Behind me the drone of the voices stopped, waiting to see if I was going to get the busy treatment.

They were disappointed. The blonde nodded solemnly at the phone and hung up. 'Mr Servo will be glad to see you. Immediately, that is.'

'I'd sooner stay here and look at you.'

'But Mr Servo said . . .'

'I know. He'd see me.' I got another frown, then her face brightened. She finally got the point. It sure was a pity.

64

I stepped inside the little gate and on in through the door marked Private. There was another receptionist inside too. This one was a big joker who sat with his chair tipped back against the wall chewing on a cigar. His thumbs were hooked under his arms and the handle of a billy stuck out his pocket.

He said, 'Go on in,' and pointed to the only other door leading off the room.

I went in.

The room was a good thirty feet with windows on two sides and whoever decorated the place must have had a blank cheque in his hand. The throne was a big, flat mahogany desk almost in the centre and the king was perched on the end of it.

He was quite a king. These days they made them in chalk-striped suits and a fresh shave. They made them smooth-looking with dark eyebrows and hair starting to silver up at the temples. They made them with two guys parked in leather upholstered chairs to make sure the king stayed safe.

Lenny Servo sat there looking at me with a face that was trying hard not to show any expression. I said, 'Hello, sucker,' and grinned at the way his mouth pulled tight and his nose showed white streaks along the side.

The weasel-faced punk in the chair couldn't seem to believe his eyes. He got up slowly, smoothed the creases out of his green gabardine suit and let his hands dangle at his sides. They were shaking. His eyes were black little slits over his thin lips and he said, 'You son of a bitch, you.'

The other guy just sat there and watched, trying to make out what it was all about. That made two of us.

Lenny's voice was a pleasant, low-pitched snarl. It was velvet, but if you looked under the velvet you saw the teeth. 'Sit down, Eddie,' he said. 'Mr McBride came to see me, remember?' He never stopped staring at me with those quizzical eyes of his.

I could feel it in the room, whatever it was. Hate. Or fear maybe. Pure, blind emotion, whatever it was. It had Lenny tight as a bow even if he didn't show it. The way everybody was watching me you'd think I was a freak. I stuck a butt in my mouth, lit it to give them time to take a good look and when I thought they had enough I hooked a chair over with my toe and lowered myself on the arm of it. I blew out a mouthful of smoke that drifted right into Lenny's face without ever letting go the grin.

The guy he called Eddie cursed me again.

I said, 'I'm back, pal. You know why I came back?'

A little muscle moved high up on his cheek. It did something to the corner of his mouth and he started to smile. 'Suppose you tell me.'

'Where is she, Lenny?'

The smile went away. 'That's something I'd like to know too,' he said.

He shifted position on the desk. I grinned even bigger. 'You're a slob. I wonder what the hell she ever saw in you.'

The insult didn't faze him a bit. He didn't turn red or anything. He just looked at me. But he was the only one it didn't bother.

The little guy couldn't stay put any longer. He charged out of it and if Lenny hadn't swung his foot out he would have come for me. His eyes were big wide things in a face that was all sucked in and he breathed in tight little gasps. 'Lemme take him, damn it! Lemme do what I said I'd do to him!'

Lenny shoved him gently with his foot. 'In due time, Eddie. Mr McBride understands that, don't you, Mr McBride?'

I took another drag on the butt and looked down at the punk. Just for kicks I reached out, grabbed him by the arms and threw him all the way across the room. He slammed into the chair, knocked it over and took an ash tray along with him.

Nobody said a word. Nobody even breathed. For a minute it was like a tomb in there and when Servo's face came back to mine it was a nasty dead white. 'Tough, aren't you?'

'Uh-huh.'

'You forget very fast, don't you?'

'Uh-huh.'

He slid off the edge of the desk, looked at me until he got his voice back. 'You should have stayed away. You really should have.'

I played it right up to the hilt. It was a brand-new game and I didn't know the rules, the players or the score, but I sure was having fun. I said, 'I want Vera, Lenny. If you got any idea where she is at all, you better produce her quick. You know what'll happen if you don't?'

Lenny didn't get it. He was the king and nobody spoke to him like that. The other guy with the knife scar on his face got it though. His mouth hung open and he watched the two of us like a farm boy at his first burlesque. Lenny's breath was hot in my face. 'McBride . . .'

I hit him then. It chopped his words off in the middle and spun him around the corner of the desk. He grabbed, hung on, then slid to the floor. I threw the butt on the top of the desk and walked back out. The gorilla was still there in his chair still chewing on his cigar. He was grinning until he saw me. It was a sure bet he thought I was the one getting pushed around inside.

'You shoulda been there,' I told him. 'It was fun.'

He was still thinking about it when I opened the door to the outer office. The benches were empty and the blonde was shrugging her bare shoulders into a bolero jacket that put her in the decency class again. She saw me and smiled. 'Finished?'

'For now I am. You going home?'

Her eyes went to the clock. It was an even five. 'Uh-huh.'

'Swell. I'll walk you down.'

'But I have to tell Mr Servo . . .'

'Whatever you have to tell him, he won't want to hear, sugar.'

'Oh, you're wrong. I always . . .'

'Mr Servo is sick,' I said gently.

'Sick? He's never sick. What's wrong with him?'

'He just had the crap kicked outa him. Coming?'

Her eyes got a little cloudy, but she didn't say anything until I took her arm and walked her outside. Going down the stairs she said solemnly, 'You're in an awful lot of trouble, Mr McBride. You know that?'

'Yeah,' I answered, 'yeah, I guess I am at that.'

There was a bar right across the street from the building and it didn't take much persuasion to steer her in and onto a stool set at right angles to the street. Her name was Carol Shay, she was twenty-six years old, had an apartment downtown someplace, a yearning to try her luck in the movies and a yen for one Manhattan after another.

After a half-dozen of the things she got giggly and tugged on my sleeve until I turned around. 'You're not talking to me, Mr McBride.'

'I was watching the office across the street. Thought maybe I'd have a chance to see my pals come out. It would've made good watching.'

She giggled again and sipped her Manhattan. 'Oh, forget them. They'll go down the back way.'

My ears pricked up at that. 'Why?'

'Keeps the car down there. All his private appointments come up that way.'

'Then what's he got you for?'

She squealed into her glass and raked her nails across the back of my hand. 'He likes to look at me. Besides, I'm dumb.' Her eyes came up and laughed into mine. 'I really am,' she insisted.

I grinned back at her. Platinum head was dumb all right. Like a fox. For a hundred bucks a week she could afford to be as dumb as they come.

She said, 'Why'd you hit Lenny? Did you really do like you said?'

'Uh-huh. A little guy too. His name was Eddie.'

'You did!' Her eyebrows were perfect parentheses, nearly reaching her hair. 'That's Eddie Packman.' Her voice went down to a lower register. 'He's worse than Lenny.'

'Swell. It'll be more fun when we meet up again.'

'You're crazy!'

'Nope, just mad. How long was Lenny in his office today?'

'All day.'

'Sure?'

'Of course I'm sure. He was in his office with the others since nine this morning. They even had their lunches sent up. Why?'

'Oh, nothing special. Somebody tried to bump me this morning and I was wondering if it could have been our boy.' I got another incredulous stare before she turned back to the bar. 'He could have gone down that back way you mentioned,' I said.

'No. He was there. I had to call in for him often enough.'

I hooked my finger under her chin and pulled her head around. 'Not that often. I bet there was at least an hour there when he never was near his phone. Right?'

'I . . . I don't know. I just don't know.'

'That's O.K.,' I said, 'all I want is enough to make it look like it could have been him. That's enough reason for taking him apart.'

'I need a drink,' she said. 'I hope to hell nobody sees me sitting here with you.'

So I got her another drink, watched her drink it and bought one more to keep it company. 'What's the score up there, Carol?'

I could see her fingers freeze around the glass. 'What do you mean?'

'You know what I mean. Is that place the headquarters for everything that happens in this town?'

She took a long time before nodding her head.

'Like what?'

Her smile wasn't so bright this time. It seemed a little sad and a little lost. 'Look, feller, I'm dumb. I'm beautiful but dumb. If you want to play any games, keep them between you and Mr Servo or Eddie Packman. I don't know anything at all and I'm glad I don't because if I did you're just the kind of a guy who could put on an act I'd go for and make me put myself in a jam.'

'Like me?'

'You're nice.'

'Say it better.'

She propped her chin in her hand and looked at me sleepily. 'I like big guys. I like the ones who can come out on top and who don't give a damn for anything. I like them smart and beefed up so they don't have to wear any padding in their suits. I like mean faces and short haircuts. I could go for a guy who could slap Lenny Servo around and get away with it. The only trouble is they never live long enough for me to enjoy.'

'You tried it already?'

'That's telling.'

'Your boss isn't a good guy to kick the crap outa, huh?'

'Nope.'

I lit a butt and blew a shaft of smoke around the glass in front of me. 'I hear he's a ladies' man.'

'Nuts! He's a male nympho, whatever that is.'

'A saytr. Who's his current?'

'Some hot number from upstate who knows that the best way to his heart isn't through his stomach. He keeps her in nylons in his apartment.'

'Look,' I said, 'what do you think will happen to me?'

A frown flitted across her face. 'I . . . don't know, really. Somebody . . .'

'Go on.'

'Things just happen, that's all. Don't ask me questions like that. If I were you I'd take the first train out of here.' Her fingers closed over mine. 'Do me a favour . . . leave.'

'I like it here.'

The glass sat on the edge of her lip a moment, then tipped sharply as she drained it. The bartender came over and made her another one without asking. It was on the house. 'You would,' she said, then knocked that drink off too. When she turned around her mouth was pulled down wryly. 'Damn all big guys. Come on, take me home.'

When she got off the stool she almost went on her nose. I got her outside, whistled down a cab and shoved her in. By the time we reached her apartment she was all giggles and insisted on me seeing her to the door.

The only trouble was, she fell asleep in the elevator and I had to carry her from door to door looking for Shay on a nameplate until I found it, then fish out a key from the bottom of her handbag to get in.

It was a tricky little three-room apartment with the bedroom opening off one corner of the living-room. I kicked the door open, dumped her on the bed and tossed her bag on the dresser.

I started to leave when she said plaintively, 'You forgot to undress me.'

And there she was grinning at me, her eyes swimming through the blur of the Manhattans, but still very much awake.

'The zipper runs all the way down the back,' she said.

'I know. And there's only one hook on the gimmick and your stockings are held up by adhesive tape.'

She giggled again and raised one leg up slowly. Her dress fell back as far as it could ever get until she was all nice bare skin and sheer nylon that sent fingers crawling up the back of my neck. 'You're so right,' she said. 'Now unzip me.'

I stuck two cigarettes in my mouth, lit them and tossed one on the bed beside her. 'Some other time.'

She sure knew how to pout. She let her leg fall and picked up the butt from the spread. 'You're mean.'

'Yeah, a real killer.' I grinned again and walked out.

She let me get as far as the front door. 'If you want, you can come back here and hide from Lenny. For ever.'

Nice kid. Obliging.

'Maybe I will,' I called back. I stepped outside, tried the door to make sure it was locked and got in the elevator.

I was all the way down on the street when I remembered that I'd wanted to ask her if that peroxide didn't sting like hell.

I expected an ultra-modern apartment house with a door-man. I got a six-storey affair with a self-service elevator. I expected a bronze doorknocker shaped like a roulette wheel. I got a brass push button. I expected a name embossed in gold and got a plain printed card in a metal frame.

I expected anybody to open the door but a sleepy-eyed vixen with flaming red hair who offered me a drink out of her glass before she said hello. I took the drink because it seemed like the polite thing to do.

When I finished half of it I handed it back. 'You always answer the door like that?'

'I like to be naked,' she purred.

'Doesn't anybody ever complain?'

She grinned at me as if I'd made a joke and finished the rest of the drink.

'You selling anything?'

'No, are you?'

'It's sold,' she said. 'You want Lenny, don't you?'

'That's right,' I lied.

'He isn't here but you can come in and wait.'

She held the door open and closed it behind me. Now it was just what I had expected. Plush. Real plush. There was a room with books, a room with a bar, rooms with all the fineries of life and a special room with an oversized bed that was ready for use.

I looked at everything there was to see, but I had to quit sometime, and there she was, curled up in an overstuffed easy chair, naked as hell, watching me over the rim of a fresh drink. You don't describe naked women when you walk right in and find them like that. They're just naked, that's all. They're kind of white and soft and everything seems to be in motion all at once. Watch 'em for just a little while and all of a sudden you're used to them and it's over with. Then you can talk.

I said, 'How long have you been around, sis?'

'Oh, a long time. For years and years. Are you a cop?' Before I could answer she shook her head, making her hair ripple down her back. 'No, you wouldn't be a cop. A cop would never have come in. A friend?' Her head shook again. 'That couldn't be it either. A friend would know better than to come in. A reporter maybe? Nope, not a reporter or I would have been raped.' She giggled and sipped her drink, making a pretence of being serious. 'You must be an enemy. That's the answer.'

I lit a cigarette and waited until she put the drink down. She had to uncurl to reach the coffee table and did it with a lazy snaky motion. She leaned back in the chair and stretched, her breasts taut, then pulled her stomach in and relaxed. 'Do you know what Lenny'll do to you if he finds you here?'

'No, tell me about it.'

Another insane giggle. 'That would spoil the fun. No, I'll wait. You can talk and look at me while we wait. All you want to.' She reached for the glass again, struggled to claw out an ice cube and held it while she sucked on it. 'Now talk,' she said.

'Ever know a girl named Vera West?'

The ice cube dropped in her lap. She got it back after a frenzied search and frowned at me. 'Lenny isn't going to like you.'

'I don't expect him to. What about it?'

'I heard of her.'

'Where is she?'

'Oh, she's gone and I'm taking care of Lenny now. Who cares?'

'I care, sis. Where is she?'

She tossed her head impatiently. 'How would I know? She's been gone so long nobody knows. One time she was here, then she was gone. Just like that. Besides, I don't like her.'

'Why?'

'Lenny talks about her, that's why. He gets drunk sometimes and calls me by her name and sometimes I hear him swearing at her in his sleep. As long as he's swearing I don't care, but I don't like him calling me with her name.'

'What would happen if Lenny found her?'

'I know what would happen if I found her.'

She plopped the ice cube in her mouth, washed it around until it was melted then swallowed it. It must have made a cold track going down because she got gooseflesh all over. There was a lot of her to get goosefleshed. She shivered as if she liked it and reached out for another. This time she really stretched out for my benefit, making sure I didn't miss anything. I think she was starting to get mad.

I said, 'What would happen?'

Her tongue toyed with the ice cube. 'I'd fix her so no man would ever want to look at her again. I'd fix her good. Someday I'll find her. I think I know how, too.'

'You do? How?'

Something happened to her eyes. They started to match her hair. 'What'll you give me if I tell you?'

'What do you want?'

'That's a silly question.'

There was no doubt about her eyes. They were simmering coals waiting to be blown into life. They were half shielded by her lids so they looked lazy, but they weren't. It wasn't the first time I'd seen eyes like hers either.

I said, 'Lenny's nuts about you, isn't he?'

'Certainly.' She dragged the word out. 'Lenny's oversexed too.'

I pushed up out of the chair. 'Excuse me. Be right back.' She didn't say anything so I walked through the room. It only took a couple minutes to find out what I wanted to find out. On the dresser in the bedroom was a small fortune in diamonds and a slightly smaller fortune in pearls was strung over the tap in the bathroom sink. Her pocketbook was on the telephone stand and there were C notes stuffed in it with a few fins like poor relations guarding the roll.

No place in the house was there even so much as a pair of lace panties.

Lenny was so nuts about his little chipmunk that he wasn't taking any chances on her leaving the nest. The only way he could keep his nymph at home was to garnishee her clothes and I couldn't think of a better way if I tried.

When I went back inside she wasn't in the chair. She was stretched out on the couch with a cigarette in each hand daring me to come over and have a smoke. I took the dare. I reached for the cigarette but I wasn't watching close enough. She twisted it and touched the hot tip to my hand and laughed when my mouth went tight.

To her it was fun. A very nice little chipmunk. She and Lenny must have had some great times together.

'You mentioned something about finding Vera West,' I reminded her.

'Vera? Oh . . . I did, didn't I?'

I said, 'Maybe I better ask Lenny like I came here to. When will he be back?'

She twisted on the couch, doing things that were supposed to make me forget what I came for. 'Oh, not for hours and hours,' she grinned.

Those kind of games I could play too. It was an awful waste, but she was too naked to be exciting. She should have used a curtain or something. Anything. I flipped the lit butt and it landed right on her belly. Her eyes popped open wide and she doubled up with a curse. It was funnier than with the ice cube.

I laughed once and started off to the door. I looked back in case she was getting ready to throw something. A dame like that can go off the handle pretty hard.

Hell, she wasn't even mad. She was grinning and her eyes were brighter than her hair. 'I have some mean things I'm going to do to you for that,' she said. The pause between her words slowed me down. 'When you come back,' she added softly.

I pushed the button and waited for the elevator to come back up. My reflection was grinning at me in the black glass window of the door. Nice having a couple of red hots throw themselves at you in the same half-hour. Some town, this Lyncastle.

The super had his apartment in the back of the building. He was short, bald and toothless, but the thousands of ash barrels he had hefted gave him arms like kegs. Before I said anything I held up a ten-spot and let him look at it.

He liked it.

He showed me his gums and picked it out of my fingers. 'Come on in.'

When he picked a couple of dirty undershirts off the chairs in the living-room he nodded for me to sit down. He squatted across the room from me still playing with the bill. 'So you're nosing for news. Who of? Servo? The whores on the top floor?'

'You catch on quick, don't you?'

75

'Nah. Them's the only two in the place anybody'd pay fer news of.'

'Who else has been asking?'

'You a cop?'

'Nope.'

'Reporter?'

'Nobody that counts. I just want information.'

'O.K. The whores pay off to the cops. They send people around to ask how business is. It's good, they pay steeper, you know?'

'And Servo?'

He let out a gummy chuckle. 'Ever hear of honest cops? We got some here. Guy by the name of Lindsey.'

'I know him,' I said.

'So he keeps after Servo. Likes to know who his contacts is, you know?'

'Yeah. Who are they?'

'For ten bucks I should stick my neck out? Mister, for a hunnert I don't even know nuthin'. For five maybe I could scare up something.'

'If you're dead you can't spend five hundred any better than ten.'

His eyes glittered at me. 'No, but with five I could clear outa this trap. Me fer the country, see? Can't make no dough around here.'

'Got anything worth five hundred?'

The glitter disappeared and he shook his head. 'Well, I ain't even got anythin' worth ten. I'm only kidding myself. It's a long time since I seen any company and I felt like talking, you know?'

I leaned back in the chair and stretched out my legs. Time wasn't that important. Talk, that was what I wanted. Small talk. Big talk. After five years talk was all you had to go by anyway. I said, 'How long has Servo been here?'

The guy seemed to relax somewhat. Maybe he felt the way I felt and knew how interesting the subject was. 'Oh, he been here almost ever since he came. Spent a fortune getting his place redecorated. You oughta see the chippy he got up there.'

76

'I did.'

I saw his Adam's apple move as he swallowed. He leaned forward in his chair tensely. 'Yeah . . . how was she?'

'Bare. She wanted to play. I didn't.'

He swallowed again. A vein throbbed in his neck. 'Cripes, what a dame! I go up there to fix a tap and she don't have nothin' on. You know what she did? I start uncorking the nut and alla time she's talking to me sexy so my hands can hardly hold that damn wrench, then when I'm not looking she grabs a ball-peen hammer outa my kit and . . .'

'What about his other women?'

His eyes lost their glaze. He stared at me, blinked and sat back, chewing on his lip. 'He always got good lookers.'

'Remember any of 'em?'

'Sure. Remember 'em all. This one is best.'

I shook out another butt and lit it, thinking through the smoke. 'A long time ago he had one named Vera West. Remember her?' When he didn't answer right away I said, 'Well?'

He was flexing the muscles in his arms, his face tight. 'Mac,' he told me slowly, 'I don't know you from nobody, but she's one dame I don't talk about.'

I didn't waste time offering him another bill. I just kept it friendly and said, 'Don't blame you. She was O.K. I don't want that kind of dope about her.'

'Yer damn right she was O.K. So she was always plenty high. She was one of them party girls or something, but even a looker gotta live. She was still O.K. and knocked Servo off'n his high horse plenty. Hell, I heard him plenty of times tryin' to get her to shack up there. She gives him the business. Lenny, he likes the treatment so he keeps her around. Maybe he gets tired of the easy stuff. But like I said, she was O.K. Time I got clipped by the car she gimme a transfusion. Hardly knew me at all, but she gimme blood.'

'She's disappeared.'

'So I hear,' he said sourly. 'I hope she had sense to get a roll together and blow this dump. That's what she did, I think.'

I let another trailer of smoke drift towards the ceiling. 'Servo didn't like that, huh?'

'He was pretty burned about it. Hell, he got another one in fast enough. They last awhile then he kicks 'em out. That redhead upstairs must be pretty good. She's sticking around. She got a temper, that one. Oughta hear her work Lenny over. She makes him jump.'

'What she's got anybody'd jump for,' I said.

'Not that kind of jump, pally. She's boss up there. Like a wife, you know?'

'Happens after awhile,' I said. I got up, stretched and stubbed my butt out in an ash tray. 'Maybe I'll drop in again sometime. If you think you have anything worth five hundred bucks, keep it under your hat until I see you.'

'Sure.' He walked me as far as the door and opened it. 'There was a fight up there last night,' he said.

I stopped and looked down at him. 'The dame?'

'No. Him and some other guy. They tried to keep it quiet, but I heard 'em. I was up on the roof.'

'What went on?'

'Beats me. He got air-conditioning and all the windows stays closed. I heard 'em yelling at each other, but I couldn't catch none of it. They was plenty sore.'

'Know who it was?'

'Just know one was Servo. He did most of the yelling.'

'Oh!' I thought it over, tacked it down in the facts-to-be-remembered department and thanked the guy. He gave me another gummy grin and let me out.

For a while I stood outside the building looking at the long slanting shadows on the street. I finished a cigarette and had another, but they didn't do much good. I tried to think, to figure angles, to put things together, but nothing clicked in place.

Try walking in a town sometime. Try picking up pieces that are five years old. Try finding a girl named Vera West without tipping your hand to the whole population, I thought.

So far it had been great. I got beat up, shot at, slapped a hood around and almost seduced. It hadn't been a bad beginning. At least I knew how important I was.

Or the real Johnny.

He was so damned important he either had to be run out of town or killed quick. But why? Damn it, why run him out of town if he could have been bumped to start with? That much was clear. It was better to have him run for it than dead. But why, damn it, why?

Did he run from Minnow's murder or the two hundred grand? Either one was a good excuse, but which one?

I threw the butt in the gutter and walked down the street. Maybe it would have been better if I had stayed with old gummy. At least the guy had wanted to talk. If I had talked it out maybe I could have thought of something.

I turned in at a drugstore and went back to the phone booth. I tried to call Logan and couldn't get him. The next nickel got me the bus station and Nick. He got all jumpy again when I told him it was me.

He said, 'What're you doing? You're all right, aren't you?'

'Nothing's wrong with me. I'm trying to think. You got any time to spare?'

'Sure, plenty. Nothing's due in for an hour. You had me pretty worried, boy. Wendy called and said you wouldn't stay at her place.'

'How is blondie?'

'Fine. She sure was sore at you.'

'Too bad.' Then I thought of it. I said, 'I'm coming down to the station. How about calling her for me. Think she'd come?'

'Yeah . . .' he slowed up a bit and added, 'sure, she won't be leaving for Louie's for a while.'

Now I had something to do. It was something I could chew on while a cab hauled me down to the station. I could pass it around in my mind and it made better sense each time. Nick and Blondie. They were right there on the end of the receiving line when I came to town. The very front end.

79

They said hello and patted me on the back. They played it sweet and low and not long after somebody was pumping a slug in my direction.

The cabbie skidded his wheels in the gravel outside the station, marked something on a report sheet and held his hand out. I put a buck in it and climbed out.

Both of them were inside the office. The window was closed, the little radio was blaring away and there was a steaming container of coffee on the table. Nick shut the door behind me, locked it and pumped my hand.

And over by the wall there was Wendy. Blondie. Beautiful blonde Wendy with the lovely legs and round hillocks that tried to peek out of the dress. She was a good-looking twist if you didn't get too close. She was smiling and shrugging out of a light trench coat and the motion shoved her breasts out for inspection. It didn't take a second look to see that if she had anything on under the white blouse it must have been painted on with a brush. The skirt part of the ensemble was too tight around the hips, but it was designed that way. There was the suggestion of a rumba in every motion she made and for good measure a slit ran up the side seam to let the flash of nylon show through, and if you looked hard enough the slippery sheen of skin above where the nylon ended.

She threw the coat over the back of a chair and sat down. Nick did too.

Not me.

I stood there with my back against the door looking at the two of them and my face must have made a picture of everything that went on in my mind. Wendy's lips moved as if to say something, but Nick cut her off. He frowned at me: 'What's wrong with you? I . . .'

My mouth pulled tight in the corners. 'Did I ever tell you what was going to happen to three people?' They looked at each other wonderingly, then back to me. 'One's going to die,' I said. 'One's going to get his arms broken. The other one is going to get the hell kicked out of her.'

Wendy's fingers locked on the arms of the chair. She was half up and her eyes were a nasty blaze. Like a fast fuse. 'Say it,' she snapped out.

'I got shot at.'

Pop let out a startled grunt. 'Johnny . . .'

'Shut up. I'll get to you.'

Wendy was a sharp little cookie. She caught wise in a hurry. So she had nice legs and a nicer bosom, but she wasn't drawing any admiration from my side of the room at all. I looked at her and looked at her, trying to decide if a sweet dish like her could bump a guy and decided she could. I said, 'Where you been all day?'

'Why?'

'Answer me.'

The eyes got brighter if anything. 'Don't be so damned domineering. I don't like tough guys . . . if you're a tough guy.'

'I'm tough enough. You can find that out if you want to. Some other people already did.'

The corners of her mouth looked strained. 'So now you think one of us shot at you?'

'Maybe, sugar, maybe. It's pretty simple when you think of it. Who else knew I was in town? I can rattle them off on my hand if you want. Nick here. You. Lindsey. Tucker. Maybe I should throw in the bellboys at the hotel and the taxi driver.' My eyes closed down on themselves and I watched her face. 'It even gets simpler. Lindsey or Tucker wouldn't have missed. Nick couldn't see that far. The bellboys and hack jockey weren't important enough to try a stunt like that. That leaves you. Funny, isn't it?'

I smiled at her.

She didn't smile back. The white lines at each end of her mouth faded. For the first time it grew soft and pretty and if I didn't know better I would have thought she was feeling sorry for me.

She said, 'At a quarter to nine the mailman awakened me. I had to sign for a registered letter. You can check on that. About twenty minutes later the milkman got me up again and I paid my bill. His name is Jerry Wyndot and you can reach him at the Lyncastle Dairy. Before he left Louie drove by with my new costume and stayed until noon. He had a friend with him from ASCAP. Then at . . .'

'That's enough,' I said. I felt a little foolish. I went over to the table and reached for the coffee. When I took a good pull I set it down and wiped my mouth with the back of my hand. Nick was shaking his head sadly. 'Sorry, kid. I never make little mistakes, only big ones.'

Her eyes came up to mine and the fire was out of them.

'That's all right, Johnny, I understand.' The little smile she gave me said she meant it, too.

I laugh when I feel good. Hell, I felt good! When do you meet a dame that lets you throw an attempted murder in her teeth and then understands why without being sore about it for a week?

I laughed, Nick thought I was nuts, but Wendy, she laughed too. In a way it was a pretty good joke. I parked on Nick's window stool and passed the butts around. 'I get in trouble a lot that way,' I told them.

Nick agreed readily. 'You'll get in too much to get out of if you do that to the wrong people. Maybe now you're ready to say what you came to say.'

'I didn't come to say, Nick. Ask is the word. I'm stuck. What do I do now?'

Wendy pulled on her cigarette. 'Stuck for what?'

'Ideas. Information. I can't go to the cops and nobody else knows anything. Lindsey has a murder charge written out with my name on it and he can't serve it. Someday he's going to find a way to do it, but before then I have to get clear of the thing. Unless I do I can't make a play without sticking my neck out.'

Nick slid his chair closer to the table and propped his elbows on it. 'You tell us, Johnny. Shucks, I know plenty of people I can go to. What's it you need?'

Things I never even thought about before started popping in my head. 'I don't like the way Minnow died. He was sitting there and bang, just like that he caught it. Neat. Clean. No fuss. And there I was with a beautiful tailor-made motive for bumping him.'

'The gun,' Wendy said quietly. Her eyes sprayed me with a cool glance. Nick looked at my hands automatically and waited to hear what I had to say about it.

'Yeah, the gun,' I repeated. The big question. Lindsey asked it. Wendy asked it. Inside, I was asking it myself. 'I wonder what Minnow was doing there that night.'

'The papers said he was working,' Nick muttered. 'It was his office.'

'It was pretty late, too.'

'What are you getting at?'

'Back to what I said first. I didn't like the way he died. He should have been out of his chair on the floor or something. If he was surprised in the office by the killer, especially me, he would have tried to make one move, at least.'

Nick pulled at his whiskers. 'You got medals for shooting quick and fast in the army, Johnny.' There wasn't any hedging about him at all.

'Not that fast,' I said. 'I like it better to think that the killer was there all the time. Maybe Minnow even went there to meet him. What about that?'

They said it together. 'Maybe.' They meant me. It was getting rougher.

'How can I find out?'

Wendy crossed one leg over the other. White, slippery white above nylon showed through the slit in the skirt. 'Minnow left a widow. She might know.'

'Know where she lives?'

'I can find out.'

I got down off the stool. 'Come on, then. Let's find out.'

She lived in a white frame house in the suburbs. It was a quiet neighbourhood and all the houses had plenty of lawn space around them. There were swings out in the back and kids playing on the lawns and people gathered in hammocks on open porches. The house we wanted had a fence around it, a bird house on a pole and a rustic sign that said 'Minnow'.

I opened the gate and let Wendy go in ahead of me. She went up on the porch, rang the bell and smiled at me while we waited. The door opened and a woman in her fifties said, 'Hello, can I do something for you?'

'Mrs Minnow?'

She nodded at Wendy. 'That's right.'

It was hard trying to find the right words. I stepped forward and said, 'If you have a few minutes, we'd like to talk to you. It's pretty important.'

She held the door open wide. 'Certainly, come right in. Make yourselves at home.' We stepped inside and followed her into the living-room. It was a nice room that told you that whoever lived there liked things orderly and in good taste. Wendy and I sat together on the couch while the woman settled herself. She smiled again and waited.

'It's about your . . . husband,' I started.

At one time it might have startled her. Not now. She sat there relaxed, but there was a question in her face.

'My name is Johnny McBride.'

'I know.'

Wendy and I stared at her.

'I couldn't very well forget your face, could I?'

'You don't seem very excited about it.'

'Should I be?'

'I was supposed to have killed your husband.'

'Did you?' Cripes! She was more like my mother waiting to hear why I got a low grade at school.

I said, 'No.'

'Then why should I be excited?'

The pitch was too fast for me. I shook my head. 'I don't get it.'

'I never thought you shot my husband either,' she said.

Wendy's fingernails made a sharp *click* in the silence. She

84

was staring at the woman, shot me a glance out of the corner of her eyes and went back to picking at her nails.

I came out of it. 'Let's do it over again, Mrs Minnow. I'm still in the fog. If you thought I didn't do it then why not go to the police?'

'Mr McBride, by the time I came to that conclusion the police had already made their decision. In all fairness to Captain Lindsey, let me say that I *did* tell him what I thought, but he didn't consider it reasonable. Since I spoke to him I've gone over the matter carefully enough to be sure I'm right. I've been waiting.'

'For what?'

'You. A man never stays away from murder. Not if he didn't do it.'

'Thanks. Or do I remind you about the fingerprints on the gun?'

Her smile was a tight knowing thing. 'That's something for you to figure out, young man.'

'Great. With a detail like that in the picture how'd you figure me innocent?'

She leaned back in her chair with something like a sigh. 'Bob and I were married a long time. Did you know he was a police officer in New York before he took up law? Well, he was. A good one, too. A better one after he was made District Attorney. Bob never put too much store in details. He was more interested in motive.' Her eyes passed over mine. 'The motive behind his death wasn't revenge.'

'What was it then?'

'I'm not quite sure.'

'The night he died . . . why'd he go to his office?'

'I'll have to go back a way to explain that. He told me that one day a girl came to his office. She was frightened and left a letter with him that wasn't to be opened unless she died. That may seem unusual, but it isn't. He had several requests like that every year. However, he forgot to put it in his office safe and brought it home with him. That night he put it in his safe upstairs and forgot about it.

'Several months later he came home quite worried and asked me about the letter. I reminded him where he had put it and he seemed satisfied. That evening when I brought his tea to his room upstairs he was sitting in front of the safe quite preoccupied and I saw him take the letter out of one of the compartments, stare at it a moment, then put it back.

'Two nights later he had a call from New York. It seemed to excite him and I heard him mention the word "verification" several times. He went upstairs and I heard him open the safe. When he came back down he put on his hat and coat, left the house for a good two hours, came back, went to his safe again and stayed in his room working on some papers. A few minutes later he had a call from his office, told me he had to leave and went out. I never saw him again. He was killed that night.'

'Who called him?'

'An officer named Tucker.'

My hands knotted into fists. 'Why?'

'A special-delivery letter came for Bob. He wanted to know if he should hold it or deliver it to him at the house here. Bob told him he'd come down and get it.'

Damn, damn, damn! I was all ready to catch the big bite and it had to turn out simple. Tucker, the bastard! I said, 'Lindsey checked on all this?'

'Oh, yes, indeed.'

She was waiting for me to ask the next question. It was right there ready to be asked, so I did. 'What happened to the letter?'

'I don't know. When I went over his effects the safe was open and I noticed that it wasn't where I had seen it before. Captain Lindsey showed me all that were in Bob's office, but since it was nothing but a plain white envelope I couldn't help out.'

'You think he died because of that letter?'

'Among other things. It was fortunate for a lot of people that he died.'

'Servo?'

She nodded.

'Me?'

She smiled and nodded again.

'A whole crooked set-up in a whole crooked town?'

The smile also got a little crooked, but she nodded.

I said, 'The motive could have been a lot of things then?'

'Anything except sudden revenge. That was too easy.'

'I thought so too,' I told her. She raised her eyebrows a trifle and her mouth made a funny arc. Something made her face look a little bit happy when it wasn't the time and place to be happy. She looked at me like a mother who knew her kid was telling a lie but waiting for him to say so first.

It made me uncomfortable as hell so I stood up and nudged Wendy. 'Thanks, Mrs Minnow. It's been a help.'

'I'm glad. If there's anything else, you let me know. I'm in the phone book.'

She took us to the door and said goodbye. I could feel her watch us all the way down the walk to Wendy's car and even after we had headed back to town. For a few minutes I didn't say anything. I just let it go through my head and find a place to settle down. When it was put where I'd never forget it, I said, 'What do you think?'

'Strange woman.' She kept her eyes on the road. 'I wonder how I'd feel if I were she.'

'She isn't stupid.'

'No, she seems quite convinced.'

'What about you?'

'Does it matter?'

'Not particularly.'

She stopped for a red light, tapped her fingers against the wheel until it changed and eased back in gear again. 'I'm not so sure,' she said.

I let it go at that. It didn't make a damn bit of difference to me what anybody thought about what as long as they didn't try to stop me. I sat back and folded my arms, still thinking about the letter. The street we were on intersected the main drag and down a half-mile or so Lyncastle was making the night look like an oversize pinball machine.

The car swung into the kerb and stopped. Wendy said, 'I'll let you out here. I have to pick up my clothes and get out to Louie's.'

'Can't you take me downtown?'

'I'm in an awful hurry, Johnny.'

I grinned at her. 'O.K., working girl. Thanks for the lift.' I opened the door and shoved my legs out.

Her hand hooked under my arm and she stopped me. When I looked at her she had that same expression the Minnow woman had. 'Johnny . . . in your own way you're a nice guy. I hope you know what you're doing.'

'I do.'

'And, Johnny . . . I'm . . . pretty sure.' She wrinkled her nose like a little kid and a laugh parted her lips.

I leaned over. I let her have plenty of time to see what she was getting. Only this time I didn't have to pull her across the seat. She met me halfway and her mouth had a tingling warmth to it as it tasted mine.

She pouted when I stopped and threw me a kiss when I waved so-long. I watched her drive out of sight, hopped a cab for town and got off in the middle of what the cab driver said was the hottest spot in the good old U.S.A.

CHAPTER SIX

I spent the rest of the evening making the rounds of the joints in town. For a couple of hours I put the beer away while I tried to get a line on Vera West and at ten o'clock all I had was two people who remembered having seen her with Servo.

At five minutes after ten I left the Blue Mirror and decided to let the guy who had been tailing me catch up with me. He had picked me up at the second joint I was in and had stuck like a leech ever since.

He was a short stocky guy in a grey suit and grey summer hat who walked with a crab and his left arm cocked at the elbow to keep the rod under his arm in place. The cops in this town certainly needed a few lessons in shadowing.

I turned off the main street, crossing over into a residential district until I found a corner nicely shrouded in shadows. From the way I was walking he must have thought I was going somewhere and figured I wouldn't be thinking of having a tail.

When I made the corner I stepped back into the hedges and waited for him to come around the bend. He walked right into my hands and I had his elbows pinned behind his back before he even started cursing. I shoved my knee into his spine and jerked him back like a bow. 'Just make one funny move and you're gonna break in two, mister.'

So he didn't move a bit. Not an inch. He let me pull his rod out and drop it on the turf then fish for his wallet. I dropped that and all he had in his pockets and what I was looking for he didn't have.

A badge.

I gave another little twitch and the scream that started up his throat got cut off in the middle. 'Who sent you, pal?'

His head came back and his hat fell off. In the dull light his eyes were a couple of big glass marbles. The spit ran down the corner of his mouth, dripping off his chin. I eased up and asked him again and that was as far as I got. Someplace far off there was a sharp crack and the night got darker and darker until it was just an empty void and I was floating in the middle of it.

After a while the floating merged into a series of hard jolts that was a hammer beating against my skull. There were voices and sounds again, coming back slowly. Moving hurt, so I sat where I was until the blasting inside my brain subsided.

One of the voices said, 'Goddamn it, he nearly cracked me in half!'

'Ah, shaddup, you asked for it. You was climbing up his back all the way.'

The first voice let out a series of curses that took in everybody. 'You wasn't supposed to be more'n a block away, goddamn it! You took your time about getting there.'

'So what? We got there, didn't we? There was a red light before we made the turn. You want we should get a ticket?'

'Ticket, hell! For a ticket I should get a broken back? Some son of a bitch is gonna pay for this. Damn 'em, this guy was supposed to be a drip. Easy, the son of a bitch said. He'd shake in his shoes if you yelled at 'im.'

'Quit crying. You found out who he was. He got medals in the army fer being a rough apple.'

'So what? The lousy bastard said he was one of them fatigue cases. He was yellow. He was scared of fighting any more. Maybe I shoulda asked him first, huh? Maybe I shoulda found out for myself before I got my back damn near broke!'

'He's here, ain't he?'

'So'm I, but I don't feel so good. For a guy what's supposed to be yellow he damn near done all right. Maybe these big guys get yellow after a while, but they don't stay that way. That war was a long way off.'

The words formed inside my head without being spoken. I felt like thanking the guy. There were a lot of people who thought Johnny was yellow. First Nick. Then Logan. Somebody else figured that way and their boys fell for it. So a guy is yellow because he gets his belly full of killing. He gets so that he doesn't want any part of killing or the things that cause it and they call him yellow. A typical civilian attitude. *Here's a gun, go get them, feller. Attaboy, Johnny, good job. Here's some more bullets. What? You've had enough of it? Why, you yellow-bellied bastard, get away from me!*

Somebody next to me started laughing at the argument and I turned my head. The guy caught the movement and the snout of a gun rammed into my ribs. 'Sonny's awake back here,' he said.

The little guy who had tailed me turned around in his seat. His arm was a blur of motion and his fist cracked across my mouth. 'You bastard, I'll show you something.'

He would have done it again if the guy beside me hadn't shoved him back. 'Lay off, jerk. You pile us up and you'll be the one getting a ride, not him. Now sit down and keep your trap closed.'

It was nice knowing what was going on. I wiped the blood off my lips with the back of my hand. I said, 'So this is it?'

The gun in my ribs pressed in a little deeper. 'That's right, sonny, this is it. Let me tell you something. You're a big boy and you like to play rough, but this gun is loaded and cocked and the first move you make you get it sideways, right across your belly. It'll take a long time to die that way. Be nice and it'll be all over with quick.'

'Thanks.'

I sat back and enjoyed the ride. Hell, what else was there to do? We were out on the highway and the city was only a faint reflection in the rear-view mirror. There were cars going by every once in a while, but going too fast to yell and attract attention before I caught a bullet in the ribs. The car was a two-door job besides, so there wasn't any chance of taking a dive even if I wanted to.

We must have been about a half-hour out of Lyncastle before the guy at the wheel pulled off the highway onto a dirt road. Until then it hadn't been so bad. Now my heart started pounding against my chest like a wild thing trying to beat its way out. The guy beside me felt me stiffen up and nudged me with the gun as a reminder that he was still there.

It was pitch black, darker than the void I had swum in, with the driver feeling his way along on his dimmers. The road curved and started to rise, then flattened out and disappeared altogether. Just before the lights went off entirely I had a chance to see the reflection of the stars in the water and knew that the road was a dead end up to a quarry of some sort.

The guy said, 'Out.'

One of the others held the seat down so I could crawl out the door. He had a gun facing me for insurance.

I started to think a lot of things right then. Most of all I was thinking what a damn fool I was for not playing it safer. Those guys had been on my tail all day waiting to get me off someplace where they could pick me up and I go and make it just perfect for them.

The gun rammed me in the spine again. 'Start walking over there to where the hole is.'

'Listen, I . . .'

'Keep quiet and walk. Don't make it rough on yourself.'

They formed a fan around me, flanking me in as nice as you please. Like Nazis, that's what. I did everything but dig my own grave. They had it just right, too . . . back far enough so I couldn't make a stab at one of the rods and close enough to see my outline even in the dark.

God, I couldn't just go easy like that! I had to do something!

Before anyone could tell me to shut up I said, 'I want a cigarette.'

A voice said, 'Give him one.'

'What the hell for!'

'I said give him one.'

Paper rustled and a cigarette came to me out of the dark, held lightly in the ends of the fingers. I stuck it in my mouth and groped for a match. The guy who complained about giving me the butt started to complain again and the other voice cut in with 'He's clean. You don't think I'd let him be packing a rod around, do you?'

I almost felt like answering him myself. I swung around so I'd be facing them and flicked the wooden match with my thumbnail. They were just stupid enough not to see what I did. My eyes were shut tight, I felt for the butt, lit it and shook the match out. Then I opened my eyes.

I was the only one who could still see in the dark and while they were still seeing a great big bright spot where the match had been I leaped off to the left, hit the dirt and rolled.

The shots came blasting out with the shouts and curses, stabbing the air where I had been, trying to search me out with orange tongues of flame. The slugs were smacking the ground, whining off into the brush splatting the walls of the quarry and tearing into the foliage with a harsh, ripping sound.

I had a rock under my hand and threw it. A frenzied yell welled out of a hoarse throat and the bullets spat in a direction away from me. The guy doing most of the shooting wasn't three feet away. I came up behind him, choked off a scream with my forearm and wrenched the gun out of his hand. I clipped him once behind his ear, stuck the gun in my pocket and heaved him as hard as I could.

One bullet gouging into soft flesh made the nastiest noise I ever heard.

There was no sound after that for a few seconds. Just the dull rumble of the echoes down there in the quarry. A guy said, 'That one got him.'

I heard their feet on the gravel, the grating of a match and there they were, the two of them, bending over the body. He was sprawled face down and one guy turned him over. 'Cripes, it's Larry!' The whole thing hit him at once and he tried to shake the match out.

I shot him in the head while I could still see him and he gave one convulsive leap that threw him over backwards into the quarry. You could hear him bouncing off the rocks until there was a faint splash. I didn't even try for the other one. He didn't waste any time about moving. The air was so still, so quiet now that I could hear his feet slipping in the soft loam and the way he dragged his breath in as he battered a path through the brush.

Just to leave a nice clean camp I put my foot under the body of the one called Larry and shoved. He went down there in the wet with his friend. Then I tossed the gun down after him.

It was nice of them to leave me the car. The plates were from out of state and there were some toys on the floor in the back, so it was a sure bet the heap was stolen. I kicked it over, swung around and took the road back to the highway.

I should have felt good. I was dirty as hell, but I was still alive. That should make anybody feel good. That is, anybody but me. A gun felt too natural in my hand, I got too much pleasure out of seeing a guy die even if he did deserve to die. I was thinking things that no right guy would ever think of, like getting the powder marks out of my hand before the police could make a paraffin test on me. I knew how to do all that and I didn't know what or who I was more than a few years ago.

A shudder pinched my shoulders together and I could feel the damp of the sweat on the back of my neck. I knew too goddamn many things for my own good, all right, but in a way I was lucky I knew them.

I found a drugstore still open on the edge of town, bought a few things and sat in the car washing my hands. When I was done I wasn't worried about paraffin tests any more. I threw the bottles and the jar of solvent out the window, started to turn the key and noticed the pad on the seat.

It was just a cheap loose-leaf job with a small pencil stuffed between the rings. Whoever used it tore the pages out as they were used up, and except for the first page it was completely empty. Right at the top of page one was the notation, 'John McBride, registered own name Hathaway House. Check both entrances.'

They had it down pat. If they had missed me in town I would have been picked up at the hotel. I grinned a little bit, ripped the page out and tossed the rest of the pad out the window.

That made two attempts to knock me off and I could damn well expect a third. I must have been some boy to be so important dead. Brother! I gunned the motor and drove into town.

The hotel was out now. There was no sense building my own trap. When trouble came I wanted to pick the spot myself. Between times I wanted someplace where I could hole up and think if I had to without worrying about who was waiting outside ready to use me for a target.

It was after two when I left the car in front of police headquarters. Hell, I wasn't trying to be wise about it. But it helps when the other guy knows you're cocky enough to pull a stunt like that. It makes them a little cautious, and in the time it takes to be cautious you can make them wish they hadn't been, if you get what I mean.

A family-type gin mill was going strong on the corner. Everybody had a package on including the bartender and they were all huddled together giving some Irish ballads a working over. Nobody noticed me slip into the phone booth and nobody cared.

I got the *Lyncastle News* office first and the night editor gave me Logan's home number. It took five minutes of steady ringing to wake him up and he wasn't the happiest-sounding person I'd ever talked to. He barked, 'Who the hell is this and what d'ya want?'

'It's Johnny, kid. Got some news for you if you're interested.'

His voice tightened up. 'Find her?'

'Nope. Somebody found me. I got taken for a ride.'

'God! What happened?'

'There's a quarry of some kind outside of town. Know where it is?'

'Yeah, yeah. What about it?'

'There's two bodies down there. The third got away from me.'

'Did you . . .' He hung there expectantly.

'I did one, friend. The other was knocked off by his buddy. The third lad is going to carry the story home and we better get our licks in first.'

'Johnny, this is going to be rough. Lindsey'll love it!'

'Uh-uh. Not if we handle it right. Whoever put them on me can't talk without exposing himself and there's no reason why I should get tied into it. Can you keep it quiet?'

'I sure can try. I'll round up the boys and get out there now.'

'Good. See if you can find out who they are. I wouldn't be a bit surprised if they were hauling in ringers now,' I said drily.

'They?'

'Yeah. It goes back a long way, friend, but it's just now paying off. Somebody is scared silly. I'll call you in the morning. By the way . . . they used a stolen car. I left it in front of police headquarters.'

'You're a damn fool, Johnny!'

'Everybody keeps telling me that. Some day I'll believe it. One more thing before I forget. Servo's got a red-headed tomato up his place. Who is she?'

'Slow down, Johnny. You haven't been fooling around with her, have you?'

'Not exactly. The pleasure was all hers.'

He said a couple of nasty words under his breath. 'You're just looking to get killed, aren't you?'

'That's not the question.'

'If you gotta know, her name is Troy Avalard.'

'The hell with her name. What about her?'

'She's been living with Lenny for a couple of years. She came through with a show one time, made a big play for Lenny and he bought out her contract to keep her around.'

'You know how he does it?'

'I've heard.'

'Doesn't she ever get out?'

He didn't answer right away. I could hear his fingernails rattle against the phone impatiently. 'When she's out Lenny's with her,' he said. 'Troy's a good hand at steering a sucker who's loaded with dough to a dice table.'

'A nice friendly gesture that helps out Lenny's friends, is that it?'

'Sort of.'

'Who held her contract, Logan?'

I hit him with the question so fast he choked over a curse. When he got his voice back it was soft with amazement. 'You should have been a cop. Sure as hell you should have been a cop. You can smell out the damndest things.'

'Yeah?'

'Lenny paid fifty grand for that contract. It was supposed to be a hush-hush deal but it got noised around. That's too much cash to hand out for a chunk of sex so I checked on it. The guy who held the contract sold it for five.'

'That leaves forty-five G's to go, kid.'

'I know. Most of it was deposited to the account of Troy Avalard a few days later.'

'She sure must have a lot to offer,' I said. 'Maybe I better look in on her again.'

'Damn it, Johnny, you . . .'

'Logan,' I laughed, 'you ought to see her with an ice cube. It's really something.'

I hung up while he was sputtering into the receiver and got back out on the street again. I kept wondering whether two hundred grand was worth a double try for a kill and decided that it was well worth it if the guy you were trying to kill was important enough.

About two blocks over I picked up a cruising cab and climbed in the back without giving the driver any kind of a chance to get a look at me. I said, 'Pontiel Road. Drop me off on the corner.'

'Right, Jack.'

He looked like the kind of cabbie who liked to gab, so I turned on the radio that was built into the side and picked up a network news commentator who did all the talking for the both of us.

I got out on the corner of Pontiel Road, paid off the cab and started walking. It was a long walk. The road started off as a residential street, kept on going with more and more spaces between the houses, passed a few acres of empty lots, wound into a wooded grove and came out in a gentle upgrade where a few more houses were in the early construction stage.

The white house on the crest of the hill had the choicest location of all. Evidently it had been built some time ago with an eye to the future, the builder expecting an expansion of the suburb in this direction. You could look down and see the whole city at a glance, yet be far enough away to enjoy some of the advantages of the country.

I walked up the flagstone path, took the steps to the porch that had 4014 in brass numbers tacked over *W. Miller* and looked around for a flowerpot. It was in back of the pillar and the key was there where Wendy said it would be.

There was an amber night light in the foyer that was enough to show me the stairs. I went up, found the bathroom with the light switch beside the door jamb, stripped off my clothes and climbed into the shower. The patch on my head got wet, so I took it off after I dried down and made a new one out of the bandage and tape in the cabinet, then hung my clothes up in the closet.

There were two doors leading off the bathroom. I opened one and it smelled of perfume and powder like every other woman's bedroom in the civilized world, so I closed it softly and tried the other. That was better.

I tossed the towel in the hamper, walked over to the window and opened it and stood there breathing in the fresh air. The moon was just coming up behind the town, a mellow, peaceful moon all red around the edges.

A benevolent moon, I thought, smiling down on a malevolent city.

I let it douse me with its yellow light a minute longer, grinned back at it, then felt around for the bed and perched on the edge for a last cigarette. The breeze felt good on my bare skin, cool and comfortable. I stuck the butt in my mouth and snapped the match on the folder.

Her voice was a gentle whisper coming out of the darkness. 'You look nice without anything on, Johnny.'

The match froze there in my fingers, dropped and went out on the floor. But not before I saw her on the other side of the bed, her body a naked splash of white before it dipped under the covers.

My benevolent moon smiled again and its light made a play of shadows over the firm sweep of her breasts, wavering gently with her breathing.

'Sorry, kid,' I said hoarsely, 'I . . . thought . . . this room was . . . empty.'

She stretched her arms out in a lithe, lazy motion, her mouth a dark oval that barely moved. 'It usually is, Johnny.'

I would have left, but her hand reached out and touched me, the tips of her fingers inviting little feathers against my skin and there was something animal-like in the way she moved under the covers.

Then she was all animal and so was I, a warm, fragrant animal who made whimpering noises until I stopped her with my mouth and who clawed and clung in a mad frenzy of motion until her breath hung in her throat and it was over.

She was still asleep when I got up in the morning, curled up on her side with her face buried against my shoulder. I tucked the cover under her chin, got dressed and went downstairs to the kitchen. I had the coffee done and breakfast on the stove when I heard her come through the door. Her hair looked like yellow hay blowing in a wind, her mouth a scarlet smile that said, 'Good morning.'

She was wrapped up in a red quilted housecoat that didn't hide a thing. 'Nice,' I grinned, 'very, very nice. Sit down and eat.'

Wendy pulled out a chair with her toe and parked. 'I wanted to make breakfast, Johnny.'

'You were domestic enough last night, girl. Besides, I'm in a hurry.'

Her eyes were curious. 'Going somewhere?'

'Yeah. I'm going looking for the somebody who wants me dead.'

Her eyebrows made two little arcs.

'I got taken for a little ride last night. That makes twice they tried.'

'Who . . .'

'I'd like to know that myself. Ever hear of a girl named Vera West?'

'Why, certainly! Wasn't she . . .'

'The one I was in love with. She worked in the bank,' I finished.

Wendy frowned and sipped her coffee. 'She was Lenny Servo's girl too.'

'Uh-huh. And now she's missing. I want to find that babe.' I tapped a cigarette on the table and lit it. 'How easy is it to disappear right here in town?'

'Not very easy, but it has been done. Do you think she's here?'

'Maybe. I heard something about where the girlies wind up in Lyncastle. You know anything about it?'

'There are . . . houses. It is possible, though it doesn't seem logical. Why would she want to disappear?'

'That goddamn tart framed me. She . . .' I stopped in the middle of the sentence. 'How good are you at keeping your mouth closed?'

The coffee cup made a faint *clink* against the saucer. She read the expression on my face and stiffened. 'That isn't very nice.'

'I don't do nice things, Wendy. But I want you to know. I may shoot off my mouth because you and Pop did me a favour, but if you sound off to anybody you'll never be able to do it again. You understand that, don't you?'

Her face was white with anger. 'You don't have to tell me anything,' she snapped.

'No, I don't have to, but I can think better when I talk. Listen all you want to, but keep it to yourself. Like I said about Vera West, she told Gardiner I was using a set of books I had no business seeing. She had it all arranged so in case she was caught she'd be able to shove everything on me. Well, that's just what happened. *She* was the one pulling the fancy stuff. *She* was dummying the books and I took the rap for it!'

'You . . . went to the bank?'

'Yeah, and saw Gardiner. He's going to look for her too.'

'You're sure about this?' she asked seriously.

'As sure as I can be without any proof. If I knew more about how the hell a bank runs its books I could have put the questions right.'

The eyebrows went up again. Higher this time. 'But you . . .'

'I never worked in a bank,' I said, 'because I'm not Johnny McBride. You're the second person I've told this to and you're going to be the last, but Johnny McBride is dead. I'm just a guy who looks like him.'

I gave it to her with as few words as possible and she sat there with her mouth open trying to absorb it all. I motioned to her to eat while she was listening and finished about the same time she did.

She took the cigarette I offered her, dragged in a light and let the smoke curl out with her words. 'It's incredible, really. Nobody has thought different so far?'

'Not so I'd notice. I'm going to play the game right up to the hilt until I find out why Johnny left like he did. If you're wondering why I bothered telling you all this it's because I'm going to need you.'

'And Nick . . . are you going to tell him?'

'No. Pop's O.K., but he's too old to help me much. I'm glad he picked me up when he did and he's got my thanks.'

'You'd better stop calling him "Pop". He hates that. You're supposed to know him well enough to know what he's called.'

I nodded. 'Thanks for reminding me.'

'What do you want me to do, Johnny? I mean . . .'

'Keep it Johnny. I want you to help me find Vera West. Women are good at asking questions right. Try the gang that comes through your place.'

'But they're all from out of town.'

'That's all right. She may not be in Lyncastle. If she changed her name she's probably still using the same initials . . . like Veronica Waverly or something. Put out a few feelers with your friends, but cook up a good story to go with it in case they start asking questions.'

I pushed my plate back and got up.

'All right, Johnny. And you can take my car if you want to. I'll use the old one. It's in the garage.'

'Yeah, I'll do that. Don't wait up for me,' I grinned.

'You'll be back?'

I looked her up and down slowly. 'What else?'

Her eyes half closed and she tilted her head up. 'Kiss?'

'Uh-uh. I wouldn't think of spoiling your paint job.'

'Rat.'

'Ain't I?'

She stuck her tongue out at me.

Wendy was a pretty head, all right. A little on the hard side when you looked close and the make-up didn't take away the brittle lines that were etched in the corner of her mouth and eyes. She was a million bucks in a green dress under artificial lights and two million in bed. A dime a dozen in the daytime though.

I told her so-long and went out to the garage.

The car was a black Ford coupé in good condition parked alongside a decrepit Model A that probably had made a reputation for itself in college ten years ago. Some of the witty sayings still showed through the finish and there were coon tails hanging from the chrome guides on the fenders.

I backed out to the street, drove down Pontiel Road and cut over towards the centre of town. At a candy store I stopped and picked up a copy of the *Lyncastle News*, then sat in the car to see what it had to say. It said plenty. Page one had a big splash of the cops hauling a pair of bodies from the quarry under the spotlights from a police car. The story was that an anonymous tip to the *News* brought out the police who recovered the bodies and made an immediate identification. The men were a pair of medium-sized hoods whose activities were usually centred around Chicago. One was wanted for parole violation and the other was wanted for questioning in a series of stick-ups in Florida.

Lindsey made the statement that it was undoubtedly a revenge killing by some gang outside the state and hoped for an early arrest. Apparently the cops and the reporters on the scene had messed up any extra footprints or car tracks because nothing more was said.

Buried on page four was a squib mentioning the fact some joker had stolen a car, taken it for a joy ride and abandoned it in front of police headquarters.

When I closed the paper I dug a nickel out of my pocket and went back into the candy store, looked up the number of the Hathaway House and dialled it. I asked for Jack, heard the desk clerk hit the bell a few times, then got my party.

I said, 'This is Johnny McBride, Jack. Can you take a few minutes off and meet me somewhere?'

His voice was guarded. 'Certainly, sir. Topps' Bar and Grill you say? In fifteen minutes. Yessir.'

I told him fine and hung up. Topps' was about six blocks from the hotel and I made it before he did. I took a table in the back, asked for coffee and waited. A couple minutes later he came in, saw me and came back to the table.

'Hiya, Mr McBride.' He sat down across from me and I signalled for another coffee.

'My room still empty?'

'Sure. You had a couple calls to see if you were in last night and this morning. Didn't leave their names though.'

'Anybody staked out around the lobby?'

He screwed his face up. 'Not now. Some character was there most of the night. I kind of thought it was a new dick.'

I peeled off two tens and a five from my roll and tossed them across the table. 'When you get back pay for my room and check me out. I left a suitcase with some old clothes in it under the bed. Throw that in the ash can. I won't be going back to the hotel.'

'You got trouble?'

'Plenty. I'm not well liked around here.'

Jack grinned broadly. 'Yeah, I asked about that. What's the story?'

'Don't believe what you hear,' I said.

'You got framed, eh?'

'What makes you think so?'

'Coming back. If you pulled that bank job you'd still be a thousand miles from here. Whatcha want with me?'

The waiter came with the coffee and I waited until he was back at the other end of the room before I said, 'Not meaning to be impolite, but since you do a little pimping on the side you might know something I need.'

'If it's about dames, sure.'

'Ever hear of Vera West.'

He let out a low whistle. 'You're working the top brackets now, ain't you, Johnny? She's one of Servo's exes.'

'Where is she now?'

His eyes lost that young look. 'Seems like a lot of people are looking for her.'

'Who?'

'Just people. A pair of chicks I have on call both were tapped with the same question. They didn't know.'

'Do you know?'

He dumped milk and sugar in his coffee and stirred the concoction around slowly. 'I only saw her once after Servo dumped her. She was just getting off the night train and she was carrying a suitcase. I remember that she looked pretty upset or something. Anyway, one of Servo's boys happened to be in the station putting some tomato on the train and when she saw him she ran like hell for a cab. I never saw her again after that.'

'Which way was the train going?'

'It was the incoming train, the express that comes in from Chicago to the state capital, turns south and goes through here down to Knoxville.'

'I see. Who was the guy she saw?'

'Eddie Packman. He's a right-hand man to Lenny Servo nowadays. Thinks he's big stuff. Hell, before he hit Lyncastle he was small potatoes. He gimme a hard time in a poolroom one day and I beat his ears off. I wouldn't try it now.'

'Why not?'

'Because now I'm small potatoes and he's Servo's boy,' he grinned.

'So you think Vera West left town, is that it?'

He shook his head. 'I don't think anything. I remember seeing her last coming into town and remember that she and Servo split up right around that time, but I never had any reason to think about her. Maybe she's right here in town.'

'The last time you saw her, what did she look like?'

'Scared.'

'Describe her.'

'Well,' he squinted in thought, 'she was usually half in the bag, and this time she had a beaut of a hangover. Her eyes were red. She sure had pretty hair. Used to keep it in a page boy, you know, down around her shoulders curling up inside on the edges. Like gold. Outside that she was medium. Guess you'd say a nice build. I never looked too close.'

'O.K.,' I said, 'now suppose she never did leave town. Where could she hide out?'

'Well, for one thing, all she had to do was dye her hair red or brown or something and that'd help. There's places she could work like the laundry and rooming houses she could live in. If she didn't move around too much she could stay under cover. I know a couple of kids who were hot, one with the Feds, and they stayed right here in town while they did some job of searching, but they got away with it.'

'I see. One more thing. Why did she break with Servo?'

Jack looked a little pained. 'You ask the damndest questions.'

'You know?'

'I got a good memory and a good imagination. I put two and two together, see? If you're going out and mess around with Servo and my name gets mentioned, me and Lyncastle will have to part company and I like it here.'

'Nuts,' I said, 'you won't get involved in anything.'

'O.K., then I'll tell you what I *think*. It ain't what I *know*, remember that. Lenny Servo's got a way with the broads. He treats 'em nice so long as they treat him nice, but he don't like any one of 'em around too long. Now I know a couple others he brushed off and they didn't like it. Life was too nice while Lenny paid for it so they put the squeeze on him. Hell, they musta seen it coming and worked up a little insurance. Anyway, they don't know that Lenny won't squeeze. He gives them the business the hard way and they scram. No fooling around. Not if they want to keep their own teeth and noses. You get the idea?'

'Yeah, I get it. So where would somebody like Vera go . . . working the houses?'

His shoulders shrugged unconcernedly. 'That's as likely as anything else. She's a tramp, she stops giving it away and starts selling it.'

'Servo got anything to do with those houses?'

'Naw, this is Lyncastle, not New York. They're on their own, pay off the cops regular and let it go at that. Hell, with all the free stuff coming through here who's going to play around in those bug mills? Me, I got some fancy women working. I catch the legitimate travelling trade, but the houses don't get anything but the low-down stuff.'

'Do I need an introduction to get into 'em?'

Jack grinned, finished his coffee and set the cup down. 'Go to 107 Elm Street. Tell the bag in charge I sent you. You'll get in.' He grinned again. 'You oughta let me fix you up instead.'

'I'll fix myself up,' I said.

'You'll do that all right, down in those joints.'

I fished a buck out of my pocket and started to get up. Jack picked the bills off the table and I waved at them with my thumb. 'Keep whatever's left over.'

'Sure, thanks. If you need me again, look me up. I'll see what I can do finding the broad for you. Maybe the dames know something.'

'Swell.' I paid for the coffee, let Jack have a few minutes start while I picked up some butts, then got back in the car. This was the day I was going to dig up my life history. Or Johnny's rather.

It didn't take long. In a way it was fun. Here I was practically a celebrity and nobody knew who I was. Five years sure go a long way with the public when it comes to remembering. I started off with the records in City Hall, found out I had been born 9 December 1917, lost my parents while I was in high school and was legally adopted by a bachelor uncle who died while I was overseas. I checked the registration rolls of my family, found out where we had lived, went back to the library and dug around in the papers and got a partial history of my service record. Along with several hundred others I had enlisted the day after Pearl Harbour, taken basic training down South, then was assigned to O. C. S. and sent overseas.

I went over all the details until I had them set in my mind and if anybody asked there wasn't much I couldn't tell them. When I left the library I didn't stop to light a cigarette on the steps. I used the side door, ducked down the back alley to the car and hopped up to the main drag for a quick lunch.

At a quarter after two I called Logan. There was something funny about his voice when he told me to meet him in the parking lot outside a bowling alley on the west side of town.

I found the place without any trouble, drove up to the fence and killed the engine. A couple minutes later I saw his car turn in the drive and I waved him up next to me. He got out, opened the door next to me and sat down.

'Any news?' I asked him.

'Plenty.' He glanced at me queerly.

'You found out who the boys were?'

'No. . . . I found out who *you* were.' He reached in his side pocket for an envelope. I waited while he drew out some clippings and a folded printed circular. 'Take a look,' he said.

I spread it out and took a look. I took a good look because it was a police circular with a picture of me on it that said my name was George Wilson and I was wanted for armed robbery, burglary and murder, and the description it gave fitted me to the screwy colour of my eyes and the tone of my voice.

CHAPTER SEVEN

All I could say was, 'Where'd you get it?'

'Our little hick paper has a big city morgue. Read the rest of it.'

I did that, too. They were accounts of the crimes I was suspected of committing. They were all dated and the date of the last one was about three weeks before I forgot who I was. I stuffed them back in the envelope and handed them to Logan. I felt like something that should be crawling instead of walking. 'What're you going to do about it?'

He stared out the window. 'I don't know,' he said, 'I honestly don't know. You're wanted, you know.'

'I could get away with it.'

'Yeah, your fingerprints. You might get away with it if they can't bring them out. You might get away with it if you throw everything on the real Johnny McBride. He's dead. He wouldn't mind.'

'Go to hell.'

'I'm just saying.'

'Say something else.'

'O.K., I will. I went further than just digging this stuff out of the files. I checked back on your story. Everything you told me was corroborated by the outfit you worked for. Maybe you were a lot of things before the accident, but those things aren't what you are now. It's quite possible that you are a completely different personality from what you were and there's no need making you stand trial for something another self did.'

I turned my head and grinned at him. It felt like it was plastered on: 'Thanks, pal. What happens if I get my memory back?'

'Let's wait until it happens.'

'You think I'll tell you about it?'

'No.'

'You're not kidding. If I have a conscience it won't bother me so much that I'll go and make a public confession of murder and do a jig at the end of a rope. Not me, pal.'

'Nuts, you're taking that chance right now.' Logan snorted derisively. 'Although it would be funny if you hung for Minnow's murder and not the right one.'

'Oh, that would be great all right.' I tapped the bulge in his pocket. 'Does Lindsey know about all this?'

Logan shook his head. 'He's much too interested in you as Johnny McBride. You'll be safer if you let him keep thinking you are.'

'Someplace you come in, Logan. You're still a reporter and if you're the right kind nothing's going to make you squelch a good story.'

He nodded abruptly. 'Nothing except the possibility that a better one might come out of waiting,' he said. He turned slowly and stared at me. 'I'm destroying this stuff. It can be duplicated, but it wouldn't do to have it on file where it might get picked up accidentally. I'm going to wait, Johnny. I'm enough of a reporter to know when a story is brewing and I think one is coming up. Don't pull anything fast on me, understand?'

'Perfectly. Now how about Vera West?'

'Not a trace. She disappeared completely. I even checked through Washington with a friend of mine in the Social Security office. If she's employed nothing is being paid into her account.'

'And my friends who tried to knock me off?'

'They're tagged, but that's as far as it goes. If they were working for somebody here in Lyncastle they didn't leave any evidence of it.'

'Something else'll happen soon,' I said. 'There were three of them and the other got away to carry the story home. It'll happen again. If it does I'll call you.'

'If you're still alive. If that happens you can usually reach me at the Circus Bar.'

My lips jerked back and left my teeth bare. 'I stay alive through a lot of things, Logan. I'm not easy to take at all.'

He grinned back at me and got out of the car. I stayed there until he had walked away then kicked the engine over. A half-hour later I was down in the red-light district looking for a parking place.

Some people might have called it a slum section, or if they saw it when it wasn't too light, an old residential spot gone to seed. There was a swamp on one side and a road that led to the smelter plant on the other, with four or five blocks nestling in the V of the two. Along the road were a dozen gin mills, a gas station and a few stores. Most of the section was given over to providing homes for the poorer element of Lyncastle, but the one block along the outer edge of the section made no bones about being what it was. Elm Street. There wasn't a tree in sight.

The houses were the same style and age, but they looked alive. There was fresh paint all around and the hedges were trimmed. Some were sprawled out with extra wings added on in ranch-type style and others had fairly new second storey added.

Hell, all you had to do was look in the garbage cans. They were loaded with booze bottles. I spotted some of the babes sunning themselves in the backyards and on the front porch of one place a drinking bout was just getting started.

No. 107 was the last place on the road. Originally it had been a two-storey job with a garage. Now the garage was part of a wing that crossed the back of the house like a T, extending on the other side into three small cabin affairs. It was a white house with red shutters, a red door and red Venetian blinds on all the windows.

Very appropriate.

I went up and rang the bell. Inside a radio was playing softly. The Moonlight Sonata. It didn't go with the business at all. I rang the bell again and lit a cigarette.

Then the door opened and the bag Jack told me to see was standing there smiling gently at the creature that was man, glancing quickly and humorously at the watch on her wrist because it was only four o'clock and not the time for that sort of thing at all.

110

But she wasn't a bag at all either. Somebody had taken a statue of Venus, patted it until it was soft, coloured it with jet-black hair and rich magenta lips and poured it into a dress that had an elastic quality of being stretched too tight, needing only one touch to burst.

I said, 'Jack sent me,' then felt like a damn fool. I must have looked it, because her smile got wider. 'If I knew you'd be here I would have come anyway and kicked the door down to get in,' I added.

She had a nice laugh. She looked even prettier with her head thrown back. 'Please come in. I really wouldn't want you to kick my door down.'

So I went in. I sat down and gaped at a room that had all the trimmings of a mansion and let her serve me a drink from a small bar built into the wall. On either side it was flanked with books and they weren't just dummy copies. There was a record library built in around a console player that held a selection of classics and only a handful of popular pieces.

'Like it?' She swayed over with a bottle and ice and put them on an end table.

'It fooled me. I've never been in one of these places before.'

'Really?' She took a sip of her drink. 'I'm alone until six o'clock. The girls won't be in until then.'

It was a nice way of putting it. Just so I didn't get ideas, you know. Venus was the owner and operator, not a hired hand. I finished my drink and the cigarette at the same time and waved off seconds. 'I'm not too early because I'm not after merchandise, kid. I'm after information. Jack thought you might be able to supply it.'

'Nice boy, Jack. Who are you?'

'A friend of his and names don't matter. Ever hear of Vera West?'

'Certainly. Why?'

She said it so coolly that I got caught short for a second. 'Where is she?'

'That I couldn't tell you. For a while she was Lenny Servo's girl, but then that isn't unusual. A lot of women were Lenny's . . . for a while.'

'You too?'

'A long time ago. For a week.' She took a deep pull on the butt and exhaled it slowly, watching the smoke curl around the glass in her hand. 'You really meant to ask me . . . if Vera was . . . one of us now, didn't you?'

'Something like that.'

'Well, fella, as far as I know, she never had anything for sale. She certainly never got this far. She wasn't the type.'

'You don't look like the type either.'

I got that laugh again. She reached over and ran her fingers through my hair. 'That's a long story and a rather interesting one. Now tell me about your Vera West.'

'Hell, I don't have anything to tell about her. I want to find her.'

'How long has she been gone?'

'Quite a while. It's a cold trail.'

'Have you tried the police?'

I let out a short snort and she knew what I meant.

'You can try the bus station and the trains. If anybody knew her there they might have seen her leave. It's possible that she might have gone to some large city and taken up her former occupation. She was something in the bank, wasn't she?'

'Secretary,' I said.

'Then she'd be a secretary or steno somewhere else.'

'You know a lot about things, don't you?'

'A little,' she said, 'I used to be married to a cop.'

I squashed out my butt and stood up. 'I'll try everything I can. This was an angle and it didn't pan out so at least I know where not to look now.'

'Have you tried Servo? He might know where she is.'

My fist kept pounding against my palm slowly. 'I haven't seen him . . . yet. Maybe I will pretty soon now.'

Her eyes went a little bit cold. 'Say hello for me when you do,' she said.

'In the teeth?'

Her head moved up and down once, and slowly. 'Snap them off. Right across the front.'

We stood there looking at each other for quite a while. Everything she was thinking came out in her eyes and I knew the kind of a deal she had gotten from Lenny Servo too. I was working up a nice feeling for that guy. 'I'll see what I can do,' I said.

'I'd like that. Maybe if you called me back later I'll have news for you. The . . . girls usually know pretty much of what goes on in town. The number's unlisted – 1346.'

She walked me to the door and twisted the knob on the lock. She was close and smelled faintly of jasmine, the way Venus should smell. Every bit of her was outlined in detail against the clinging fabric of the dress. She caught me studying her and smiled again.

'How do you get into that thing?' I asked her.

'It's a trick.' She handed me a silken tassel that was suspended from a gimmick on her shoulder. I held it in my fingers a second, she kept on smiling, so I gave it a pull. Something happened to the dress. It wasn't there any more. It all came apart and fell on the floor with me still holding the tassel and Venus looked like she was supposed to look. She was tall and lovelier than when she had clothes on.

'Now you know,' she laughed. 'What do you think?'

'Baby,' I said, 'on some people skin is skin . . .'

'And on me?'

'A beautiful invitation in black and white.'

I opened the door, stepped out and closed it behind me. Venus had made it too plain that I didn't have to wait until six o'clock if I didn't want to, but I just couldn't afford the time. Later maybe.

I drove back downtown and picked out a joint that didn't look too flashy and went in for a beer. The bartender set one up, took my change and stood by until I finished, then got me another. The slots were making music all around the walls and over the noise there would be an occasional yell from the back room when a number came up on a wheel. The two guys next to me were spending some of their winnings

113

from the craps table and getting ready to go back and give it another whirl.

One of them tried to talk me into making it a threesome and I turned it down and had a beer instead. I had just started on it when somebody moved into the space they left at the bar and said, 'Hello, tough boy.'

I said, 'Hello, flatfoot,' and Tucker's beefy face got real nasty.

'I've been looking for you.'

'I'm not hard to find.'

'Shut up and pick up your change. You're going for a ride.'

That was nice. I wanted to tell him I already had one and didn't feel like another, but I didn't. I said, 'You arresting me?'

'If you want it that way.'

'What for?'

'A little double murder out at the quarry. Suspicion, you know. Captain Lindsey wants to talk to you.'

I picked up my change and went for a little ride.

It was silent all the way. Nobody said anything until I was back in that same office where it all happened before. Lindsey was behind the desk and two other guys in suitcoats were sitting beside him. Tucker leaned back against the door and let me stand in the middle of the room.

When I pulled out a cigarette Lindsey barked, 'No smoking in here.' I put the butt back and walked over to a chair. 'McBride,' Lindsey said, 'you stand there until I tell you to sit down, understand?'

I picked the chair up by the legs and looked at him and the rest of them. 'I don't understand a thing, you goddamn pig, you! I'm making it nice and plain so there won't be any mistake about it. There's four of you here and some more outside, but just get wise and I'll smash your lousy head in. I'd like to see who's got the guts to try and take me.'

Tucker would have tried it. He had his gun out and was moving in when Lindsey stopped him. 'Cut it, Tuck. When it comes this guy is mine. He's talking big and I'll let him talk big, but by God he'll be talking mighty small soon and I'm going to show him the kind of gadgets we got in the cellar and let him see how they work.' He nodded to me curtly. 'Sit down, sit down. I have some questions to ask you.'

I put the chair down and sat on it. Tucker got behind me and stayed there playing with his gun. 'What is it now?'

'I suppose you have an alibi for last night?'

'I got a beauty,' I lied.

It turned out better than I expected. I was doing some fast thinking when Lindsey gave me credit for really having one. I could tell it by his expression. He took in the men beside him with a glance. 'We recovered two guns that had several prints on them. Over one was a peculiar sort of smudge. That make any sense to you, McBride?'

'Sure. The killer was wearing gloves.'

'No, the killer had no prints.'

'Good for him.'

'Not so good for him. These men are from Washington. They specialize in that sort of thing. They're going to take you downstairs and check your fingertips.'

Then I saw why he wasn't too concerned about my alibi. Hell, he didn't care about the two at the quarry. He wanted to get me for Minnow's murder. There he *had* a set of prints to go on, not a smudge.

I shrugged like I didn't give a damn and that much was the truth. *I didn't give a damn.*

For two years I had had experts work those same fingers over just to find out who I was, and now I was damn glad nothing came of it. The two guys got up, led the way, I got in the middle and Lindsey and Tucker followed along behind me.

The whole thing took better than an hour. I let them play with their gadgets, do things to my fingers that left them raw and bleeding, take sample impressions one after the other and never squawked when I got blisters from holding my hands too near the ultra-violet lights.

I was the most co-operative subject the boys had ever had and when it was over all they had was a bunch of smudges and a brand-new case history for rookie cops to study because I was the first one who ever had his fingerprints removed completely. The boys were shaking their heads when I left, Lindsey was cursing to himself trying to hold his temper in check and Tucker was watching me like he was glad because he might be able to even things up with me his way.

I went in the barbershop off the lobby and picked out a chair along the wall. Looth Tooth had a customer in the chair and was fidgeting over him like an old woman. A bellboy came in and handed the guy two telegrams and a telephone message slip and when he got a fat tip said, 'Thanks, Mayor.'

Two men came in after me, gave the mayor a fat hello, then parked and talked shop. One was a councilman. I was in the Waldorf of Lyncastle. Where the élite meet for a shave and a haircut and some choice cuts of local gossip. Logan should hire Looth Tooth, I thought. It would be better than taking a poll.

When the mayor climbed down I took his place in the chair. Looth Tooth had the apron around my neck and was about to pin it shut when he met my eyes in the mirror and turned white. His hands started to shake when he put the towel around me and I was beginning to think that it wasn't such a good idea after all.

When he had about five minutes of it, I said, 'Look, quit being so nervous. You gave me a treatment with the cops and I got back at you in that bar. It's over. Finished. I'm not mad any more.'

The sigh he let out whistled through his teeth. 'I . . . I'm awfully sorry about that, sir. You see . . . I thought . . . well, I *do* have quite a memory, and I thought the police . . . well, it was sort of a public duty and . . .'

'Sure, I would have done the same thing myself. Forget about it.'

'Oh, gladly, sir, gladly!' He laid a hot towel across my face and began to massage in the heat. It felt good. I lay there stretched out in the chair while he went through all his tricks. My eyes closed and the sounds from the street got dimmer and dimmer and the brush was a gentle thing floating across my cheeks.

It was nice for thinking. Johnny and I used to make a habit of being barber-shaved on Saturday afternoons. We'd sit next to each other and crack jokes under the towels and make plans for the day. We sure had a hell of a good time together. It wasn't so nice without him any more. Wherever he was, I hoped he'd keep an eye on me. Maybe he'd like what I was doing . . . or maybe he wouldn't. It wasn't too nice to bring things back that were better off forgotten, but as long as he was dead now he was going to have died honourably. Somebody else didn't want that past brought up again . . . they were scared silly when I came around, enough to try to have me bumped. And somebody else was looking for Vera West too, according to Jack.

I wondered about that.

Looth Tooth rattled something I didn't hear, something about getting slicked up for tonight. I said, 'Make me pretty, mister. Tonight's a big date night.'

The stuff he patted on my cheeks bit in. 'You mean, Miss West? Yes, I remember. You and she . . . oh, I . . . I'm sorry, I didn't mean . . .'

'Hell, man, that's O.K. All over the hill now.'

He was smiling when he dusted me off and I handed him a buck tip. He did everything except kiss me goodbye when I left and he was glad to see me go. The poor slob probably figured he had talked his way out of a smearing and would have something else to gas about to the rest of his customers.

A light drizzle had put a slick on the streets. Off in the west, sheet lightning turned the sky a dull orange momentarily and seconds later there was a faint rumble of thunder. I stepped up my pace until I got back to the car, then sat there deciding where to go. A kid in a green sweater came along with a batch of papers under his arm, turned into the gin mill and made the rounds. When he came out I called him over and asked him where the Circus Bar was. He told me it was straight down the avenue and I couldn't miss it because there were pink elephants

117

painted across the windows. I bought a paper, flipped him a quarter and rolled away from the kerb.

The Circus Bar was back-to-back with the *Lyncastle News* building and for all its fancy name, it was strictly a place for reporters and linotype men. There must have been twenty phones on the bar with half of them in use. It was between shifts and everybody but the reporters were either having one for the road or a pre-work quickie.

It didn't take me long to find Logan. He was all the way down at the back of the bar with a phone pressed against his mouth, shifting around every second or so to keep from being overheard. He saw me the same time I saw him, slammed the phone back and grabbed me on the run.

'Come on, if you want to see me you can do it while we ride.' He yelled so-long to a couple of people and hustled me outside. I climbed in the Chevvy with him and waited until we had backed out to the street and turned around.

'Where we going?'

'Item for my column. Some jane got bumped.'

I let out a whistle. 'Who?'

'Don't know. A guy that tips me to these things just called in about it. There's a dead woman in a hotel over by the river. The way Lindsey and the coroner operate, they won't give out any details to the Press for a week unless we're right on the spot when they arrive. What have you been up to all day?'

'I've been visiting with friend Lindsey,' I said. Logan's eyes drifted to mine for a second, then went back to the road. The wipers buzzed steadily, keeping time to the hum of the wheels.

'What'd he want?'

'He had a couple of experts with him. They wanted to bring my prints out.'

'So?'

I hunched my shoulders in a shrug. 'So they couldn't do it.'

'George Wilson's as dead as Johnny McBride then, isn't he?'

'Looks that way.'

Logan wrenched the wheel over and sent the car skittering around a curve onto a gravel drive. Up ahead was a ramshackle wood frame building with a veranda that ran completely around the place. He stopped, backed into a parking area and nodded for me to get out.

Over the door a sign read 'Pine Tree Gardens.' There was an old pick-up truck around the side, but nobody seemed to be around. Logan started up the steps and pushed the bell. 'This used to be a fairly decent boarding house. It's next door to a flophouse now.'

The dirty curtain that stretched the length of the door inched to one side and a pair of eyes took us in. Something like relief showed in the face and the door creaked open. The guy standing there biting his lip said, 'Geez, Mr Logan, this sure is trouble. I don't know whatta do.'

'Did you call the police yet?'

'No, no, no! I didn't do nothing 'cept tell Howie and he said he'd call you. Geez, Mr Logan . . .'

'Where is she?'

'Upstairs. Second room on the front. You want to look, you go ahead. I ain't going in no dead room.'

We went inside through a foyer, up the stairs and the guy waved towards the only door on the floor. Logan said, 'There?'

'Yeah.'

I went in behind him. It was a shabby room with an old-fashioned brass bed, a couple of ratty chairs and a dresser. The closet doors were open, the windows were open and the dead woman lay stretched out in the middle of the bed with her head still cradled on her arm. Somebody had planted a knife in her back right through the bedclothes and she died so fast she didn't even bother to bleed.

Logan let out a coarse shudder. 'Right through the heart it looks like. Neat job. Missed the ribs so there was no trouble working the knife out.'

'All that in one glance,' I said sarcastically.

'I've seen as many of these as Lindsey has. Where's that guy?'

'Waiting in the hall.'

Logan swung around and went back to the door. He yelled, 'Who is she, Mac?'

119

'Name's Inez Casey. She and some other broad have that room together. They're waitresses someplace. Work shifts in the same joint.'

'You stay here?'

'Downstairs. Yesterday they told me they wanted a window fixed so I came up to fix it. I found . . . her . . . there like that.'

Logan grunted something and came back in the room. I was on my knees looking at the babe's face and he knelt down beside me. 'She wasn't a bad-looking tomato,' I said. 'What do you make of it?'

He got up with a shrug and felt her arm. 'Hell, who knows? Things like this keep happening in this town now. Probably a love angle in it. The dames they get for waitresses in the joints around here are never too careful who they fool around with. Good knife job, though.'

'Yeah,' I agreed, 'it has a regular professional touch. Whoever did it knew right where to place that shiv. Didn't even have to feel around for the spot.'

Logan shuddered again. 'I'm going to call Lindsey.'

'I'll wait outside,' I said. 'He won't be too happy to see me around.'

So I sat in the car and Lindsey didn't see me. Neither did Tucker nor the two plain-clothes men nor the fat little coroner. The D.A. came in last and left first. He didn't see me either. Almost an hour later Logan came back and got in under the wheel. I asked, 'What's the decision?'

'Stabbed. Unknown assailant. Lindsey was on the phone most of the time and picked up a few details. She worked in the ABC Diner out along the highway. Her room-mate is there now. There's a couple of guys involved but nobody knows their names.'

'Not even the room-mate?'

'Nope. It's a fairly recent thing and they don't seem to get much time together to talk over love affairs. Evidently she met them both in the diner and has been playing them along. The past week she's been going strong for this one joe and broke off with the other one after some sort of a fuss. Lindsey'll track 'em down. Won't take long.'

'Not much of a story, is there?'

Logan wrinkled his mouth. 'Not for my column.'

'I was doing a lot of thinking while I waited for you,' I said. He looked at me without speaking.

I said, 'She didn't move when she was killed.'

'Hell, she got it right through the heart. She died instantly.'

I made like I hadn't heard him at all. 'She was on her belly with her face buried in her arm.'

'What about it?' he demanded impatiently.

I grinned at him, then let out a short laugh. 'Don't pay any attention to me, Logan. Wild ideas, I guess. I wish I knew where the hell I get them.'

He turned the key and started the engine. Tucker was pulling away in a police car and we stayed behind him to the highway. On the concrete the police heap turned on the siren and picked up speed. Logan didn't bother to keep up with him.

Right on the edge of town Logan said, 'Hey . . . almost forgot. You see the paper tonight?'

'I bought one, but I didn't read it. Why?'

'Take a look in the personal column.'

I scowled at him then pulled the paper out from behind my back. When I found the personal section I held it under the dash light and fingered my way down the column. Next to last from the bottom were two lines that read: J. Mc call 5492 at 11 P.M. Urgent.

I tore the spot out and tucked it in my pocket. 'Could be me, couldn't it?'

'Could be.' Logan nodded. 'It came in just before the paper went to bed. I happened to catch it in the proofs accidentally. A boy brought it in and paid for it.'

'What time is it?'

He looked at his watch. 'Ten-thirty. Want to stop for a beer?'

'Sure,' I said.

There wasn't any trouble finding a roadhouse. The trick was in finding one that had room to spare in the parking lot. We had to cut back away from town to a dump that was supposed to look like a log cabin and the only reason there was a half-empty parking place was because of the lack of gambling facilities inside. There wasn't any blue sign in the window, either.

It was almost eleven by then so I told Logan to order for me while I put in a call. I could see the clock on the wall and held my nickel back until the time was right, then spun my number. It rang once and a voice said, 'Yes?'

It was a woman's voice, a nice deep, controlled voice that painted pictures of what was on the other end of the line.

'I'm calling about a certain piece in tonight's paper.'

She didn't offer any information except, 'Go on.'

'I'm a "J. Mc" . . . if it helps.'

'That helps some.'

'Johnny McBride is all of it.'

'Yes, Johnny, you're the one I meant.' There was just the slightest pause between her words. 'See Harlan, Johnny. You must see Harlan.'

Then she hung up. It happened so fast I turned the receiver around and stared at it before I put it back. On second thought I took out another nickel, dropped it in and dialled the operator. When she answered I said brusquely, 'This is Tucker, city police. I want a number traced. 5492. Want me to wait?'

'Just a minute please.' I waited, then: 'That number is a pay station on the corner of Grand and the boulevard.'

'O.K., thanks.'

I didn't get it at all. I went back to the bar and had my beer. Logan was curious without asking questions so I told him that it wasn't for me and he seemed satisfied.

We had another beer and halfway through it the door to the men's room on the other side of the bar opened and a little guy with a funny walk came out. He kept his head down and edged in to where he left his drink and started working it over.

Logan wanted another round, but I shook my head. The little guy over the way was collecting his change and I did the same thing. Across my back the muscles were lumping up into

122

hard knots and my fingers wouldn't hold still. Not ten feet off was the son of a bitch who tailed me last night, the same boy who had gotten away from me up at the quarry.

I made it look casual as possible because I didn't want Logan in on it. I gave the guy about thirty seconds, got outside in time to see him stepping into a car and hustled over to Logan's Chevvy. I managed to mumble something about never having driven a late model like his and he told me to go ahead and try it.

That was nice because I was able to tail the guy all the way back to town without Logan getting wise. And for a change I even got a break. There was a red light showing when we came to the Circus Bar and the guy had to stop for it. I had a chance to say good night to Logan, hop out and make my own heap before the light changed and picked the guy up as he drove past.

He swung down the main drag with me right behind him and he never got wise to the tail job for a minute. When he slowed up and started to crowd the kerb I knew he was looking for a parking place, so I pulled ahead of him, found an empty slot before he did, and backed into it. About a half a block down he got a place too, parked the car and walked back towards me.

I let him pass. I gave him a hundred feet of space between us then took up the tail again. This was even easier than driving. The drizzle was steady now, blowing in from the west, but neither that nor the flashes of lightning in the sky were doing anything to hamper business.

Place after place was a madhouse of noise that overflowed to the sidewalk. People were changing spots constantly hoping for a change of luck. Most of them had a slight edge on and were in a hurry to get back to the bars and the tables. I had to weave through them to keep up with the guy and finally stayed on the outside near the kerb where there was a narrow open lane.

He turned into the gaudiest spot on the street. It had a canopy extending from the doorway to the kerb with an admiral in full dress uniform helping the patrons from the cabs. It had a fancy French name with tiny gilt letters on the windows that proclaimed, 'Edward Packman, owner.'

123

And Eddie Packman was the guy Vera West had seen at the station just before she ran. Or so Jack said anyway.

The bar was fifty feet long with the crowd four deep behind the rail. A dozen bartenders tried to keep up with the orders, moving with short, jerky motions like comedians in old-fashioned movies. The rest of the room was just one big gambling casino jammed to the rafters with more people than the fire laws allowed trying their luck on anything that came along.

They even had mouse games. The women screamed, the men cheered and the live mice ran into holes that paid off at six to one. But there were about two hundred holes in the board and only three mice to each game so the house could not lose at all.

My little guy was half the bar away finishing a beer. When he set the empty back on the bar he backed through the mob and walked down the back. A flight of stairs went up and disappeared into a dimly lit alcove. I watched him until he was out of sight and took it easy with my drink.

A half-hour later he was back. This time he didn't stop for a drink. His face had a peculiar set to it; pleased, but still showing the signs of recent anger. He went past me, out the door and started back to his car.

I was right there again when he pulled away. He turned right at the corner, right again on a street that was without much traffic and kept going until he intersected the highway. You could see that there wasn't a car in sight going either way and I didn't expect him to make a stop just because the sign said to. He jammed on the brakes and I had to yank the wheel to cut around him and for the first time he saw my face. His mouth dropped and he let the clutch out so fast the car hopped ahead like a jackrabbit.

I gave the Ford all it would take and screamed out on the highway. His tail light was a tiny red eye going like hell, but the Ford was up to it and closed the distance down fast. We were both up past the eighty mark, taking the turns with the tyres whining and I was getting edgy enough to curse myself for not having taken him sooner. On the straightaways I could pick up on him, but the Ford was too light to make the turns and he was holding his own.

Then there was a nice long straightaway and I pushed the gas pedal all the way to the floor and crouched there trying to keep the Ford on the road. I would have had him if I hadn't seen the lights of a truck sweeping around a curve about a mile ahead. I knew damn well I wouldn't make it and eased on the brakes, but the guy in front of me tried to take it wide open.

He went into the turn skidding, started to recover, lost control for a second then all he was was a blur tumbling end over end through the fields in a horrible screeching noise of tearing metal and breaking glass. I overshot him by a half-mile, turned around and pulled off the road where he went into the weeds.

Fifty yards away I found the wreck upside down with one crazily bent wheel still spinning foolishly. He was half out of the car because that was all that was left of him. The top half.

It was still alive, too.

It kept saying, 'Doctor . . . doctor.'

I bent down and said, 'Who sent you after me? Listen to me . . . who sent you?' I lit a match and held it up so I could see his face, cupping my fingers over it to keep off the rain. 'Tell me, feller. It's too late for a doctor. Who sent you after me?'

The eyes got some recognition in them briefly. He mumbled, '. . . Doctor . . . need . . . doctor,' then the rain put the match out anyway, but it didn't matter because the guy was dead.

Tough! Ha!

I flipped open his jacket and lifted out his gun. I took the shoulder harness off too and tossed it as far as I could. The gun I dropped in my pocket. Then I found his wallet. There was one thousand bucks in hundred-dollar bills tucked behind two fives and a one. The grand went in with the gun and I put the rest back in his wallet and stuck it in his coat.

Now the cops and the papers could blame the accident on a guy who had too much of what was for sale in Lyncastle.

Now I could go back and ask Eddie Packman what the guy did to earn a grand and maybe squeeze him a little to make him talk.

So I went back to the joint with the fancy French name and made some discreet inquiries concerning Mr Packman's whereabouts. Only that man wasn't around. He had left twenty minutes before with a party and was someplace in town having himself a time.

Nobody knew where.

I said to hell with it and had a drink. The lousy beer sat there in my stomach and growled at me because I had too much to drink and not enough to eat. That, at least, I could take care of. I got back in the car, drove out past the bus station to the highway and kept on going until I came to Louie Dinero's place. The gun made a bulge in my pocket so I slid it behind the cushions and went in.

Wendy was just coming on with her number and the patrons were letting out a long 'Ahaaa' of satisfaction. I let out one myself and watched her step up to the mike. There was a baby spot behind her that shone right through the white dress she had on and the only thing you couldn't see was what was on the other side. She was real pretty to look at, especially with all that skin showing. I slid into a table, told a waiter to bring me a steak, rare, then had a butt while Wendy made with some gentle spasms here and there until the dress seemed to crawl right off her.

I looked around at all those jerks, watching the frozen expression of their faces, the too-plain lust in their eyes and all of a sudden I got mad – at Wendy. I didn't like for a babe to show off to a pack of stiffs what she showed me in private.

Then I felt like one of the jerks myself and dropped it. She was just another sugar cutie, a little better than most, but her hair came out of a bottle and up close her eyes were hard around the edges. So she liked to play games and who the hell was I to complain about it? The waiter brought my steak, I ate my way through it, paid my bill then caught Louie's eye and he waved me over.

The guy had a memory like an elephant's and gave me a regular glad hand. When I asked him if it'd be O.K. for me to see Wendy backstage he told me sure and showed me where the entrance was to the dressing-rooms. So I went back, found the door with W.M. lettered on it, turned the knob and shoved the door open.

I should have knocked first.

CHAPTER EIGHT

She was just slipping out of the dress, a tan velvet animated thing partially hidden by the swirl of the translucent fabric. The lights from the dressing-table behind her brought out the strong surge of youth in her body, the firm, sweeping curves of her breasts underlined by a stomach so flat it looked almost sucked-in and held in place with a play of muscles that danced as she moved.

This is the way her act should have ended, I thought. It would have been pure art. She almost had the thing off when the band outside hit a chord and she knew the door was open. The second she saw me she looked like a frightened fawn ready to bolt, then she had the dress up in front of her and backed away from me with her eyes wide.

I grinned because she was worried about the inevitable and it had stayed hidden. I said, 'You *do* remember me, don't you?'

She licked her lips and a frown worked its way into her eyes.

'O.K., kid, don't drop dead from fright on me, will you? I've seen you like that before only it was better in the moonlight.'

'You . . . startled me, Johnny. You should've knocked.'

'It occurred to me too late.'

'Well, if you don't mind, play the gentleman for a second and turn your back. Moonlight and unshaded bulbs are two different things.'

She threw me one of those funny smiles and I turned around. Women can sure get some screwy ideas. I said, 'Got any plans for tonight?'

I guess she took me wrong. The way she said no was as if I'd just slapped her across the jaw.

'Not those kind of plans, Wendy. I meant were you figuring on doing anything tonight.'

'Just go home to bed. I'm pretty tired.'

'Like to take in the town some?'

She didn't say anything. I turned around and she was bent over peering into the mirror with a lipstick in her hand. The harsh light of the naked bulbs made her hair look like it had been painted on, but not deep enough. It was showing dark down around the scalp. I said, 'Well?'

'Not . . . tonight, Johnny. I'm too tired.'

'It's pretty important.'

The lipstick poised an inch away from her mouth. 'Go on.'

'The last of the unholy trio who tried to dump me in the quarry is out on the main highway in two pieces.'

Her face made a grimace of horror before she spoke. 'Did you . . .'

'I would've if I coulda caught him. He wrapped his car up.'

'But what's that got to do with tonight?'

I looked at her and grinned a little bit, then slid into a wicker chair and lit a butt. 'He had a thousand bucks in his pocket. All nice, new bills. It was pay-off dough.' I blew a finger of smoke into the lights and watched it roll up towards the ceiling. 'He got that dough from a guy named Eddie Packman. I want to find that boy. Tonight.'

'And you want me to go with you?'

'Uh-huh.'

'No.' She turned back to the mirror and drew the lipstick across her mouth slowly. Our eyes met in the mirror and held. 'Johnny . . . look, I know how you feel and all . . . but I like to live. You're trouble, bad trouble. You haven't been here any time at all and already three people are dead.'

'It's only the beginning, kid.'

'I . . . know.' She dropped her head, then turned away from me quickly. 'Do you . . . mind too much?'

I shrugged carelessly. 'Not that much, sugar. A guy can do more when he's not solo, that's why I want company. Hell, half those fancy clip joints won't even let you on the floor when you haven't got a babe under your arm.'

She slipped the lipstick back in its case and stared at it. Her head came up in a slow arc and she let her eyes roam over my face. 'Sometimes . . .' she began.

'Yeah?'

'Maybe it would have been better if you had stayed away, Johnny.'

'Better for who, sugar? Better for a slob of a killer who's out enjoying himself?'

'I didn't mean that.'

Maybe it was the light that made her eyes look so misty. I couldn't be sure so I stepped up to her for a better look and it wasn't the light at all. They were misty and getting wetter until they swam in their own sadness. She smiled a little crookedly and reached for my hand.

'I'm a sad sack, aren't I?' she said. 'I haven't got any shame . . . any sense. I'm sorry I'm silly, Johnny.'

'You aren't silly.'

Outside, the band swung into a slow waltz, a tired song that drifted in through the walls like a vapour and wrapped around us. She had the light behind her like the sun filtering through a haystack and a tear was ready to roll down each cheek. 'You aren't silly,' I said again.

'I was doing fine until you came along. There's a hundred men out there who'd love to make love to me and the only one I want is you.'

I wanted to answer her, but there wasn't any room for words. Her mouth was a fiery cushion against mine, her body a warm curve that melted and flowed into mine, pressing so tightly I could feel every tremor that ran in excited little ripples from her lips to her feet.

My fingers caught in her hair and pulled her head back. 'You're a good kid, Wendy,' I grinned at her.

She didn't grin back. The corners of her eyes tilted with an obscure humour, but that was all. 'Good? You know how good I am. I was good then I grew up. By the time I got smart it was too late. I was a tramp and I'm not making any bones about it. Take a long look, Johnny, and you'll see it all, every bit of it. You'll see a gal who's been kicked around and did a lot of kicking herself. Now I put on an act that shows a little skin and I'm some sort of a success and until you came along I was pretty contented. I have a house, a car and a couple of good friends and I thought I had enough. See what you did to me?'

'Nuts, you're still a good kid.'

This time she did grin. Just a little. 'I can't be. If I was I wouldn't be so stupid and so perfectly frank as to stand here telling you that I was a tramp and almost in love with you to boot.'

I tried to say something, but she wouldn't let me get in a word. 'Don't worry about it, Johnny. Let me be stupid, but don't feel sorry for me. If there's any loving to be done, let me do it. I'm not that stupid. I won't tie you down no matter how many kisses you want. Is that plain enough?'

For a good ten seconds I did nothing but stand there and look at her. It was the first time her soul was in her face and it wiped out all the hard lines around her eyes. I said, 'Yeah . . . I guess it is.'

'By the way . . . I have news about your Vera West.'

I hardly heard her. 'Tell me.'

'I asked around like you told me to and one of the entertainers saw her up at the state capital a few years back. She was playing around with some local character.'

'How'd they know it was Vera?'

'Because she had seen her with Servo when she was booked in some of the clubs in Lyncastle.'

I grunted something and nodded. When I thought about it I said, 'Was that before or after she broke up with him?'

She pinched her tongue between her teeth, then, 'When she vanished she vanished completely, didn't she?'

'Looks that way.'

'Then it must have been before.'

I thought it over but my mind couldn't fit it in anyplace. So she took a flyer on Lenny and so what. Maybe she was tired of his games. I shoved her away gently, holding her out where I could look at her. 'Keep asking. Maybe something good'll turn up. Sure you won't change your mind about tonight?'

'Please . . . not tonight.'

I liked that about her, too. I tossed the butt into an ash tray and opened the door. The tail end of the waltz rushed in on a wave of applause, echoing off the walls. When I looked back she was still standing there watching me. 'Kid,' I said, 'I'm not so interested in virgins that I'd trade a real woman for one.'

Her smile was beautiful this time. Then she stuck her tongue out at me and I shut the door.

Louie met me coming out and waved me over to the bar for a drink. Without being told the bartender shoved something that bubbled under our noses and we raised the glasses in a silent toast. Louie smacked his lips and crooked his head at me. 'Tell me something. You take Wendy away from here?' He caught the question in my glance and added, 'I see her watch you alla time. Me, I know. I have the wife. Lots of pretty girls before that too, you betcha!' He let out a series of grunts and patted himself on the belly in pleasure.

'Look, Louie, you don't *want* to lose her, do you?'

'Hell, Wendy goes and my trade goes too.' He grunted again. 'Maybe not. Men, they like to see the naked women. Sometimes I don't think they care what she's like as long as she's female.'

'You're quite a philosopher. Wendy's not a naked woman.'

'Sure, that's even better. She's better'n a stripper. Let her show one extra inch and these men think they really see something. Not so good to show it all at once. Wendy, she's a good girl.' He peered at me knowingly.

'That's what I told her, Louie.'

'She's had it rough, you know.'

'Sure.'

'But she's a nice girl. You understand?'

'I understand.'

'You treat her rough and you know what happen. You understand that, too?'

If he hadn't been so damn serious he would have sounded

funny. Like her father or something. I raised the glass and drained down the last of the bubbly water. 'Don't worry, Louie, she won't get treated rough. I kind of like the kid, see?'

'Sure, Johnny. I know. Me, I guess I worry too much. She's here long time now. We two good friends. Old Nick, he's good friend too. In that town back there . . .' he waved a thumb over his shoulder, '. . . is all kinds of no-good things. Here it's pretty good and we like it that way. You know.'

I played with the glass a little bit. The bartender tried to fill it up but I held my hand over the top. 'You know much about those bad things, Louie?'

'Some. I don't shop for trouble. I see who goes in and who comes back. Lotsa trade goes through this place.'

'You know a guy named Eddie Packman?'

At first I didn't think he was going to answer me, then he said, 'Why?'

'He's a wise guy.'

'He's a tough guy too.'

'Not that tough. Know where I can find him?'

'He's gotta joint . . .'

'Nope. He's on the town tonight.'

'Then he's gotta woman. You go to the Ship'n Shore. You find him there. He's a big stuff with a woman. Always he has one two feet bigger than him. You taking Wendy?'

'No.'

'That's good. You find trouble with somebody else.'

'Yeah, Wendy suggested the same thing. O.K., Louie, thanks for the info. I'll see you later. Take care of my girl.'

I slid off the stool and waited for a couple to unblock the aisle. Louie's beefy fingers snagged my arm. 'Johnny . . . you ever kill anybody?' His voice was almost lost in the hubbub.

My face tightened up all by itself and my stomach felt hollow. It was something I didn't like to answer, but the answer must have been right there because he added, 'You get tough with this Packman . . . somebody die all right. Somebody get killed quick.'

133

I nodded and he let go of my arm. 'It won't be me,' I said.

'No, it won't be you, Johnny.'

The band started another noisy piece that cleared the bar of dancers long enough for me to squeeze through. I stopped by the door and lit another smoke, trying hard to unscramble the ends and put them together long enough to lead me somewhere.

Somebody wanted me out of the way. Somebody put a thousand bucks in the pocket of a guy who tried to do it. That somebody could be Packman, and if it was Packman he could supply a lot of answers. Like where was Vera West, for instance.

My mind started turning over fast and I dug some change out of my pants. There was an empty row of phone booths off to one side and I grabbed the one on the end. The operator took my nickel for the unlisted number in the red-light section, then rang it twice until that voice sounding like a tall, cool drink said hello.

I said, 'I'm the guy who pulled the tassel, remember?'

Her laugh was the drink spilling over. 'Yes, I certainly remember. You seemed startled.'

'I never pulled a tassel before.'

'What a pity.'

'Look, you said you'd ask around . . .'

'That's right, I did. Do you . . .' she hesitated a moment, 'think we can discuss the matter in say, a half-hour?' In the background I heard the low murmur of voices and the *chink* of ice in a glass. I caught it fast.

'A half-hour's fine. Do we talk there or some other place?'

'Yes . . . please . . .'

'O.K., I'll be parked down the street from your place in a half-hour. I'll have the dimmers on. You'll see me.'

She was saying goodbye when I hung up.

It didn't take me long to get there. Both sides of the street were lined with heaps from battered pick-ups to flashy convertibles, out-of-state licence plates predominating. A black Buick was pulling away from the kerb and I slid into the slot it left.

I still had fifteen minutes to go, so I dragged out the butts and lit up. The second one was down to my fingers when a shaft of light hit the sidewalk as the door to the house opened. Venus in a tailored suit was framed there for a brief second before the door closed and the darkness swallowed her again.

Her heels made little tapping sounds on the pavement as if they were keeping time with some inaudible music. I switched the dimmers on and off twice then left them on and watched her walk into their soft glow. When she was opposite the car I pushed the door open and waited.

Then Venus with her heavenly aroma slid in next to me and plucked the butt out of my fingers for a last drag before flipping it out the window. 'I feel like a schoolgirl,' she smiled.

'Sneak out?'

'More or less.'

'Sorry if I interrupted something.'

'Oh,' her eyes slanted a little and grinned at me, 'it wasn't that important. As a matter of fact, I was looking for an excuse to get away when you called.' She leaned over and turned the switch on the radio, then fiddled with the dial until the throbbing beat of a symphony filled the car. 'The Philadelphia . . . mind?'

'Not at all.'

Venus was quite a woman. Quite. Red light de luxe but loved her symphonies. She sat with her head back on the seat, her eyes half closed, breathing in every note.

I let her listen to the last of it. Fifteen minutes of sitting there not saying a word until only the echo was left then I shut it off. She dreamed on for a minute longer before her head came up and another smile leaned in my direction. 'You're a pleasure to be with, man.'

I said thanks kind of drily, waited, then: 'You didn't come out to listen to that, did you?'

This time she laughed deep in her throat and without any kind of coyness slid her hand under mine. 'You don't know much about women, do you?'

'Enough, I guess.'

'I said women.'

'Is there a difference?'

'You'd be surprised.'

'Then I guess I don't know much.' She didn't know how much truth was in that statement. You don't learn much in just a few years. Not even a lifetime.

'You're about to learn, man,' Venus grinned. Her hand squeezed mine just enough so I'd know exactly what she meant. Not that it was necessary. The devil had been there in her voice and her eyes warming me with the thought. She reached for the cigarettes in my pocket without taking her eyes from mine. 'Not now of course,' she added. 'Later. In style.'

'Of course,' I tried to say knowingly.

It sounded like a croak.

She pulled the dash lighter out, held it to the tip of her cigarette a moment and stuck it back. Through the smoke she said, 'You wanted to know about Vera West?'

The warm feeling I had went away. Fast. 'That's right.'

'Everybody wants Vera, don't they?'

'Jack tell you?'

She nodded. 'I didn't learn much until he did. The girls were a little afraid to talk about it, but I gathered that they had been approached by several men and quizzed.'

'Who?'

'The men weren't identified. Frankly, I believed the girls when they said they didn't know them, but from what was said, the men weren't exactly strangers in town.'

I mulled it over a minute and she anticipated my next question. 'No description. The girls were tanked at the time and weren't paying any attention to the men. They . . . see a lot of men, you know.'

'Yeah, but hell, why pick on them? How would they know about Vera?'

'One,' she told me softly, 'happened to be a girlhood friend of Vera's. The other happened to be a pet flame of Eddie Packman's when Vera and Servo were making a big thing of it. At the time they were quite friendly.'

'You question them?'

'Without any results. When Vera went she went completely. Nobody seems to know what happened to her.'

'Any chance of her being . . . dead?'

'You know . . .' her lip went under her teeth momentarily, 'I thought of that and would've considered it a possibility if it hadn't been for one thing.'

'Yeah?'

'Servo didn't break with Vera like he did with the others. It was the other way around. In fact, Lenny Servo was pretty upset about it from what I heard. He had it pretty hard for that girl. Later, of course, he acted like it was all his doing. The guy's neck-high in pride especially where women are concerned. No, I don't think Vera's dead at all. I think she disappeared of her own will.'

'Why?' I asked.

'That's something I haven't figured out yet. If she had something on Lenny and proposed to use it she certainly wouldn't have gone off like that. That is, if she was smart enough to protect what she had so Lenny couldn't touch her. No, I don't think that was it at all. She had another reason for leaving.'

'She could have been afraid of somebody,' I said.

'Maybe, but it would have had to be Lenny. Nobody else could scare her into leaving.'

'Why?'

She shrugged her shoulders eloquently. 'Lenny Servo is still boss in this town and as long as you're on his side nobody bothers you. Lenny would take care of them quick. Certainly if someone was after her for some reason she would have told Lenny and that would have ended it right there.'

She was right. She had it down pat, every bit of it, and it all made sense. I flipped my butt out the open window and stared at her. 'There's only one catch to it.'

'There is?'

'Don't you see it?'

'Well . . . no.'

'Maybe Lenny isn't the boss.'

Her lips parted in a faint sarcastic smile. 'Man, you just don't know Lenny Servo.'

'No, but I will, chicken, I will. In fact, I'm very anxious to know Mr Servo. It's going to be one of the big moments of my life. The second big moment.'

'What's the first?'

'Finding a crumb named Eddie Packman.'

'Brother,' she whispered, 'have you got a case.'

'Like to come along?'

'I'd love it, man, just love it. I'm really interested in finding out whether you're a jerk or not.'

'And if I'm not?'

'Then you'll find out what a real woman's like. In style, of course.'

This time I said, 'Of course,' and it didn't come out a croak. I kicked the starter in and pulled away from the kerb. Behind me a little coupé grabbed the space before my fenders cleared the car in front. Business was good tonight.

Down at the corner I made a U-turn and headed back towards town. My lovely zombie turned her head questioningly in my direction and asked me, 'Where are we going?'

'To a place called the Ship'n Shore. Know where it is?'

'Umm. We're really going fancy. Stay on the River Road. You can't miss it. That where you expect to find Eddie Packman?'

'Maybe.' I switched the radio back on again, only this time no symphony. Just a nice sexy rumba instead. 'By the way, what do I call you?'

She looked at me sleepily. 'Oh, any pet name will do.'

'Don't you have a real one?'

'I did, man. That was a long time ago.'

'O.K., Venus.'

'O.K., man.'

'The name is Johnny. Johnny McBride.'

'O.K., Johnny.' Her eyes touched my face speculatively a second and something like a grin pulled at her mouth. 'I'm in fast company,

138

aren't I?' She mused. 'I *thought* there was something familiar about you. That picture in the paper didn't do you justice.'

The grin got very real. 'But never mind, a lot of my best friends have had overnight accommodations in our official hostelry.'

This time she curled her arm around mine and pulled herself over closer, leaning her head on my shoulder. I liked it that way. Her hair was so black it was invisible in the darkness, but I could feel little feathers of it brushing my face and smell the flowers that seemed to be growing there.

A signpost told me where to cut off on the River Road and a neon-trimmed sign said the place we were after was only two miles ahead. Long before we got there the aurora of the lights showed up like a false dawn while the breeze carried the throbbing rhythm of 'Bolero' through the air.

It had been another long day and it wasn't over yet. Logan with that back history of mine. Lindsey and Tucker and the boys from Washington with all their science and gadgets. My hands were still sore. A murder I didn't have anything to do with for a change. A screwy ad in the paper and a screwier phone call then a dead man I did have something to do with.

Thinking about the phone call was what got me. Who the hell was so interested in me and why? I gave Venus a poke with my elbow. 'You awake?'

Her hand squeezed my arm.

'You know anybody named Harlan?'

First she didn't do anything. Then she tilted her head forward and glanced at me with her face wrinkled up. 'Just Harlan?'

'That's as much of it as I know.'

'There was a girl once . . . a long time ago. That was her name. Funny you should mention it.'

I took my foot off the gas and let the heap slow down some. 'Go on,' I said.

'She was a dancer . . . we were in a show together. I know that Harlan was her stage name, but I never knew her other.'

'When was this?'

139

'Oh, a long time ago. Ten years. Both of us were new at the time. When the show closed I never went back on the stage, but I remember reading about Harlan occasionally. For a while she was pretty successful, then I never heard any more about her. Why, Johnny?'

'That's what I'd like to know. Why. Why a lot of things? Remember what she looked like?'

'Dressed or undressed?'

'Both.'

'Dressed she was very beautiful. However, like most of the show-lovelies, she was a very plain base upon which make-up showed to the best advantage. There was nothing to hide; everything added was an improvement. Understand?'

I nodded to show that I did.

'She was about my size, brown hair, no distinguishing features that might set her apart after all these years. Oh, yes, she was dumb. The genuine beautiful-but-dumb type. She was quite a doll as long as she kept her mouth shut. When she voiced an opinion all her admirers got sick to their stomachs.'

'She sounds great. Would she be in Lyncastle?'

'Not if I know Harlan. I've never seen her around.'

'Maybe it's a different woman. That is, if Harlan *is* a woman.'

I let out a couple of dirty words under my breath and shoved the gas pedal down again. There was the answer all right. Harlan was either a man or a place. Great. I was doing fine again. And for a couple of minutes it all looked so good, too.

Venus lost herself in thought before she spoke again. 'Someplace at home I have a picture of the old chorus line-up. The Harlan I knew is in it. Just for kicks I'll dig it up.'

I muttered an O.K. and pulled the Ford around a curve. Up ahead was the Ship'n Shore looking like a grounded houseboat, alive with lights and sound. On the near side was a two-acre parking lot crammed to the fences with not a sign of anybody even thinking about going home.

A coloured attendant waved me into a slot near the gate, took the four bits for his wave with an unconcerned nod and went back into his stuccoed cabaña. You didn't need a guide around the place, not with all the neon fixtures that told you just what was where. The bar was in the front of the place with the main lounge directly behind it protruding out over the water. Every table was packed, the dance floor was a blur of motion and out over the water on the open deck you could see the flashes of white that were faces merging with other flashes of white.

But the gimmicks were upstairs. The place had a second storey that had windows all around except for a section in back and nobody tried to hide the chant of the croupiers or the whir of the wheels. You could even see the clusters of people hovering over the tables, straightening up when the throw was made, reaching for more moola to keep in the game.

Venus didn't give me any choice. She nudged me into the bar, smiled a smile that got us a rail position and immediate service and ordered up a pair of highballs. They were two bucks each, but I wasn't bothering about money. Not with those nice, crisp bills tucked away in my wallet.

I laid a new hundred-buck bill on the mahogany, watched it get changed into some old ones, shoved the bartender a fin for his trouble and downed the drink. Venus was about two swallows behind me. We had two more quickies when I noticed the gang lined up at the bar giving me and Venus the business with the eyes. I gave her a second look myself. Before, it was dark and she looked good.

Under lights she was really something.

Ever see a babe pass on the street who was all smooth curves with enough skin showing in spots to make it exciting? The kind you wanted to whistle at but couldn't get your mouth puckered up fast enough? That was Venus. To make it rough on the boys she didn't bother to wear anything under the jacket and where it dropped off in a long V before the buttons grabbed it together was something that made your breath catch in your throat. It wasn't what you saw, but what you knew was there, and the business I was getting with the eyes was because it was there for me.

But that wasn't all.

They knew damn well who she was all right. You could tell that. The boys weren't above dropping down to her block occasionally. So tonight they were here and supposedly respectable, and the eyes made the business you'd give a slut when she walked into a church social. When I caught the angle I felt like knocking them all on their lily-white tails.

I guess the bartender took me for a hick on the town with his harvest wages because he was giving Venus the big look that meant she had a sucker in tow and upstairs was the place for the suckers. He waited until a quarter of the hundred was in the till then angled over in our direction polishing glasses.

He looked at me with a faint grin and said, 'You can double that roll upstairs, friend.'

'I can?' I must have played it innocent enough because he nodded solemnly.

'Sure thing. Guy came through here last week and left with twenty-five grand.'

'Say now.' I nudged Venus with my knee. 'That sounds pretty good, chick. What say we give it a try. You know, I'm pretty hot with the cubes, mister. Think there might be any big-money men up there who like to gamble? *Really* gamble, I mean?'

My boy played it cute. He leaned over confidentially. '*All* the big boys are upstairs, friend. All, I said. You'll get your money's worth.' He winked at Venus. 'The lady too. Drinks on the house upstairs.'

That was all I needed. I shoved the change in my pocket and the two of us edged back through the mob and followed the waiter who had come up at the bartender's nod to show us the way. I gave him a fin, too.

It was fancier than I expected. A million bucks' worth of chrome and pine panelling and not a cent of it going to waste. A bar ran the entire length of the room with tables along the other side if you felt like taking a ten-minute break. Every other inch of space was taken up with some kind of game with the biggest play being given the roulette that occupied the centre position.

Up here Venus wasn't so undressed. Most of the dames in evening dresses were going to catch cold in their lungs tomorrow. I changed another hundred for a stack of chips and started edging in on a dice table.

Venus grabbed my arm. 'Ever meet Lenny Servo?' I didn't like the quiet way she said it.

'We've met.'

She looked at me first, then her eyes went across the room to a faro spread. The background was supposed to be Western and the single light bulb that dangled inside the reflector over the table made the mouse under Lenny's eye seem to take up the whole side of his face. He was talking to the dealer and when he looked up he saw Venus standing there and waved casually. Just as casually she waved back.

Me, I had two dames in front wide enough to block me off. Lenny didn't see me and I wasn't about to go over and shake his hand. Eddie Packman I wanted first. Then Lenny. I'd always find time for Lenny.

Nobody had to tell me about guys like him. Everything was written on his face and if something was left out you saw it in the way he strutted standing still. Servo was a little general, a brain, a whip, a sloppy son of a bitch and I felt like smearing him right there.

That gives you an idea of the kind of guy he was. A mug. A mug from way back. But a smooth mug with money to buy what he didn't have even if it was somebody's death.

When he turned back to the table again I pulled Venus over to me. 'Now show me Packman.'

'I don't see him yet.'

'Think we'd do better circulating around?'

'Perhaps. He can get lost in a crowd pretty easily.'

I reached in between a couple of hips and covered a number on the table. The wheel went around, the voice chanted and I lost. I tried again and lost again.

I had better luck at the dice table playing the field numbers. At least I recouped what I lost. We made our way around the room trying to act like just part of the crowd, but it didn't do much good. Venus didn't locate the guy and I didn't see any tall babes who could have been his dish. By the time we made the complete circuit I had dropped a couple of hundred and was tired of playing tag with Servo. Every once in a while she'd point out a couple of prominent joes in the mob and give me a quick run-down. One was the mayor. He wasn't with his wife, either. Two members of the city council were at the bar talking politics with what appeared to be a couple of businessmen. In each of the four corners were oversized lugs in tuxes that didn't fit. Standard accessories in any joint, only two of them happened to be city cops picking up a few bucks in off-duty hours.

I had about as much of it as I could stand. I grabbed Venus and said, 'Let's get out of here.'

She tossed a couple of bucks on the table. 'One more roll.' I waited, watched the cubes spin out and heard the stickman call it off. Venus turned around and grinned at me. 'See, last rolls are lucky. Let me lose this then we'll go.'

'Go ahead,' I told her. Hell, it wasn't my dough.

She didn't lose. Ten minutes later she was raking in the cabbage like dried leaves and half the room was over watching her do it. She got up past the twelve thousand mark and I started to get interested and if my damn head hadn't been up and locked I would have seen what was coming.

He was a big guy and he wasn't kidding. He had another guy just as big along to back him up and when he tapped me on the shoulder and said, 'The boss wants to see you,' I played rube and fell in the middle between them and lock-stepped through the crowd. I had to stop once to let a dame swish by and what prodded me in the back wasn't the end of a finger.

We went out through a pair of swinging doors, down a corridor to a walnut-panelled door and the guy in front knocked twice sharply, waited until somebody called out to come in, then shoved the door open.

'You first.'

So I went first.

Lenny Servo was in the same position he had been in his own office, perched on the end of the desk. The guy in the swivel chair beside him was a greasy little fat boy with no hair and pig eyes and he looked like he was all set to enjoy himself. The other guy was a pimply-faced brat hardly out of his teens and he was having a great time testing the action on an oversized automatic, trying to make like he was tough.

With a motion he must have studied in front of a mirror, Lenny plucked a cigarette from a gold case, edged it into his mouth and lit up without looking at it. It was very neat. When he took a drag on it he said, 'Hit him,' soft and easy like, and right on cue the three pair of eyes in front of me went a little bit to my right and behind me.

There was that much warning and it was enough. I turned under the swing, yanked the bastard off balance and kicked his buddy in the guts before he could get the gun out of his pocket. The puke spewed out of his mouth, but I was in back of him by then and didn't worry about it. In fact, I wasn't worried about anything. I had his gun in my fist and hoping like hell somebody would try something.

Lenny was funny. He couldn't believe it had happened. His face was slack with surprise and he turned around to look at Pimples who still had the automatic in his hand. Pimples wasn't so tough after all. The rod made a 'thunk' on the carpet and little beads of sweat formed on his head and ran in crooked rivulets down through the maze of pimples.

Only the big guy on the floor tried something. He was so damn mad he was all set to take me, gun or no gun. His mouth was pulled back showing more gums than teeth and he crouched in front of me like a tackle ready to charge. Maybe he didn't appreciate it, but I saved his life. I kicked him right in the neck and he went out like a light.

Pig eyes said, 'Cripes! Lenny, you said . . .'

Lenny's butt dropped on the carpet and the stink of singed wool filled the room. He was watching me with the surprise all gone, the skin over his cheekbones a little tighter than usual, but that was all. I had the gun pointing smack at his belly, but he wasn't a bit scared.

Curious was the word.

'You needed enough help, Lenny,' I sneered.

He didn't answer me.

'How many times are you going to try before you get smart? You better start reading the papers. There's a lot of dead men lying around lately.'

The muscle in his cheek twitched. 'It's pretty hard to teach you a lesson, isn't it?'

'Damn hard, pal.' I let the gun come up until it was pointing at his head. 'I asked you a question the last time. Where is she?'

The colour seemed to drain out of his face. He was absolutely white, a crazy mixture of impotent rage and bewilderment that held him tight as a bowstring. 'Damn you, McBride,' he grated, 'I'm going to get the both of you if it's the last thing I do!'

I let him get it out of his system then wiped the muzzle of the rod across his jaw with a crack that knocked him on his knees. He squatted there, moaning softly, covering his face with his hands.

Fat boy behind the desk couldn't keep his lips wet. His tongue was a pink streak licking out of his mouth while his hands were white blobs gripping the edge of his desk.

I said,' You don't want to try a stunt like this again, do you?'

His jowls flapped as his head jerked from one side to another. I looked over at Pimples and grinned at him. It must have been a hell of a grin. He fainted.

The two boys on the floor were making signs of getting up. I opened the gun, kicked the shells out and threw it beside the one I took it from. Lenny's head came up out of his hands and he stared at me with all the hate he could muster up.

'You'll die for that,' he said.

I felt like kicking him in the teeth. I should have instead of telling him, 'That'll be the day, Lenny.'

When I got back to the room Venus was still at the table, but the crowd was gone. She only had a little pile of bills left and the stickman had stopped sweating. I poked her in the ribs with my thumb and she jumped to attention. 'From rags to riches and back again, huh?'

'Damn it, where'd you go? If you had stayed around I could have left with a fortune.'

'Sorry. What I had to do wouldn't wait.'

'Oh!' She raked in what she had left and stuck the bills in her pocketbook. 'Ready to go?'

'Any time.'

I steered her to the door and we had a nightcap in the bar downstairs. One of the off-duty cops spotted me and wrinkled his face as if he were puzzled. I wasn't for sticking around long enough for something else to happen, so we took a quick tour of the dance floor just for luck. But if Eddie Packman was around he wasn't where we could see him and they didn't have rooms for rent in that joint.

Venus looked as disappointed as I felt. 'Lousy try, huh?'

'Stinking,' I agreed.

'Want to try anyplace else?'

'Where?'

'Ah, there are a lot of places he might be. I think you'd do better to try the hotels. Unless he's with a woman who's giving him a hard time, he won't be wasting the night floating around the clubs.'

'Ah, the hell with it. Tomorrow's another day. I'll find him.'

'But I wanted to see it happen,' she pouted.

'You're a bloodthirsty devil.'

'Aren't I though?'

She laughed up at me, her teeth flashing in the night. I bent over and let my mouth lean against hers. She didn't kiss me. Her fingers grabbed my arms and she bit my lip then took the sting of the bite out with her tongue.

All so damn fast it was like being struck by a snake whose venom was a vicious, poisonous pleasure that left you rigid and trembling in your shoes.

Her breath came so fast the words tumbled out. 'Don't . . . ever do that again. Not you . . . not when there's people around!'

I knew just how she felt. I slid my hand under her arm and made her walk to the car, feeling her leg touching mine, deliberately keeping pace with me, knowing her eyes were crawling over me. Venus knew how to make it rough on a guy.

When I got behind the wheel the boy came out of his little cabaña, waved me out for another four bits and I turned back towards town.

This time he earned his four bits. For a curious second he flashed his torch on the car that came roaring up behind me with the headlights off and I caught the reflection in the rearview mirror. I didn't have the chance to jump the Ford into high when the big job slammed into the back bumper then darted past on the right with the roaring slam of a heavy gun spitting holes in my windshield.

I did the only thing I could; tried to duck and wrench the wheel over as hard as possible, then jarred forward into the wheel when the tyres hit the sand on the shoulder of the road. The rear wheels went up into the air as the nose tipped forward, then smashed back and bounced the car around in a quarter-arc before coming to a shuddering standstill.

Venus was jammed against me covered with splintered glass, the marks of it traced in blood on her cheeks. I couldn't get my voice to say anything except 'Damn, damn!'

The blood was there on her chest too, a dark trickle moving into the V of her jacket. I grabbed the lapels and tore them apart. The button held, then ripped loose and she was shamefully naked from the waist up and I was screaming mad because such beauty had to be wasted. My hand went out to stop the bleeding . . . do anything to keep her alive. My fingers probed for an ugly hole that should be swelling and didn't find any so I wiped the blood away with the flat of my palm to look for it.

And it wiped away clean. There wasn't any hole. I said, 'Damn!'

Then her eyes opened and she whispered, 'You can say that again.'

So I said it again, only this time with a grin.

'But you can keep looking if you want to,' she added softly.

I did that, too, looking and thinking how nice and round she was where it seemed so necessary, and so damn glad she was very much alive. Just why, I couldn't figure. I could still hear the hum of those bullets passing in front of my nose.

She didn't want to, but I made her close the jacket again.

CHAPTER NINE

'You all right?'

'I . . . think so.' Her hand passed over her face and brushed a fragment of glass away. 'Who . . . was it, Johnny?'

'Somebody who's so damn anxious to see me dead he doesn't give a hoot who else dies in the process. It's not very healthy to be around me any more, baby.'

'No. That's a fact, isn't it?' She looked around at the holes, her face blank with astonishment as she visualized how close she'd come to getting booted out of this land of the living. She fumbled for a cigarette, lit two and stuck one in my mouth. When she had a deep drag settled in her lungs she asked, 'How did he miss? I don't understand.'

'I do,' I told her. 'The jerk misjudged his distance. If he hadn't ploughed into us I probably would have kept going straight ahead and been a lovely target. At least I know one thing: he was alone, that's why he stayed on the right, so he could shoot through the driver's side instead of firing across the seat. With all his plans he muffed it anyway. Well, we can't just sit here. Climb out a minute.'

When we were both outside I dug out the jack handle from under the seat and knocked out the rest of the glass in the frames. Venus found a whisk broom in the glove compartment and cleared off the cushions and we were ready to get moving. Luckily, the rear wheels were still on the pavement, so it wasn't any trouble hauling the front free. Just about the time I got the heap rolling the headlights of the first car turned out of the parking area back down the road. When he saw we were moving the car stopped, turned around and went back to the parking lot.

Either the wind wasn't right or the people in this section weren't very curious when other people started popping away with a rod. Hell, maybe they thought it was a gag. Yeah!

The breeze whipped in through the blank space in the windshield, kicking the dust around our faces. Venus waited until we had reached the main highway before she finally broke down and let herself cry. When the spasm passed I said, 'Feel better now?'

'Much, only I need some coffee. Stop someplace, all right?'

'Sure.'

I pulled in at the first all-night joint I came to. It was a regular Hollywood affair, a fancy dog palace sprawled along the highway with tables inside and out, car-hop service and a small bar if you wanted one for the road. The place was packed with couples heading home after a big time in Lyncastle and there were more drunks around trying to sober up than anything else.

Venus wanted to go inside so I found a table, signalled a waitress over and ordered two coffees and a foursome of hot dogs. My eyes were hungrier than my stomach. You don't get almost shot up then try to get your insides to take things calmly. The dogs wrinkled up on the plates, but the hot coffee held me together somewhat.

Or almost did anyway. Just before I finished the cup I saw something happen to Venus's eyes and looked where she was looking. There was a table in the far corner completely dominated by a red-headed bundle of curves who would have gone six feet in her stocking feet. She almost completely obscured the guy who was leering across the table at her.

Venus's mouth made silent words that said, 'Eddie Packman,' and something went crawling up my back. The little bastard's hair shone over a face that should have been peering out of a cage. There were muscles built into the hundred-buck suit he wore and I could see the flash of the diamond on his hand all the way across the room.

The redhead must have loved him because she was holding his hand while her finger kept fiddling with the brilliant hunk of ice enviously. I could have sat there and watched for one minute or thirty. Time didn't make a bit of difference any more. All I knew was that when he paid his bill and walked out I was right behind him.

What I wanted most of all was to see the kind of car he was driving. In my mind I could still see the black hulk of the sedan with the winking red eye sticking out the front window. I wanted to see if they were the same before I tore his arms and legs off.

The car was big and it was a sedan. It wasn't black, but the colour was close enough. In the dark there isn't any difference in colours to talk about anyway. I said, 'Hello, Eddie,' good and slow and watched him turn around. He almost said hello, but it never came out. His narrow eyes looked propped open momentarily then came down to meet the sneer that was twisting his mouth out of shape.

And you know what the little bastard did? He came for me! He didn't wait. Hell, no. He shoved the redhead away, took a jerky little step forward and winged his right at me without even bothering to make a fist of his hand. The lousy little punk tried to slap me across the jaw and damn near did it, too.

Not quite.

I grabbed that open palm, twisted him right off his feet, watched him come up off the ground screaming until my fist smashed the yell right back down his throat again. He lay there face down in his own blood and I was just going to give him another taste of it when I felt my skull get parted down the middle. It didn't even hurt. It was just a big blanket of noise that rolled in like thunder. The animal reflexes a man is born with kept me standing and seeing long enough to catch the shine of polished brass buttons and see the barrel of a gun come down again and make another sharp crack across the top of my head.

Things weren't all white this time. There was a funny smell in the air, but it wasn't antiseptic. No mummy, either. Everything was painted an ugly efficient green and the light that streaked in the windows seemed to be slatted. After five minutes of looking at it I realized why. There were horizontal steel bars built right into the frames.

The cop said, 'Awake, eh?'

I grunted and touched my head. It would have been better if I hadn't. The top of my skull was soft and squashy, held together by strips of tape that went down to my ears. My body seemed to throb all over, trying to explode.

'Want something to eat?'

My stomach started to heave at the word. I said no, but he brought in a tray anyhow so I managed to get some of the coffee down. It helped things enough so I could swallow some limp toast.

Then a doctor came in and probed around, checking what he found against a pair of X-ray pictures. I said, 'Look good?'

'Looks lucky.'

'That's what the last doctor said.'

'If either one of those blows had landed a half-inch on either side you'd be dead.'

'That's nice. I saw brass buttons behind the gun that nailed me.'

The cop in the corner lowered his paper. 'You was disturbing the peace. You committed assault with intent to kill.'

'You should live to be a hundred; but right away,' I said, 'I want a lawyer.'

'The court'll assign one.'

'The hell it will. I'll pick my own. Who's in charge of this rat trap?'

The doctor shook out some pills on the table-top beside the bed. 'I don't think you're in a condition to be excited at this moment. You're going to have to stay quiet a few days.'

'Nuts! I'll pick my own doctor too if I want to and you know damn well I can. I want out of this trap.'

I saw the doctor look at the cop and shrug. 'It's up to him,' he said. The cop put down the paper and walked to the door. Five minutes later he came back and he wasn't alone. Lindsey was with him. The guy looked happy again. Real happy. I called him a son of a bitch and tried to kick him in the stomach. He leered at me and stayed out of range. All I did was make my head hurt worse.

'You know why you're here, don't you?' Lindsey grinned.

The cop muttered. 'He knows. I told him. He thinks he's pretty wise.'

'Yeah, I know,' Lindsey agreed. He pulled a pad out of his pocket, leaned back against a chair and waited for me to say something.

He'd still be waiting if the Press didn't walk in as nice as you please. The cop at the door looked at Lindsey kind of puzzled-like, waiting to see if Logan would get tossed out or not.

My boy handed an envelope to Lindsey and said tonelessly, 'It's a writ. Very legal and all that. McBride's free on bail so you can put your pad away, copper.'

Remember how I told you Lindsey looked the first day I saw him at the hotel desk? How his eyes went all the way up and the red came into his face? He looked like that again. Maybe a little worse.

But you'd never know how mad he was by the way he spoke. His voice was calm as still-frozen water and just as cold. He said, 'I heard you were mixed up with him, Logan. I didn't want to think so because you used to be a nice guy.'

'So did you, Lindsey.' Logan had ice of his own.

The chief's head made a slow turn until his face was pointed at me. 'Now you got friends, Johnny. Now you got friends who can pull writs out of a hat early in the morning because a judge is afraid of getting in wrong with the Press. Somebody even went to the trouble of putting up ten-grand bail, so you have some very powerful friends all of a sudden.' His eyes shifted to Logan a moment before coming back to me. 'You're going to need them, feller, but they'll never be able to help you enough.'

The doctor and the other cop edged out the room and closed the door. I went to sit up, managed it after the second try and perched on the edge of the bed. Lindsey took a step closer to Logan, the hate oozing out of every pore. 'Don't ever come near me, Logan. Never again, understand?' Then he swung on his heel and reached for the doorknob.

Logan said, 'Lindsey . . .'

The cop barely looked back.

'We used to be friends,' Logan said.

'No more.'

'You used to be a good cop, too.'

'No more,' I put in, and Lindsey looked all the way back, his hand still on the door.

'When you finally realize that it's possible for even a brain like you to be wrong, maybe we can be friends again. You're not much smarter than me in police business and I say McBride never killed Minnow. Think about it sometime.'

He thought about it. For at least three seconds. Then he opened that door and slammed it behind him so hard it almost came off the hinges.

Logan shrugged sadly and turned back to my remains. 'Feeling well enough to clear this place?'

'I certainly don't feel bad enough to stay. Give me a lift, will you?'

He came over and hooked his hand under my arm, half dragging me upright. When he was sure I wasn't going to topple over he got my clothes out of the closet and helped me into them. The whole operation took a while, but I was fairly presentable except for the patch over my skull. The boys at the desk downstairs handed me a manila envelope with my personal effects and that was the end of that. Logan had his Chevvy outside and got me into the seat next to him, then lit up a brace of smokes and handed me one.

He had to say it sometime. I was waiting for it and he said it. 'Of all the lame-brain stupes you take the cake. How much trouble can a guy get into anyway?'

'A lot more than this.'

'Feel like talking?'

'Not especially, but if you're curious, what would you like to know?'

'A few things the cops don't seem to know. First about a dead man outside of town. He was a very special kind of dead man. He and two friends were part of an out-of-town team who specialized in rough stuff. The other two were found very nicely killed.'

'So?'

'He made the third. It might have been accidental but the chances are it wasn't.'

'It was. At least he wasn't murdered. I was chasing him and he ran off the road. He died without talking. Next question.'

Logan took another drag on the butt and nodded. 'Same guy was seen in Eddie Packman's place only a short time before. Then you beat up on Packman while the cops are looking and get tossed in the can. Why?'

'Because said dead man had a grand in new bills on him, that's why. Eddie paid him off for the job he didn't do. There must have been trouble about it because the guy came away mad.'

'So that's why you went after Packman this morning.' He made a nice neat statement out of it.

I shook my head carefully. 'That was only half why, friend. About a half-hour before that somebody fired a hatful of bullets at me and they weren't kidding. Whoever it was waited for me to come out of the Ship'n Shore, barrelled up and let loose. Nobody got hurt, but I got pretty mad. I checked Eddie's car and that could've been the one.'

'It wasn't,' Logan said.

'What?'

'Eddie had been at that road stand for a good two hours before you came along. I checked.'

I remembered every curse word I had ever learned and strung them out in a row. When they were out of my system I dragged the butt down to my fingers and tossed it out to the sidewalk. 'Logan,' I said, 'this whole thing is a screwed-up mess if ever I saw one. Everybody wants me dead but the wrong people. A killer wants me dead. The cops want me dead. Not Servo or Packman, pal. Servo was behind me in the joint when I left and Packman was in the other place. Whoever shot at me this time was the same one who tried it from the roof top the last time, and if it wasn't Servo or Packman this time it wasn't Servo or Packman then. No, they don't want me dead.'

Logan's face tightened up until it was white. 'Who says they don't?' He kept staring out the windshield.

'Finish it.'

'Packman's threatening to kill you on sight and Servo's going to be in a blue funk when he finds out you aren't where you can be gotten to easily.'

'Like in the clink?'

'Exactly.'

'Where he has men on his pay roll?'

'You got better eyes than I thought you had.'

'Then to whom do I owe the debt of putting up ten grand for my bail?'

Logan dropped his butt on the floor and stepped on it. 'This'll kill you. Your old boss put it up. Havis Gardiner.'

'Fine, but I don't get it.'

'You will. Your direct-approach system seems to have had its effect. The guy thinks you're innocent. Or at least your buddy was. His insurance investigators have uncovered a lead on Vera West.'

'Fine,' I said again. This time my voice shook.

'Not fine, kid. They think she's dead.'

'Oh, hell, when's it going to end!'

He turned around and glanced at me absently. 'When somebody finds out why Robert Minnow died, that's when.' His foot went down on the starter and churned the engine into life.

'I've been looking into that angle. I saw his wife.'

'Yeah?'

'It was a pretty good story.'

'Tell me about it.'

I told him. I gave it to him in detail right down to the last minute Robert Minnow had spent on this earth and all the while I was talking his face kept getting tighter and tighter. His eyes seemed to sink deeper into his head and he didn't ask any questions. When I finished I let him mull over it for a while,

157

hoping he'd make a break, but nothing happened. After he thought about it ten minutes the scowl turned into a puzzled frown and stayed there. Hell, if that's the way he wanted it, good enough. I wasn't going to pump it out of him.

I said, 'Where to?'

'You're going to stay with me until I deliver you to Gardiner.'

'O.K., pal, whatever you say. But how about letting me get my car back. I wouldn't want the friend it belongs to worried about it.'

It didn't take more than an hour to collect the Ford and park it at a garage where they promised to have it ready before noon. All the slugs had gone through the glass and since I had knocked out what was left of it nobody could tell what happened. Logan let me get finished then hauled us back to the *News* office where he went in to see about some business.

When he came back I asked 'Where to?'

'No place special for a while. I'm still on that murder case.'

'The dame?'

'Yeah. The cops are up a tree too. They're trying to run down the truckers she was friendly with.'

'What about her room-mate?'

'She took a powder when she heard about it. Got skunky drunk right after she identified the body and was last seen climbing into a truck for a necking party outside a joint on the highway.'

'Didn't show up yet?'

'Naw, probably still on a binge. She's just the type, according to those who knew her. Right now she's probably sleeping it off if she isn't already back at work. I'm going down there now and see what the score is. Look, if you don't feel like running around I'll drop you off at my place.'

'Hell, I'm O.K.'

So at nine-thirty-five we pulled into the ABC Diner and I waited in the car while Logan went inside to ask his questions. He didn't take long. Five minutes later he was back shaking his head. He got back in the car and started to pull out just as a

158

prowl car drove up. Logan grimaced at the driver through the windshield. 'You won't get anyplace either, copper.'

'No soap?' I asked.

'Hell, she's still missing. At least it isn't anything new. Her boss said she took off like that a couple times before. Didn't show for a week.' He reached in his pocket and flipped a snapshot out at me. 'There's what she looks like.'

I said, 'Umm,' because she wasn't bad at all. It was taken at a beach and she was oozing out of a bikini suit like toothpaste out of a tube. She was some hunk of stuff if you didn't mind a face that was too much lipstick, too arched eyebrows, too wide eyes and too little sense than to try to wear an upsweep in a stiff wind. I gave him back the snap and settled down against the cushions. It was his working day, not mine. My head was putting up an argument against staying awake and I didn't have anything to say about it. I closed my eyes and fell asleep.

I kept dreaming about a blonde, a real honey blonde with a soft curving body and a beautiful face that had a wonderful radiance about it. She came close to me, smiling, her eyes telling me she loved me, then when she was only an arm's length away the hands that had been reaching for my face grew sharp, curved talons and she raked at my eyes viciously. I batted them away and tried to grab her, but she stayed out of reach and laughed at me. I said, 'Vera, I'll kill you when I get you, so help me!'

The elbow that rammed my ribs wasn't trying to be gentle. Logan gritted, 'Wake up, damn it.'

'Where are we?' I came out of it fast, trying to see everything at once. The day had drifted into dusk and the cars coming towards us had their dimmers on. We were nestled against the kerb beside a six-foot field-stone fence in a section of town I hadn't seen before.

Logan let me get the sleep out of my eyes first. 'Gardiner's place. He wants to talk to you.'

'I been asleep all day?'

'You're not kidding. Come on, snap out of it.'

So I snapped out of it. Logan locked the car then took me for a short walk around the field-stone fence to a wrought-iron gate that might have been swiped from Buckingham Palace. He rang a bell, we waited, then a tall gent in riding breeches did the honours of opening the gate. The guy was the type who could turn politeness on or off and since he had it on right then I gathered that we were expected.

There was a long walk up a flagstone path that curved through a series of gardens, ending abruptly at the foot of a gently sloping lawn that encircled a fine old house. A three- or four-car garage was set back in the shadows under the trees and behind that the faint outlines of a tennis court probing the sky with metal fingers of its fence corners.

'Some dump.'

Logan nodded curtly. 'Some have and some don't. I'll let Gardiner have it. Taxes on this place must cost a fortune.'

'Yeah, it's rough having to be a bank president and live in style. I feel for him.'

'Quit being class-conscious,' he said.

Evidently there was some communication between the gate and the house. The door opened as we were going up the steps and an elderly woman in a severe black dress smiled and ushered us in. She took Logan's hat, escorted us into a walnut-panelled room lined with books and said, 'Mr Gardiner will be right with you, gentlemen. Make yourselves comfortable.'

We didn't have time to do that. Havis Gardiner came in before we had gotten seated, nodded hello and pulled a chair up for himself. He was as distinct as the men of distinction come. Strictly sharp in a hundred-buck pin-stripe suit and looking like he just stepped out of the pages of a magazine. His greying hair was freshly trimmed around the edges and for a minute I was wishing it was me sitting over there instead of here with a bandage for a hat and a headache to keep it company. He waved for us to sit down and crossed his legs carefully enough to show he was teed off about something. Logan and I shared the couch and lit up a pair of cigarettes.

'You have something on your mind, Mr Gardiner?' I asked.

'That's a mild way of putting it. The way you seem to move events around to suit yourself is quite disturbing.'

'Like last night?'

'Like last night. Do you realize what you did?'

'Sort of. Maybe you better explain in case I missed a point.'

Gardiner looked at Logan. 'Tell him, Alan. You're more familiar with conditions than I am.'

'Hell, he won't listen to me.'

'Tell him anyway.'

Logan tapped his butt into an ash tray. 'We're after two things. Robert Minnow's murderer and a couple hundred thousand bucks. Your coming back here has spread this case wide open again as far as we're concerned. Until now you were tagged for both jobs, now there's reason to believe that you never pulled anything.

'Let's look at it this way. Minnow, as District Attorney, wasn't concerned with the law-abiding element . . . it was the gang making Lyncastle a criminal paradise that he was after. He was doing fine until he happened to get called in on a routine case of suspected embezzlement, then all his good work was washed out when the embezzler killed him out of pure revenge. That embezzler was supposed to have been you.'

'Great,' I said.

'Shut up. However, after you ducked out of sight it made the case certain, and in one respect, even if it *wasn't* you, the heat was directed away from the guilty party. Now, we know this much. Vera West could have done the actual embezzling, though the details of it aren't clear yet. The money involved was worth killing for, especially if the murder could be directed away from herself. We know too that after it happened Vera and Lenny Servo, who we'll unofficially class as part of the criminal element of town, were pretty chummy until Vera disappeared.

'Now for the reasons for her disappearance. She might have stuck close to Lenny as long as he could afford her some protection, and there's no doubt at all that he's influential enough to give plenty of protection. She had enough dough to pay for that

161

protection and enough to make the proposition interesting to him, too. But remember this, it was still big dough and if you could get away without splitting it, a couple hundred grand could make for some pretty fancy living. Vera might very well have taken that cash without cutting Lenny in and taken off for somewhere.'

Gardiner nodded approvingly. 'Or,' he added, 'Servo could have kept the money and killed Vera.'

'I like it better the first way,' I said.

Logan's butt poised over the ash tray. 'Why?'

'Because Servo was in love with her, that's why. She left him flat somewhere along the line.'

'Where'd you hear that?'

'I get around,' I grinned. 'You mentioned something about Vera being dead. What about it?'

Gardiner looked at me squarely. 'The investigators for the insurance company have managed to trace Vera West out of the state. There's no need going into detail of how they did it, but they found that she had spent some time in the state capital then moved on to New York. Her last known address was a small uptown hotel off Times Square, but after she left no further trace of her was found. The investigators went on the premise that she might have died, and checked with the New York police. Their morgue records showed two cases of drowning, both suicides, either of which could have been Miss West. Since both bodies had been buried in a pauper's grave an exhumation for purposes of facial identification wasn't practical. After so long a time decomposition would have made identification impossible.'

'So?' I said.

'So there's still the money to be accounted for,' Logan said. 'There was no indication of Vera's having lived high.'

Gardiner saw the frown on my face. 'The point is this, Johnny, the case is not exactly a local one any longer. Since it has been reopened, the insurance company for the bank has its own men assigned to the case working in conjunction with the Federal Bureau of Investigation. I am quite aware of the situation that exists as far as our local police force is concerned, which is to say that in their minds the case is already settled except for a positive means to identify you. Now, you have been a sort of a centre of the controversy. You can upset things if you aren't careful.'

I stood up and flicked my butt into the fireplace. 'In other words, I'm to pull in my horns?'

'Until the proper authorities have reached a conclusion.'

I could feel Logan's eyes on me, waiting to see what I'd do. I said, 'The insurance company and the F.B.I., what are they looking for?'

After a moment's pause Gardiner said, 'Primarily a murderer, then the stolen funds.'

'That's very good,' I told him, 'very good. Me, I want a killer too. But that doesn't come first. I want a whole town of people to know that Johnny McBride didn't have anything to do with anything. I want to prove that there's still something to be proud of in a name and you know how I'm going to do it?'

They were both waiting for me to tell them and I didn't. Instead, I said, 'Nope, the horns don't get pulled in. Not even a little bit. Maybe the cops'll trip over me some, but there's more of a chance that somebody else will trip over me first.'

I expected an argument and didn't get any. Gardiner shook his head in a slightly puzzled fashion. 'I . . . understand quite well how you feel, Johnny. Please understand this. I'm not trying to interfere with your . . . crusade. I know the kind of people you're dealing with and I don't want you to be in further trouble before we come to the truth of the matter.'

'Like getting myself killed?'

'Yes.'

I looked down at Logan. 'You feel the same way too?'

'More or less. You're screwing the works up pretty nicely.'

'Then if Vera's still alive and she pulled this stunt you're willing to see her pay for it?'

He got mad first, then dropped his eyes. 'If she's behind it.'

I said, 'Nuts,' and was going to say more. The words were there in my mouth but they didn't come out. My mind was going around in cute little circles making ends meet here and there and a picture started to form that was vague in a way but with definite outlines that could paint a picture of murder.

So instead of all the words I had stored up I said, 'Any chance of seeing the reports of the investigation?'

Gardiner reached into his jacket pocket and pulled out an envelope of official documents with COPY printed across the face of them. Everything he had told me was there in black and white all signed and stamped with an official seal. When I looked them over I handed them back with a nod. 'O.K.,' I told them. 'I'll pull in my horns.'

Gardiner saw us to the door personally. The housekeeper handed Logan his hat and we went back down the path to the car. The poor guy looked pretty upset and it didn't help his face any. He climbed behind the wheel, made a U-turn and picked his way back to town. When he got on the edge of the lights he said, 'Where do you want to go?'

'Get my car back first. Take me over to the garage.'

'Then where?'

'Someplace you can't go, chum.'

'A dame?'

'Natch.'

'That'll probably keep you out of trouble more than anything else I can think of.'

'It will?'

'As long as you don't marry one.' Logan sounded too damned sour.

He wheeled the car over to the garage, waited until I had paid the bill, then waved me over. 'If you want me for anything I'll probably be at the Circus Bar. I hope you don't want me for anything. I'm going to get stinking drunk and I want to do it alone and without having you in my hair, understand?'

'You're the one who's got woman trouble.'

'Shut up.'

'O.K., O.K.' I started to go back to the Ford then remembered something. 'You know anything or anybody by the name of Harlan?'

'No. Is it important?'

'It could be. How about finding out? It may be a woman.'

'I'll find out,' he said. I watched him roll up the window then pull away. When his tail light had turned off down the street I climbed in my heap, went about a hundred yards to the first diner I came to, parked, had something to eat, then found a phone booth around by the men's room.

The operator took my number, rang and the velvet voice said hello.

'Johnny, Venus. I've been wondering how you staged a disappearing act last night.'

The voice kept its velvety tone, but that was all. 'I'm awfully sorry, but I'm afraid it will have to be some other time.'

'No, you don't understand. This is Johnny. You remember.'

'If you care to I'll be glad to make arrangements later in the week.'

It finally came to me. I said, 'Trouble, kid?'

'Yes, that's right.' There was no hesitation at all in her answer.

'Bad trouble?'

She even made it sound good. 'Certainly.'

'Cops?'

'No . . . no, of course not.'

'Hang on, Venus. Give me five minutes. I'll be there in five minutes.'

I slid the phone back in its cradle, slapped a bill on the counter to pay for my meal and got out of there in a hurry. For a change I was lucky. Traffic was light enough for me to edge by on the outside lane and there weren't any stop lights to hold me up. I cut across town at an angle, picked up the road I was looking for and came out on the street I wanted. It must have been too early for the customers because the cars weren't bumper to bumper along the kerb. I counted four on the one side and two on the other, then picked a spot behind a new Buick and killed the engine.

The house was completely dark. Not that it was any different that way because more than half the others were showing blank spaces where the windows were. But somebody *had* to be home. A short stocky girl came out of a place that was still lit up and walked towards me. She was whistling under her breath until she saw me then stopped. Her smile was as friendly as it was professional. 'Looking for somebody special, stranger?'

'Sort of. What happened to everything? The last time I was here everything was lit up.'

The smile flashed again. 'Please, it's supper time. Everybody has to eat, you know, even us.'

'Oh!'

'Give you a ride to town if you want. You can come back with me later.'

'No . . . thanks anyway. I'll stick around.'

She shrugged and crossed over to a small coupé. I watched her drive away before going up the walk to the house. I didn't even bother checking around the place first. I didn't give a damn if somebody was standing right inside the front door and in a way I was hoping somebody would be. I tried the knob and it didn't turn so I gave the window alongside it a tentative shove. That didn't budge either. But it did when I slid a knife blade between the crosspieces and pushed the lock open.

I couldn't see a damn thing. Oh, I heard them all right, but I couldn't see anything so I had to stand there until I could. Then things began to take shape and I walked across the room to the stairs where I could hear them fine, even the muffled sobbing of a woman and a sharp, ratty voice of a man. I heard them better at the top of the landing, and outside the room that opened off the end of the hall I could even make out their words.

When I kicked open the room I could see them too. Both of them.

Servo and Eddie Packman. And Venus.

She lay across a couch crying into her hands while Eddie tried to prop her up so he could slap her again. Servo was watching with a wise sneer twisting his mouth up on one side.

If he hadn't tried to go for something he had in his pocket he might have ducked the first wild swing I let loose. It caught him right on the mouth and the remains of his teeth tore jagged holes through his lips into my fingers and he went into the wall with a sickening smash and lay there. Eddie was a kill-mad face looking at the blood on my hand and the wild expression I wore. A whole mouthful of yellow teeth bared in a crazy grimace and he did the same thing he had done the night before.

He came right for me and in that one second I saw two things . . . Eddie was just the right size to fit those impressions on the roof top where somebody had tried to turn me inside out with a slug and the other thing was a nasty switch-blade knife in his hand held the way a pro holds it, low and with the blade up ready to make one final swipe across a stomach or throat.

You don't use your hands against a blade. You don't kick or punch or rush cold steel. You do things and wonder later how you knew those things but don't really care because they worked.

I had the pillow off the couch between my fingers and let him come. He was too mad to see what I was going to do until it happened. When the knife whipped out I went into it, caught the blade in the pillow and tore the damn thing out of his hand.

He tried to run. Sure, he made a good try, but he ran into my foot and fell face down on the floor and I jumped on his back. His mouth was bubbling out a scream when I pulled his arm up over his head and broke it with a snap that was the loudest thing I ever heard.

Maybe it was just my imagination, because just as it popped Venus let out a short, hoarse sound and something laid my scalp open again.

This time it was better than the other two times. There were flowers in the air and my head was on a soft warm pillow that was a leg attached to a face that had the red imprints of a hand on one side, but a mighty pretty face just the same. A lot of black hair tumbled down where I could reach up and feel it and when Venus saw I was still alive she smiled and bent down and kissed me.

'He hit you.'

'Hard, too.'

'He used the ash tray. I tried to yell, but he didn't give me a chance.'

'What did he look like?'

'He didn't have any teeth and his mouth looked like he was eating an apple.'

'Eddie . . .?'

Venus gave me a grin of sheer pleasure. 'You broke his arm. He was still screaming when Lenny dragged him out. He wanted to kill you and was cursing Lenny out because he thought he had already done the job.'

I wanted to grin myself, but my head hurt too much. The ash tray was still there on the floor, a heavy metal job that would have made a pulp of my skull if it hadn't been for the layers of bandages that softened the blow. The tape was torn and soggy with the blood that seeped through, but as far as I could tell I wasn't any worse off than before.

I rolled my head and looked up at her. 'Chick, how come our friends left me for dead and didn't try to knock you off too?'

'Now you're not thinking, man. In this town you could have died and it would have been self-defence, especially with a witness on hand to tell how you atacked them first.'

'You'd tell a jury that?'

Her mouth made a smile again. 'There wouldn't be much else I could tell, could there? Living is fun. I'd like to live it without Lenny Servo around sometime.'

She was right. I put my head down and closed my eyes. 'What'd they want with you?'

'Information. Why I was fooling around with you. They thought I had something to do with it.'

'Oh!'

She ran her fingers across my face, stroking it gently. 'Feel pretty bad?'

168

'Not much worse than usual.'

'Sure?'

'Uh-huh.'

This time both her hands went under my head, lifted it, then laid it down gently on the cushions. She did something to the lamp, turning it so that its brightness diminished until there was nothing but a faint hint of light like that of dawn in the room. For the first time I saw how she looked, not trim and tailored like last night, but smooth and sleek in a clinging black dress that swept to the ground.

She moved languidly, turning on the record player, standing in front of it swaying to the faint but deep rhythm of a chorus of drums. She said, 'I know things you might want to know.'

'What things?'

Her feet took two rapid steps and she spun gracefully so that her skirt lifted and swirled around her legs, the white of her thighs flashing momentarily against the black of the dress.

'About Lenny Servo and his Business Group. Do you know how powerful his organization is?'

'I have a good idea. He's the money man behind the boys, isn't he?'

The drums went into a single throbbing beat and she stood there with her legs apart, stiff at first, then melting slowly into a gentle undulation. I could see her half-closed eyes watching me, her mouth faintly smiling as her hands went to the buttons at her back.

Each word was timed with the drums, keeping pace to the motion of her body. 'It's more than that, Johnny. It's a place like this and other places down the street. It's places like the back rooms of night clubs where men have smokers and girls are hired for the occasion. It's places where very candid pictures can be taken and casually shown to the right people afterwards so they know that a club doesn't have to be made out of wood or iron.'

She had the dress in her hand and curled it over her arm so that it was a curtain that parted briefly every now and then, a black curtain she stepped through and disappeared behind so fast you thought your eyes were playing a trick.

There was a glistening black wedge around her hips. Another crossing her breasts. Tight. Sensual. It wasn't easy to speak. I finally said, 'What else?'

'Servo was broke when he came to town. Somebody put him on his feet again.'

She smiled, turned her head and made the gesture of covering her eyes coyly. Her hips went back and back, then jerked forward. She did it again, laughed and tightened up so that every muscle in her body seemed to be working at once. 'I used to be good, man.'

My mouth felt dry. 'Who backed him?'

'Somebody said you must have. Nobody else in town had that kind of money. He couldn't have gotten it any other way.'

She stopped dancing. She moved and dipped quickly and something fluttered to the floor. When she took up the rhythm again I saw through the curtain and the glistening black was only around her hips this time.

'That makes Lenny the boss . . . and me the sucker.'

The drums got louder and faster. The curtain whirled and parted too fast, much too fast. 'Definitely,' I heard her say. Then, 'There may be a pair of suckers. There's more.'

'Spell it out.'

'I was told he came with a woman. A very possessive woman. She disappeared before he got to be a big shot.'

'Who told you this?'

'Don't ask me that. There wasn't any more information and she isn't important enough to be dragged into anything.'

'O.K., kid,' I said. 'You did good enough.'

Venus smiled again, did something too quick for me to follow, but I had a chance to see through the curtain before the music ended in a crazy, strained beat. The black around her waist was gone too. Then she threw the curtain at me. It missed.

It was supposed to cover my face so I wouldn't have a chance to see her before she snapped the light off, but it missed and there she was, a symphony in black and white, lithe and graceful with sharply rising breasts that swelled with every breath she took, the muscles of her stomach a predatory ripple, quivering and dancing above the luscious taper of her legs.

Then the light was gone and I could only hear her moving towards me in the darkness. 'I liked what you did to them, man,' she said.

'I'm glad of that.'

'Now I'll show you what a real woman's like. In style, of course.'

I said, 'Of course,' and my voice sounded weak like it did the first time I had said it.

She showed me.

CHAPTER TEN

The Ford was still there, but now it was wedged in between a couple of seedy old cars that bore college stickers on the windshield. It was eight-thirty-two by my watch, but by my head it was time to hole up someplace and die. There were lights on in the house now, every window except one a yellow square and at that one I tossed a half-hearted salute and said good night to my Venus.

O.K., so I'm a jerk sometimes. I get the rest of my brains damn near knocked out all for something in style from Venus. But hell, they give medals to soldiers for the same thing, and I'd take Venus to a medal any time. Besides, she was handy to have around for inside info if I needed it.

I climbed behind the wheel and poked the key into the lock. It took some tricky juggling to get out of the spot, but I made it and started around the corner when I heard the wail of the sirens coming up behind me. Don't ask why I did it, but my hand hit the light switch and kicked off the lights as I jammed into the kerb and made like an all-night parker.

There were three of them. Two were official and the other was a coupé, but they all had sirens dying to a low growl and seemed to spill out cops by the dozen. It was a nicely planned manoeuvre if you were on the outside looking in. They covered the house in pairs so that there wasn't a chance of a mouse getting through, then Lindsey and Tucker went up the front steps and rattled the doorknob.

Inside, somebody screamed, a door opened and slammed and a couple of guys started swearing and telling the cops off. Then more screams of indignation. None of the voices belonged to Venus.

I grinned to myself in the darkness.

If Tucker had come to pick up a corpse he was going to be a mighty upset copper. I knew two other guys who were going to be a little bit upset, too. It was funny as hell to watch because the cops weren't taking any chance on having a corpse run out on them. Or maybe Lenny Servo wasn't too sure about being fully a corpse and hoped I'd be made one if I tried to get out of the trap.

The more I thought about it the better it looked and the madder I got. They were playing it cagey and weren't taking any chances at all. Not even one. The bastards were angling for my death harder than they were at the beginning only now they had the cops ready to pull the pay-off so it would have a nice legal wrapper on it and there wouldn't even be the trouble of an investigation or trial.

I said to hell with it and started the car up again. If they saw me they could chase me. Just to keep luck on my side I didn't turn the lights on until I was all the way down the block and heading back towards the city.

Nobody saw me. They were all too busy looking the other way.

The Circus Bar was my first stop. I didn't see Logan's car around anywhere so I looked around inside. When I didn't see him anyplace I cornered the bartender. 'You see Logan tonight?'

'Yeah. Yeah, sure. Said he was going on a bat, only his office called and he had to stay sober to see a couple of men.'

'Where'd he go?'

'Gosh, pal, I wouldn't know where any of these joes go. One minute they're here an' the next they're tearing around the city. You know reporters.'

I said I knew and let him get back to work. I did better on the phone. The city editor told me that a couple of insurance investigators had wanted to see him and had left their phone number for Logan to call so he probably had met them.

After I thought it over a minute I thumbed through the directory until I found Gardiner, Havis, called his number and got the housekeeper. She sounded curt and was starting to tell me that Mr Gardiner wasn't in to anyone at this hour, but I heard the echo of footsteps and Gardiner himself telling her that he'd take it, then his voice said, 'Gardiner speaking. What is it?'

'McBride, Mr Gardiner.'

'Yes, Johnny.' He sounded annoyed at being called so late.

'I'll only take a moment,' I said. 'Look, Logan had to meet a couple of investigators tonight. Were they your men?'

'Why, yes, as a matter of fact, they were. Both represent the National Bank Insurance Company. May I ask why you want to know?'

'Sure, I want to find Logan. I thought you might know where he is.'

'You might find him someplace in the newspaper office. The insurance men were looking for some recent pictures of Vera West to take back to New York for identification purposes. They thought the paper might be able to supply them.'

'Oh! O.K., thanks. I'll shop around.'

I hung up and tried the paper again. This time I was connected with the file clerk in the morgue and a voice as old as parchment and just as crackly told me that yes, Logan had been in with a couple of men, yup, they did get some pictures, sure 'nuff Logan had left and said he was going to finish getting canned. And oh, yeah, he was so potted already he had a crying jag on.

I felt like telling the guy to go shoot himself. Crying jag hell, Logan was crying all right, but it wasn't the whisky coming out. Try being in love with a dame while you're working to get her hung. Just try it. That's what Logan was doing.

When I backed out of the booth I was ready to give up and find a sack someplace. It had been another one of those nights with everything happening, yet meaning nothing and my head was starting to pound so much I couldn't think straight. I was all set to leave when I saw the bartender waving at me and went over to see what he wanted.

'Damn near forgot,' he said. 'Your name Johnny?'

I told him it was.

He slid an envelope across the bar at me. 'Logan told me you might come in looking for him and to give you this.'

I picked up the envelope and slid my finger under the flap. 'Before he left he gave you this?'

'Yeah, not five minutes before. Want a drink?'

'Beer.' I waited while he drew a tall one and carried it over to the table. I put the drink down in a hurry before I pulled the two sheets out of the envelope. Across the top of the first one was the notation: Harlan . . . name of several counties and cities in the US: Harlan, Inc., manufacturers of electrical appliances. Harlan, paint supply house in Va. Harlan, stage name of actress copyrighted. George Harlan, hold-up, murder, life sen. and escaped, captured, killed in attempted escape Alcatraz. Harlan, William, prominent South American financier. Harlan, Gracie, worked con game. Convicted NY 1940. This sounds interesting. See clipping.

Logan had stapled the news account to the sheet underscoring a couple of lines. The gist of it was that Harlan, Gracie, was suspected of being a partner to a con game in which prominent out-of-towners were fleeced. It was the usual thing, a dame and a small-town playboy shacked up in a hotel room with a blackmail aftermath. None of her victims stepped forward to accuse her, but it wasn't necessary because she had talked too much and a smart DA got enough of a confession out of her to send her up a few years. The inquiring reporter who covered the affair added that the sum extracted from her victims was suspected to be considerably more than she let on and that she had worked with a confederate or two who steered the victims her way. However, this was not established at the trial.

The note that Logan had added stated that these were all the Harlans he could uncover, and if it was a place, the nearest Harlan was better than a thousand miles off, and if it was a person, Harlan, Gracie, was the only one with a criminal record. He said he'd try to get further details from a news source in New York by the name of Whitman and would let me know more about it when he saw me.

I looked the list over again, grinning at the copyrighted Harlan because she was the one Venus had told me about. At

175

least my tall lovely wasn't handing me any baloney. I folded the stuff back into the envelope, tucked it in my pocket and drained off the dregs of the beer. It was a whole hatful of Harlans, but I'd give every one to know who the hell it was who bothered letting me know about them in the first place.

I didn't stick around the Circus Bar any longer than I had to. Logan was someplace getting tanked up and I wanted to get to him while he was still able to do some good. He'd probably be sore as hell about my little fracas with the boys and if he was it was too bad.

By eleven-fifteen I had traced him through seven bars. In the first one there had been two men with him and they had talked awhile over a drink. The bartender saw them taking notes about something or other. Logan hadn't seemed happy. In the next six he had been alone and from what I could gather he was pretty well in his cups and brooding hard.

There was one thing that seemed peculiar. None of the bars he had been at belonged to Servo's Business Group. Maybe it was because he didn't want a lot of noise and people intruding on his thoughts or maybe it was something else again. At least the bars were still fairly empty with the bartenders standing around ready to pick up the late trade getting squeezed out of the places with the wheels and dice tables. The last bar was a ratty place on a side street called The Last Resort. The bartender said he had been there for about ten minutes, talked to a couple of hustlers, made a phone call, had a few more drinks and left. Wherever Logan went from there he didn't know and couldn't even guess.

That's when I gave up. Logan could wait. Let the guy enjoy his drunk and maybe he'd feel better tomorrow. I told the bartender to make me up a whisky and ginger and sat down to watch a redhead operate on a reluctant prospect.

She was doing good, then all of a sudden she stopped and moved over a seat. The bartender looked at the door and scowled a little bit, automatically reaching for the Scotch bottle on the back bar.

The guy who came in was middle-aged, lanky and in plain clothes, but he had might as well been wearing a sign around his neck that read COP. He said, 'No drink, Barney,' and pulled a photo out of his pocket and slid it across the bar.

'Ever see him before?'

The bartender studied the picture, read the caption underneath, then shook his head.

'Sure?'

'Positive.'

'You see him around, call in, understand?'

'Yeah, I know.'

'O.K.' He put the picture back in his pocket.

'Want a drink?'

'Not now. Maybe I'll come back.' The cop started to go when he saw the redhead. His smile was a dirty twisting of the mouth. 'Hello, Ginger.'

The redhead didn't bother answering. She barely glanced at him and went back to her drink. 'Stay off the streets,' he said.

The redhead flushed, but she had a lot of nerve. 'You can't make pay-off dough when you don't work someplace, copper.'

His smile kind of warped a little before he got out through the door.

I looked at my hand and it was white around the knuckles from squeezing the glass so hard. The bartender saw it too but didn't say anything. He glanced back at my face and mentally compared it with the wanted circular the copy showed him. 'Your name really George Wilson?' he asked.

I let him keep a fin out of my change. 'Could be, friend. Could very well be. Thanks.'

'No trouble. If that dumb dick had eyes for something else except what comes easy he coulda spotted you quick. I ain't helping him out none.' He leaned forward confidentially. 'I been in stir once myself.'

So I got out of there in a hurry before the cop came back for his drink. There wasn't any sense in giving him a second chance. Nice, I thought, now the door is shut right in my face.

They want me by day or night and there will be a price on my head to make it interesting.

Before I went back to the car I ducked around the corner into a drugstore. I got my number, heard it ring about a dozen times before the receiver lifted off the hook, then a hesitant voice said, 'Yes?'

'I want your boss, honey.'

The background hum muffled out for a few seconds and I knew she had her hand over the mouthpiece. A minute later she said, 'I'll put her on.'

The next 'yes' was a little different. Scared.

'Johnny, sugar.'

'Oh!' That was all she said.

'Somebody there? Can you talk?'

'Yes . . . go ahead, please.' In the background was the grating sound of a man's voice, but there was no click or dimming out that would indicate an extension being lifted.

I said, 'Did the cops come looking for me?'

'Yes . . . I'm sure . . .'

'Did they expect to find me alive or dead?'

'Oh, no . . .'

'Alive?'

'Certainly.'

'O.K., pretty girl, you can tell the copper bedtime stories. I'll see you again when there's no watchdogs around.'

I hung up slowly and dug in my pockets for a cigarette. So the cops had come looking for a live man and right after that they were on the prowl for a certain George Wilson.

Somebody had talked.

That somebody had to be either Logan or Wendy and they were going to have to talk a lot more when I caught up with them. And since Logan was dead drunk someplace there wasn't any use looking for him.

Only Wendy was left. Lovely bottle-blonde black-background Wendy.

I sat there on the corner seat of the booth staring at the phone. When I stared a pretty long time I dropped another nickel in the slot and punched out the number the card said to if you wanted the cops.

Then I asked for Captain Lindsey.

At first he didn't believe me when I told him who I was. I added real quick, 'Don't bother tracing the call, friend. I'll walk in if you want to see me.'

'I want to see you,' he said. He sounded like a tiger ready to pounce.

'Swell. Then I'll walk in and see you. Just tell me one thing, Captain.'

The phone was quiet. I could hear him purring. He liked it fine this way. He liked for me to be so damned cocky I'd put my head under the knife without being prodded. 'Sure,' he said. 'Shoot.'

'How'd you find out?'

'A little birdie told me. Cops have a lot of little birdies flying around. We call 'em stool pigeons, but they like to be known as anonymous phone calls. This little birdie called the turn right on the nose.'

'The little birdie got a name, Captain?'

'No, not this one. He was very careful to disguise his voice.'

'He?'

I could feel his frown come over the wire. 'It could have been a she. I didn't ask. You can come on in and talk to me now.'

The laugh trickled out of my chest. 'Oh, Captain, not right this minute.'

'Damn you! I . . .'

'Uh-huh, Captain, I said I'd be in. I didn't say when. Pretty soon, maybe, but not right this second.'

'You get your ass down here right . . .'

I hung up on him.

Two minutes later I was back in my car with a ten-second start over the police car that came screaming up the avenue. It was enough.

When I found enough traffic to cover me I loafed along in line and ran over it in my mind. So far there had been two anonymous phone calls and I was wondering if the same party made them both. I kept trying to bring back the voice who had told me to look for Harlan. It was feminine enough then, but now I couldn't be sure.

It could have been a he or a she.

Harlan could be a he or a she or an it.

Harlan. Harlan, Harlan. Son of a bitch, there was something I should know about her and couldn't think of. The damn thing was knocking against the inside of my head trying to make me see that it was there sure enough if I'd only use my brain.

It took a long time, then my fingers went cold around the wheel and I saw it. I had seen the name right after I had gotten the phone call and it hadn't registered. Harlan was a name that had been scrawled across one of the envelopes the D.A. had on his desk the night he died!

My foot touched the brake at the next intersection. I made a U-turn and drove back through town. I stopped at a bar for five minutes and made a phone call, then drove on to a certain street and parked.

I didn't have to wait long. The sedan came up behind me, a door slammed, then the one on my right was yanked open. I said, 'Hello, Lindsey.'

He wasn't taking any chances. There was a gun in his hand. 'Wise guy.'

I was too tired to argue with him. The gun came up when I pulled out my pack of butts and went down hesitantly when I offered him one.

He took it, waiting.

'You can get me any time, Lindsey. I'm not trying to get away.'

It was the tone of my voice that brought his head up. 'I'll get you now. I'm sick of gags. Maybe we don't have your prints, but George Wilson and Johnny McBride are both wanted for murder. The lawyers'll have fun with it, but you'll swing.'

'First wouldn't you like to find out who killed Minnow?'

An impotent rage choked him. He kept fiddling with the gun trying to decide right there whether he ought to kill me himself or not. 'I'd like that.'

So I told him who I was and why I was there, but that was all. He didn't believe it. I didn't care whether he did or not. I said, 'Stay off my back for a week. Can you do that?'

'Why should I?'

'Because I may be right, that's why. If you had a decent police force you would find things out yourself. You can't. You're just like me. One guy, hoping to come across something, only you're too blind to look in more than one direction. You're tied hand and foot by rules and regulations. Your cops make more in shakedowns than salary so they take orders from somebody else. Servo runs the boys who run you so all you can do is hope. Let me have a week. Hell, it isn't much. One week and if I don't get what I want you can take me in and let the lawyers have their field day.'

'You're nuts.' There was indecision in his voice. 'Or I'm nuts for listening.'

'I could have gotten away any time, Lindsey,' I reminded him.

He put the gun away. I watched his fingers wrap around the butt and send it spinning out the window. 'What do you want, Johnny? Say it before I change my mind.'

I leaned back and stared at the ceiling. 'The night Minnow died . . . had his office been searched?'

His breath hissed out slowly. He said one word. 'Yes.'

'What was taken?'

'I don't know. The killer didn't look far because things weren't too messed up.'

'And you were the only one who noticed it.'

He looked out the window and spat disgustedly. 'I didn't notice it until two days later when I went back to his office.' His shoulders moved under a sigh. 'I was so damned mad it took me that long,' he explained.

'There was a letter there. It had "Harlan" written on it.'

He got the pitch right off. 'You saw his wife?'

'Yeah.'

'I checked on that angle.'

'Without finding the letter. There was nothing.' He held out his hand. 'Give me another cig.' I shook one out and lit it for him. 'I checked every movement he made that night. His wife was pretty excited about the whole affair . . . thought he contacted the girl or something, but he didn't.

'He went out and bought a paper. He drove downtown, stopped in Philbert's where he made a few purchases, went across the street to a bar and had a few drinks and went home. The bartender said that while he was there he was deep in thought. He didn't do anything special and nobody noticed anything special.'

'But you never found the letter?'

'No.'

'Did you ever think about what could have happened to it?'

'I think I know. The person came back and claimed it.'

'Maybe,' I said. 'Mrs Minnow said Tucker called him about a special delivery letter.'

'That's right.' He took a long pull on the cigarette and filled the car with smoke.

'What was it about?'

'Hell, how do I know? He picked it up at the desk and stuck it in his pocket. He probably filed it away somewhere.'

'Find that letter, Lindsey. Go through every damn cabinet and drawer in the place, but find it.'

'Just a minute . . .'

'You said you wanted to find a killer.' I looked at him coldly. 'I'm not ordering you around. I'm giving you something that might tie in. Find that letter.'

His mouth clamped tight. 'And what will you be doing?'

'Finding out who wrote it and why.'

He smoked that cigarette right down to the tip without saying anything. When it was finished he threw it out after the other one, squinted his face into a snarl and climbed out. Behind me I heard his car turn over, then pull away from the kerb.

A week I told him. Seven days. It wasn't very long. I rolled the car forward and turned the corner. I travelled slowly and kept my eyes on the street signs until I found the one I wanted.

I parked in front of the building, took the elevator up and pushed the bell that had Servo on the nameplate.

Nobody answered.

I tried again, waited and still nobody answered. I went back downstairs to the super's apartment and pushed his bell too.

The guy was all smiles at the prospect of company even if he was in his shorts. I said, 'Servo come in?'

He shook his head. 'Hell, I dunno. His babe went outa here in a hurry awhile back, I know that. Just as I was coming up from fixing the hot-water burner.'

'She have clothes on?'

'Yeah.' He showed his gums again. 'They didn't fit, neither. You know what? She had on a green dress with spangles. Them whores upstairs . . . one of 'em got a dress just like it.'

'O.K. I got it.'

He squinted his eyes at me and kept his voice down. 'Somebody kicked Servo around.'

'That was me.'

'Thought so. Give it to him good?'

'Uh-huh. Why?'

'I was wondering. Him and somebody been doing a lot of arguing up there. For a while I thought maybe there was a fight in his place only I didn't hear anything like that. Just arguing. They was sore as hell about something.'

This time I gave him a ten. He folded it up and kept it in the palm of his hand. 'What floor are the babes on?'

'Top. 7E. They're alone tonight.'

I went back to the elevator and let it haul me up. At 7E I rapped on the door until somebody told me to cut it out, they were coming and to take my time.

The brunette that opened the door had on a housecoat and nothing else. She gave me a surprised grin and said, 'Well, if it isn't our tired playmate. So you finally woke up. Come on in.'

She was one of the pair Jack had sent up to me in the hotel.

I said, 'I'm not in the market, sugar. Right now I want some information. Downstairs there's a girl . . . Servo's girl. She left awhile ago.'

Her professional smile disappeared. 'So what?'

That was the sister-in-trouble act. This was another wall I had to break down fast. 'She came up here and borrowed a dress. She lammed and I want to know why.'

'Maybe she wanted to see the town. How'd I know. Look, feller, you go . . .'

'The kid's in hot water up to her ears. If you want her to get in deeper then clam up. I can find out someplace else, you know.'

She didn't like it a bit. Her teeth fastened to her lip while she tried to make up her mind. Maybe I looked honest enough to suit her. 'She was scared, that's why.'

'Servo?'

'She didn't say. She was damn near hysterical and wouldn't talk. All she wanted was some clothes. You know what the matter was?'

'No. Did she say where she was going?'

'As far as I could make out she was leaving town. She was scared stiff about something and we thought that maybe Servo had worked her over. He's good at doing things that don't show any marks. Good at doing it so it does show too.'

'Just that?'

For a second she chewed up her lip again. 'No . . . there was something else. She was babbling about something in the paper tonight. She said she'd be next or something like that. I was running around too much to notice.'

I let it sink in, then reached behind me and opened the door. 'Thanks. I'll find her.'

'I hope so. If anybody asks where she got the clothes, you don't know, understand?'

'Don't worry.'

'That crazy bastard was afraid to let her out without him. He did everything but keep her on a leash.'

'She liked it that way, didn't she?'

'Hell, why not? She got everything she wanted. She went out often enough and she kept talking of going away for good next year. That's all she lived for . . . a little place in California all her own.'

184

'Tough,' I said. 'Thanks again.' I shut the door and let the elevator take me downstairs again.

I found a news-stand not too far off and picked up a copy of the *Lyncastle News*. It was a good copy for my scrapbook. My picture was on the front page with the story of George Wilson, the one-man crime wave, and how he was someplace in Lyncastle. The reporters must have been right on hand when Lindsey got that anonymous phone call and he let them go to town on it. There was a paragraph at the bottom of special interest. It said the F.B.I. was interested in George Wilson too and were looking for him.

Big deal. I get Lindsey to give me a break and Uncle Sam takes over.

But the item I really wanted was on the back of the second page. It was a small squib about four inches long and recounted the details of a woman who committed suicide early that evening. Two kids had seen her jump into the quarry and by the time help arrived she was dead. An autopsy showed she was drunk at the time and a close check on her activities disclosed that she had been making the rounds of the highway taverns. Her fingerprints were on file with the local Board of Health and identified her as a waitress in the ABC Diner. The cause of death was remorse over the recent murder of her room-mate. They gave her name as Irene Godfrey, her address at the Pine Tree Gardens and that was all.

There was a picture coming out now. It was like walking in at the middle of a show and wondering how it started. If you stayed long enough you could pretty well guess the cause by seeing the effect. But not quite. You were still guessing. If you asked somebody in the next seat who had been there all along you might find out. If he wanted to tell you.

I folded the paper up and stuck it under the seat. My hand brushed the cold butt of the gun I had put there earlier, so I took it out, checked it and stuck it back. It might come in handy.

I was twenty minutes getting down to the bus station. The lights in the ports were out, but on the train side two handcars loaded with mail sacks and packages were standing together

185

waiting for the next connection. I parked the car, got out and walked down the end without getting out of the shadows.

Inside, two men were asleep on the benches. There was another woman with a wailing baby in her arms. The ticket grill was shut on the inside, but through the screened window I could see Nick perched on his stool shuffling papers into a drawer.

Tucker was all the way around the other side, just standing there with an unlit cigar in his mouth trying to be part of the night. I looked again and saw the other guy, a dark blob sitting on a crate. Tucker struck a match and held it to the cigar and I saw his face. He was young, well dressed. Like a lawyer. And F.B.I. agents have to be lawyers.

I made the round trip once more but I still didn't see what I came to see. Troy wasn't making any connections out of Lyncastle by bus or train. I slid inside the door nearest the office, yanked the knob and damn near scared Nick off his stool. He slammed the drawer shut with a bang that knocked over a stack of books and turned eyes on me that were ready to fall out of his head.

'Good gosh, you don't have to scare a man half to death, do you? Get over there and squat down till I get the shade down.'

He reached up and tugged at the partition that covered the grill. When he had it down he shot the bolt through the hasp and turned around. His hands were shaking.

'You got company outside, Nick.'

'Sure. All day I've had company. You know who's out there?'

'I can make a pretty good guess.'

'Damn 'em.' He reached in back of him and pulled a sheet of paper from the top of the pile. 'Look here. I have to post it.'

I took it out of his fingers and looked at it. The likeness was perfect. It was the same one they ran in the paper, but this one had a reward notice tacked on the bottom.

I handed it back to him. 'Funny place for those things.'

Nick shook his head and stared at the photo. 'Law says in public places and this is a public place. Out where you can't see it is a whole bulletin board of these things.' His fingers gave

186

a sharp snap to the sheet before he folded it out and stuck it in the drawer behind him. 'You're wanted pretty bad, son. You shouldn't have come down here.'

'I'm looking for a dame, Nick. She was Servo's girl until something scared her and she took off. She was red-headed, wearing a green dress and probably bawling her head off . . . or looked like she had been. Seen anything of her?'

A frown made furrows in his forehead. 'No, not that I remember.'

'Any other way she can get out of town?'

'Buses stop almost any place along the highway to make pick-ups.'

'That's the only way?'

'Uh-huh. Unless she has a car.'

'I doubt if she has. O.K., that's all I came for.' I started to get up.

Nick shoved me back in the chair. His moustache was working hard around his mouth, a hairy frame for the pink tongue that kept going over his lips. 'Easy, son. You can't be batting around any more. You see the paper tonight?' I nodded. 'The same thing on the radio too. I've had all sorts of cops in here telling me to be watching out for you. Suppose one of 'em grabs you?'

'Suppose they do?'

'Johnny boy, look. You have to get away. Tomorrow morning . . .'

This time I got up. 'Some other time, Nick. There's too much I have to do first.'

I got back to the car and managed to get it away from the station without being tailed. My head was starting to pound again and I was getting sick to my stomach. Tomorrow. I'd finish it tomorrow if it didn't finish me first.

I racked the Ford around a turn and lit a cigarette. It tasted lousy, but the smoke curling up around the ceiling was company. It was funny in a way. What Makes Johnny Run? Nearly like the title of a book. He had a good reason to. A long green reason or a long bloody reason, but on top of it all somebody had to run him out because he didn't want to do it himself.

A lot of people had told me things. I'd seen a lot of those things myself. I was part of them now. They were all there in a lump, slipping out of the pile one at a time to string out with big gaps between. When the gaps were filled I'd have the answers.

There was a lot I could see now. You don't play at being a detective. If you are one you work at it, but you have a knowledge of the science and details that goes in back of that work to help you along. No, I wasn't a detective. I was only a guy trying to dig up a five-year-old body long since fallen apart with decay. It wasn't easy. There weren't clues lying around. Just things happening that didn't seem to have any reason except that they all happened after I came to town.

I was a face that made trouble for somebody. They tried to kill me first. They tried to let the cops do the job instead and when that didn't work they tried to kill me again. Not the cops. I was so important dead that George Wilson had to be brought out in the open.

Answers. I needed answers. I wasn't going to be able to figure it out until I had the whole story right there in front of me. And that wouldn't be tonight.

No, tonight I'd sleep off the big head. It was hurting pretty bad.

I headed west, watching out for Pontiel Road, found it and drove up to the house. I stacked the car in the garage and got the key out of the flowerpot then went upstairs.

When I took a shower and got rid of the last of the tape that was keeping my scalp puckered together I looked in the two doors that led off the bathroom. I was too tired for games so I picked the one that smelled of bath salts and powder, dumped my clothes on the back of a chair and crawled into the sack. If Wendy tried crawling in that other bed tonight she was going to find my half of it empty and she ought to be smart enough to take the hint not to go looking any further.

188

The sheets were cool against my skin, the pillow a soft cloud ready to take me off to sleepy-town. I closed my eyes and climbed aboard.

The song seemed to come from far away. There weren't any words, just a hum with a deep, bouncy rhythm throated to sound like words. My eyes pulled open slowly and stared into the dark, just a little too heavy with sleep to be fully aware of where the song was coming from.

Then the dark seemed to dissolve into something white and flexible that moved along the edge of the room. It snapped me wide awake. Her dress whispered over her head and her slip made static crackling noises when she took it off. The humming paused for a second and I waited to see her go through the double-jointed contortions all women go through to unhook a bra. I was fooled. She did something to the front of it and peeled it off like a vest. There was another whisper of silk, almost inaudible this time, and she threw the last whisper across the chair and stretched her arms up reaching for the ceiling. Like a pagan moon-worshipper. Her body a nude shimmer in the dark, absorbing what little light seeped in the window. Her back bowed slowly, making every curve stand out in sharp relief. Then she relaxed into a sultry pose, ran her fingers through her hair and came over to the bed, still humming the wordless tune.

'Beautiful,' I said. 'You're beautiful.'

She sucked her breath in so hard it caught in her throat and froze her there. I reached up for the light over the bed, but before my fingers found the pull-chain her hand grabbed my wrist and forced it down. 'No lights, Johnny,' she said.

Her mouth came down slowly. Her lips were moist and parted. Warm. I could feel their warmth before they even touched me. I ran my hand up the small of her back and she shivered deliciously, making those animal sounds in her throat again.

The outlines of her face and body were tenuous things in the darkness, all the hardness obliterated until she was nothing but beautiful. And warm. And hot. Fiery hot. Her mouth a live, grasping thing squirming on top of me. The darkness closed in around us like a blanket until it exploded and left us there, tired and close, talking about tomorrow.

Tomorrow.

When she would do something for me.

Find out all she could about a cop named Tucker.

CHAPTER ELEVEN

Wendy was gone when I woke up. There was the impression in the pillow her head had left, the mark of her cheek on my arm. I could still smell the spicy sweetness she left behind.

I didn't like the way I felt. I didn't want to feel that way about any woman. Not yet. There was something about her that was different from most women, something direct and honest. Something that made a guy feel like he had lost an arm when she was gone.

I shook the thought out of my head and got up. There was a note on the dresser that said for me to take the car and she'd see me that evening, signed with love from Wendy. The marks of her lips were overlaid on the signature.

After I had had something to eat I backed the car out of the garage, filled it up at the nearest gas station and picked up a road map. I marked out a route up to the state capital, skipping all the main roads in case the cops had decided to throw up a road block and picked the macadam road that started the run.

At least I didn't hit any traffic. I barrelled the Ford along at a steady seventy, slowing down for a turn here and there and making up the loss on the straight stretches. Ten minutes to eleven I was on the outskirts of the city.

The public buildings were grouped in a towering grey huddle that stuck up above everything else like a sore thumb. In the rear of the mess was a parking area. I left the car there, went inside and scanned the directory until I found what I wanted. The State Auditor. His offices were on the fourth floor.

A very tall, very thin girl peered at me through her eyeglasses and told me to have a seat, so I flicked off the dust with my handkerchief and sat down. She didn't like that a bit and sniffed at me. All the seats were dirty. Visitors were probably at a premium here. The phone rang on her desk and after she answered it said, 'All right. Mr Donahue will see you now. Go right in, please.' She sniffed again disapprovingly. They weren't the friendly type here like in Lyncastle.

Mr Donahue beamed at me and shoved out a pudgy little paw. 'Sit down, sir, sit down.' He tried to give me the big squeeze that said he was a handball player every Friday at the gym. He was a little round guy with a big nose and a bigger smile, but you didn't have to look twice to tell that there was a lot of brain power behind the light blue eyes that seemed to dance in his head.

I took the seat and one of his cigarettes. I said, 'Mr Donahue, do you like excitement?'

He paused in the middle of lighting a butt and raised his eyebrows in surprise. 'Well . . .' he chuckled and pulled on the butt, shaking the match out. 'That's an odd question. Yes, might say that I do. In moderate doses, of course. Never find excitement around here.' His hand swept the room. 'Unless it's an error in bookwork. That's my only form of excitement. Why do you ask?'

'Because you're going to be able to kick up a lot of it in a few minutes if you want to . . . unless you're not the kind of a guy who likes a little fun.'

His face said he was interested. 'I . . . don't quite understand. Perhaps . . .'

'According to the police, Mr Donahue, I'm a bank absconder, thief, murderer and a few other things. One word from you and I'll be in the jug.'

His eyebrows really did nip-ups this time.

'The name is McBride. Five years ago you checked the books of the National Bank of Lyncastle that proved me an absconder.'

'I remember.'

'How much do you remember?'

Mr Donahue was nervous. The cigarette shortened in a series of jerky little puffs. He didn't know whether to look at me or not and was afraid to make a move towards the phone.

I said, 'I'm not here after you, friend, so stop worrying.' He showed his teeth in a smile, but didn't stop sweating. 'I . . . remember the details quite . . . clearly.'

I sat back and folded my hands behind my head. 'Give.'

He stamped the butt out, paused, then raised his face to mine. 'That information is confidential, you know. I'm sure the bank . . .'

'I can't go to the bank. I can't go anywhere. Cops are all over the damn city looking for me now. I was framed, Mr Donahue. I didn't have a thing to do with that business.'

'My job wasn't to prove you guilty, young man. I only checked the books. There was complete evidence of a fraud. The books had been juggled in a neat, but not uncommon manner.' He stopped and stared out the window a moment. 'Some time ago I had another request similar to yours. A young lady. She made a point of cultivating me until she openly asked the same thing you did.'

My mouth went into a sneer all by itself. 'Vera West.'

'That wasn't the name she gave.'

'A blonde. A real honest-to-goodness blonde a little on the tramp side.'

'Er, yes. She managed to extract the information from me. I thought you'd know about it.' His face reddened and he wouldn't look at me. 'I never mentioned it before. Perhaps I should have.'

'No,' I told him. 'You did right. It wouldn't do to open your mouth when she had something on you that could turn you upside down. I'm not blaming you. What I want are the details.'

His fingers picked up a pencil and tapped it against the desk. 'There really isn't much to it. The District Attorney of Lyncastle, the one who died later, called me in. I made a routine check of the bank's books and found the error.'

'Two hundred thousand dollars' worth?'

'Approximately. A shade over to be more nearly accurate.'

'You found something else, too, didn't you? Something you might have mentioned to the blonde.'

Between his eyes a shaded V formed. It deepened until he was squinting at me. 'You certainly have a wealth of information. I did tell that young lady something else. It was a mere suspicion. It couldn't be checked. In my opinion you . . . I mean, whoever was responsible, took out considerably more than that amount, but managed to pay back all but two hundred thousand of the total.'

'Interesting.'

His tongue flicked over his lips. 'There was a matter of eighty-four dollars in an account that by rights should have been cleaned out. It would have been just as easy to take the whole amount as part. In fact, easier, and the books would have been easier to balance out. I speculated on it and arrived at the conclusion that at the time of the investigation a theft was not in evidence as much as a replacement of the theft. Money was being put back into the bank with the intention of eventually making up the theft. Whatever was put back filled up the last account eighty-four dollars' worth.'

'A sort of no-interest loan on my part, you mean.'

'It's been done successfully before, I imagine. More often not enough.'

'I see.' I dropped my hands to my lap and tilted back on the chair. 'You couldn't noise your suspicions around very far either, could you?'

He knew what I was getting at. The red crept up in his face again and he shook his head. 'Actually, it didn't occur to me until I returned home and thought it over. It was too nebulous a thing to bring out without absolute proof. I forgot it until I was, ah, approached by this young lady. I realize that I never should have said anything, but under the circumstances it couldn't be helped. She made what I took to be a veiled threat if I ever mentioned the subject to anyone after that.'

'Why bring it up now?'

Mr Donahue seemed to be a little pained. 'Because I've had a nagging worry about the matter ever since and I'll be damned glad to see it come out in the open.'

My chest coughed up a laugh that startled him. 'Don't worry about it then,' I said. 'A lot of things will be out in the open before long, but you won't be dragged into it. You can forget the blonde, too. She's going to have more on her mind than trying to shaft you.'

'You . . . know who she is?'

'Yeah, I know who, but I don't know where. She'll turn up.'

I let the chair down and stood up. He shook hands again but without as much force as the last time. I caught him looking down at the phone once so just before I left I said, 'You can make up your own mind about it, but you'll do better if you keep this little visit under your hat too.' He licked his lips. 'And if you're interested enough, read the *Lyncastle News.*'

At three-thirty I got back to Lyncastle. I put the car in the garage and went in the house. Wendy wasn't there and no sign that she had been there earlier. I tried the bus station, and somebody on duty said Mr Henderson had taken the afternoon off. No, he didn't know where to locate him.

The next call went to the Circus Bar and over all the background noises I finally got it across that I wanted Alan Logan. The guy on the other end yelled back that he wasn't there and hung up. I tried his office.

A girl answered the call and I said, 'Alan Logan, please.'

'I'm sorry, but he isn't here.'

'Know where I can find him?'

'No, I don't. We've been looking for him all day ourselves. He hasn't called in at all. Perhaps you can suggest . . .'

I hated like hell putting him on the spot with his office by telling them he was out somewhere on a bat, so I said, 'Last I saw of him he was on a story. I'm calling because he had some information up there for me. It was from New York, a memo from a Mr Whitman.'

'Oh, yes. It's here on his desk.'

'Could you read it off to me?'

I heard whatever it was crackle in her hand. 'Gee . . . I don't know. We're not supposed to . . .'

'It's O.K. It was some personal information I needed.'

'Well . . .' The paper made a tearing noise and crackled again when she unfolded it. 'It isn't much. It says, "Gracie Harlan and Harlan Incorporated identical." It's signed, "Whit".'

'Thanks,' I said. I hung up and stood there playing with the phone. The blank spaces were filling in gradually. There was a little more sense to it now. The cover was coming off the picture, but I had to be sure of what I saw.

I went downstairs and backed the car out again. Someplace across town would be another piece of the puzzle picture.

It was just like the first time, quiet, with the overtones of 'The Moonlight Sonata' drifting through the door. She even had on the dress with the tassel. I said, 'Hello, Venus.'

Her eyes made one quick sweep of the street. 'Get in here, man!' She said it with an urgency in her voice that made me hop. I slid in the door, shut it and watched her lock it.

'Alone?'

'I haven't been.'

'What's the score?'

'Servo's boys. They've been here off and on ever since you left. What the devil have you been doing?'

'Plenty. Where are they now?'

'I don't know. They left, but they'll be back again.' She fumbled for a cigarette on the table. 'The police have been here too. Oh, not the local police. These were Feds.'

'Yeah?'

'Things are popping in town. The city council convened and passed an all-out resolution to find you.' She pulled on the cigarette and walked to the window. When she was satisfied nobody was watching she tugged the curtains together. 'I sent a couple of girls out to see what was going on. They made good contacts.'

'Nice. Spill it.'

'George Wilson, Johnny McBride, whoever you are . . . those Federal boys decided you have been in back of everything that went on in this town. You financed Servo's operations for the sheer hell of it and when things got too quiet to suit you, you went off on a spree of your own. You're back because things outside of Lyncastle got too hot for you. They even tagged you with a long scientific name that means you're chronically anti-social ever since you came back from the war.'

'So I'm the big wheel,' I mused. 'I'm the guy they want from here to Washington. That doesn't count in Lenny Servo.'

Her eyes narrowed cautiously. 'He has a personal score to settle. I know all about it. But there's more than that. There's a rumour that he's been splitting the take with you all along the line and now he'll be glad to see you under wraps so he can have the whole works.'

'Rumours. They have to start someplace.'

She nodded. 'You've been flush ever since you came to town.'

'That I have, kid. Rumours are funny that way; there's always an element of truth in them. A little thought will blow a hole in it though.'

'How?'

'If I'm behind Servo and I get picked up isn't it logical that I cut Lenny in on half the guilt as well as half the take?'

The cigarette went down another notch. Her face lost the cautious expression and became blank. 'Who are you, man?'

I smiled at her and let it go at that. I said, 'Once you said you had a picture to show me. Did you ever find it?'

Without answering she got up and left the room. She was back a couple minutes later with a wrinkled display-size photo that had evidently been stored away for quite a while. She handed it to me and sat down.

There was a fresh pencil mark around the girl she wanted me to see. Her name was Harlan. She was incorporated. I had seen a later picture of her not so long ago. She was a waitress who worked in the ABC Diner outside of town and had committed suicide because her room-mate had been killed. Before she came to Lyncastle she had worked a con game in New York. She had served time.

Now I knew. Or at least had a good idea.

197

I handed the picture back to Venus. 'Mind if I use your phone?'

'Go ahead.'

It was getting so I could remember the numbers now. I tried Logan's office first. He wasn't there. Wendy wasn't home and Nick still wasn't at the station. The next number was the police station and somebody answered. I asked for Lindsey and he was put on.

'Captain Lindsey speaking.'

'Johnny, friend.'

His breath got loud in my ear. 'Go ahead.' He said it through his teeth.

'What about that letter?'

'Nothing. It doesn't fit. I found the envelope and that was all. Not a thing anyplace.'

'It's around.'

His voice was a hoarse rasp. 'McBride, I think you're stalling. You won't get out of this town alive if you are.'

'I've been out and back already, Lindsey. Now listen to me. Servo's girl is loose somewhere. You know her?'

'Yeah, Troy Avalard. Why?'

'She's on somebody's kill list, Lindsey. Pick her up. I think she may be the key to this thing. Pass the word around and see what you can do.'

He said something dirty under his breath. 'You gave me the answer to that one last night, McBride. Suppose I do give orders. Somebody else'll change 'em.'

'You're not scared, are you?' I asked easily.

Lindsey was silent a moment, then I heard another muttered curse. 'I'll look for her,' he said.

'Fine. Call the bank and see if she made any large withdrawal. I'll call you back in a few minutes.'

I slapped the phone back, chain-lit another cigarette and went over to the window for a quick look down the street. There was a truck parked behind the Ford and a light green sedan behind that. A postman was sorting letters as he went up the steps to a house across the street. A kid came by on a bicycle. A kid in a sleeveless sweater was ambling along checking the house numbers.

I closed the curtains and went back to the phone. Lindsey had made his check. Troy Avalard hadn't made any withdrawals at all. The cashier had given him the information and was instructed to call Lindsey back if she appeared.

Venus was taking it all in silently, sitting there in her chair playing with the tassel on her dress. 'You're big trouble, man. Real big. Things are getting ready to blow, aren't they?'

'Soon. It should have happened five years ago. It would have if a guy named Robert Minnow hadn't been killed.' I stopped and looked at her. 'You'll be here right along?'

'I'm not going anyplace.'

'If Servo's boys come back . . .'

She smiled and reached down behind the cushions. There was a gun in her hand. A long-barrelled revolver that wasn't a woman's gun at all. You could poke your finger down the hole in the end. 'They won't bother me, man. Not again they won't, not even Servo himself.'

'Where'd the rod come from?'

'My husband's. I told you I used to be married to a cop, remember? He taught me how to use it.'

'What happened to him?'

She jerked with a short laugh. 'I shot him.'

The gun went back behind the cushions and she took me out to the door. Like I said, it was just the same as the first time. The tassel was dangling there and I pulled it.

Not quite like the last time. It was a different dress. Just the top fell off. She said, 'Skin is still skin to you, isn't it?'

I agreed that it was and closed the door while she was picking her gimmick up from the floor.

The street was empty and I climbed in the Ford. While I angled back to town I switched on the radio and picked up the local station. It was right on the half-hour and the news commentator was giving a recap of daily events. It was too late to get the details, but in brief, he said that John McBride, alias George Wilson, had not been apprehended and was somewhere at large in the city. All efforts were being made to locate him and an appeal had been made by the city council and the mayor for the citizenry to join in the search. A description followed that was a good one and changed my mind about breezing through town like I was.

Sometimes a crook is safest standing in front of a cop. Then nobody suspects he's a crook. Everybody expected me to be in hiding, so when I went in the dry goods store nobody bothered looking at me twice. I had left my shirt and jacket in the car, walked in in my T-shirt and asked the lady behind the counter for a work shirt, size 16, a size 44 leather jacket and a couple of handkerchiefs. To make it look good I bought a pair of blue jeans and a pair of brogans.

She rang up the sale on the register, smiled and thanked me, then went back to her paper. There was another picture of me on the front page. A little smaller in this edition. I changed clothes in the cubicle in the back, threw my other stuff in the rear of the car and started towards town again.

That's when I saw Wendy. She was coming out of a beauty parlour on the next corner with a package under her arm, glancing down the street for a bus. I slammed on the brakes and yelled to her. She came across the street on the run and got in beside me.

'That where you've been all day?'

I didn't mean to make it sound like it did. She looked hurt and shook her head. 'I just stopped in to make an appointment. I was on the way home.'

I could have seen that if I had looked first. She was still dark around the roots even if her hair did look custom-tailored. I looked some more and grinned. Wendy was an O.K. chick. I tapped the package. 'For me?'

'For you.' She did that trick with her mouth again and opened the top of it. 'Want me to tell you about it or read it off?'

'Tell me.'

'Tucker lives in a big house in the suburbs. He has a bar in the cellar with a game-room and a poolroom. There's a two-car garage behind the house with a new Caddy in one side. He uses the other when he's working.'

'Nice going on a cop's salary.'

'He isn't the only one. Most of the police work a shakedown racket on the side. Tucker does better than most though.'

'He's in with Servo?'

She shrugged her shoulders. 'At one time Tucker was a few grand in the hole to one of the big boys. It's been said that Servo had the debt cancelled. I have statements from seven people who saw him lose thousands in one of the joints in town.'

'Try again. He can always say he won the money on another wheel.'

Wendy fingered through the tops of the papers in the pack.

'He hires a man to make out his income tax. The guy talked with a little persuasion. He said that Tucker declares everything.'

'He's smart. Capone should have thought of it. What else?'

She closed her eyes and leaned back against the seat. 'I went back to see Mrs Minnow. The last time she didn't tell us everything. Her husband had Lenny Servo in court several times.'

'I know. It was in the papers.'

'The important part wasn't. Bob Minnow had evidence that would have broken the racket down . . . or at least put Servo where he would have talked. Twice, on the night before he went to court, somebody broke into his office and rifled the safe. Each time his evidence disappeared.'

'Tucker,' I said. 'Damn it, Tucker would have had the way and the means.' I slammed my fist against the wheel and cursed some more.

Her voice sounded like it came out of a fog. 'Not Tucker,' she said.

I stared at her. 'Who?'

She leafed out a brand-new poster of me, the kind you see in post offices. She had circled the paragraph that said I was wanted for jobs that involved robbing safes. I was an expert at it.

And not so long ago I had sat across a table from Logan telling him about the safe I had pulled from the dump heap and used to experiment on.

'You,' she said. It was soft, but it cracked like a pistol shot. Her eyes were dark with distrust, yet she sat there waiting for me to explain it away.

I didn't bother. 'That's a lot of work for one day, kid.' She pulled back as if I had taken a swipe at her. There were sudden tears in her eyes and I wondered what the hell I could have said that would do that to her.

I said, 'Oh, quit getting sore at me.' I reached out and pulled her under my arm, burying my face in her hair. She smelled pretty. 'I'm just a born lout, Wendy. Always forgetting my manners. I should've said thanks.'

My thumb tilted her chin up until her mouth was under mine. I felt her lips quivering, then her hand went around my head and held me there until I finished apologizing.

The lines she had around her eyes when I first met her were all gone. Coming out of the hardness was a new kind of beauty she let me see only briefly before she pulled back in her shell.

I hit the starter button. 'I'm going into town. You want to come along?'

'No. . . . I have things to do.' She tapped the package. 'What shall I do with this stuff?'

'Leave it in the house. Sure you don't want to come?'

She shook her head and opened the door. When she was out she stood there holding it open, her eyes going over me curiously. 'You're dressed funny.'

'Disguise.'

'Oh!' She grinned at me. 'You'll be careful?'

'Does it matter?'

She nodded and there were tears in her eyes again. A bus came along and she ran for it, leaving me wondering what it was I said that time.

CHAPTER TWELVE

Philbert's was bustling with activity. Signs pasted on the windows blared 'Anniversary Sale!' in fat red letters with the usual business about how prices had been slashed in half. I got behind a stout woman with a shopping bag under her arm and went in after her. I looked around, but as far as the customers were concerned, I was just another one of the crowd. I bought another work shirt just to have something to carry around, made my way through the aisles while I looked over the hardware, then slipped into one of the phone booths along the wall.

The operator got me my number and I could see the guy in the back answer the call. He had a habitual stoop that made his glasses seem to be ready to fall off his nose and he wasn't too polite when he barked hello.

I said, 'I know how you can pick up a quick hundred, feller.'

They always get polite when you use that approach even if they think it might be a wrong number. There's always the chance that it isn't. I watched him look around quickly then muffle the mouthpiece. 'Who . . . you know who this is?' He sounded hopeful.

'Yep. You're in the printing end at Philbert's.'

'Why, that's right! 'Now he was surprised. He turned his back to me and I couldn't see his face any longer.

'Can you get off for a few minutes?'

'Sure.'

'Swell, go outside and start walking south. You got that?'

'Well, yes . . . but . . .'

I hung up and watched him. First he stared at the phone, licking his lips, then must have decided that nothing could happen to him in the daytime. He waved over a young fellow and went in the back. He came out with a coat over his arm and threaded through the mob.

I stayed right behind him.

Outside, he took a look around, shrugged and started walking south. Slowly. When he was directly opposite the Ford I touched his arm and said, 'In the car.'

The guy twitched, shot me a look over his shoulder, then let his mouth fall apart. I said, 'In the car,' again and he opened the door without a sound and shimmied over against the other side. He was pop-eyed with fright and couldn't swallow his own spit.

It was about time somebody recognized me.

I was getting better at the game. I stuck a cigarette in the corner of my mouth, lit it and leered at him. 'You can make that hundred if you feel like it, friend. You can start yapping and just make it rough on yourself. What do you think?'

He got his spit swallowed, but he still couldn't speak. His head made a jerky nod and nothing else. 'Five years ago. Do you remember that long?'

Another swallow and another nod.

'Bob Minnow was the D.A. then. Before he was killed he went to your place and left something there. Remember that?'

'I . . . wasn't there,' he managed to say. 'Lee . . . he mentioned it. I remember . . . now.'

'What did he leave?'

This time he shook his head nervously. 'I . . . dunno. He left something. Lee gave him . . . a ticket. Maybe it's still in the files.'

'Can you find it?'

'Not . . . without the ticket. I already . . . looked.'

The cigarette almost fell out of my hand. I could feel my eyes turning into nasty little slits that blurred everything I looked at. 'Who told you to look?'

He was flat against the door, his eyes wide, showing white all around. 'Just the other day . . . Logan, that reporter. He came in and . . . asked me the same thing.'

So Logan had figured it out first. He remembered before I did that Philbert's did photograph and photostat work. Nice going, Logan.

I said, 'Why can't you find it?'

'Hell, mister . . . we handle thousands of jobs like that. All the companies, they take us their work. Maybe I can find it. I'll look if you want. It'll take a couple of weeks, but . . .'

'Damn it, I haven't got that long!'

'Golly, without a ticket . . .'

'Shut up.'

I pulled in on the butt and flicked it out the window. It landed on a guy's foot and he was going to say something nasty when he saw my face. He kept on walking.

When I reached for my wallet the guy followed my hand every inch of the way and he relaxed when he saw it wasn't a gun. My pile was going down. I slipped out a crisp hundred and passed it to him. 'Mac, keep something in mind. Every cop in town is looking for me, so it's no secret that I'm around. You mention one word to anybody that I've seen you and I guarantee you that for the rest of your life you'll be afraid to walk home alone at night. You understand that?'

He got all white. His hands shook so bad he almost lost the bill.

'How late do you stay open?'

'Until t-twelve.'

'Good! You stay there until you hear from me.'

A frantic nod said he would and he almost broke his neck getting out the door. I was back in traffic before he reached the store, cut down a side street and turned north.

Fifteen minutes later I was driving past the white house with the fence around it. Mrs Minnow was on the porch in a rocker with her head going up and down the street every few seconds. She rocked too fast. Mrs Minnow was nervous.

There were two of them, one on each end of the street. New sedans with a man behind the wheel. They were young men, not smoking or reading. Not doing anything. If there were more I didn't see them and wasn't about to go looking. I kept on going until I found a soda store that served snacks, went into a booth and ordered a sandwich and coffee. When I finished I ordered the same thing again, bought a magazine and dawdled over it until it was dark. The owner of the joint was coughing and looking over my way trying to let me know he wanted to close up, so I paid my bill. An extra buck made him smile again. For luck I tried Logan's office. He still hadn't showed up.

I hung around the street for a while smoking the last of my butts. I picked up another pack in a delicatessen and started on that. Overhead, a rumble of thunder rolled across the city and the sky lit up in the west. I took my time drifting back to the car and made it just as the rain started.

It wasn't too bad, sitting there watching it roll down the windows. It kept time with everything I was thinking, a nice background to dream against. In a way I hoped it would keep up. Later, perhaps, I would sit someplace listening to it slam against the roof while I put all the pieces where they belonged.

My watch read nine-twenty. I kicked the engine over and turned around at the corner.

Smart. I had to be smart. The boys with the badges were thinking along the same lines I was and expected me back at the Minnow house. Or else they were bodyguarding the old lady in case the Johnny McBride they wanted had further ideas of revenge.

This time I parked on the street behind the house. I left the key in the lock in case I had to get away fast, rolled up the windows against the rain and pulled on my jacket. I went back a few houses until I found a driveway, turned in and walked back to the fence line that separated the yards.

I wasn't worried about being seen. My clothes blended with the foliage and if anybody was staked out behind the place they weren't out in the open in this weather. When I reached the garage behind the house I huddled in the shadows until I had every detail in my mind.

The guy I was looking for was just inside the enclosed porch and for an instant I saw his hat silhouetted against a night light in the kitchen. It was enough. He probably was being very careful, but not quite careful enough.

I followed the hedge line, moving slowly with my body down low to the ground. I was all the way up to the house before I realized how mechanically I had done it.

Almost like I had done it before.

Something was there like a battery of floodlights winking on and off in my brain while cold hands pulled at my back. Just like that the sweat started to move down my shoulder blades. I hit my belt with my hands and felt for something that should be there, damn near going crazy when I couldn't find it.

It passed. It took a little while and left me with the shakes, but it passed. I was cold all over because something that was buried years back in time almost came back to me. I cursed and tried to think of what it was.

The house was a ghostly wall pressing against my back, the vine on the trellis wet fingers against my hand.

This.

Had this been what I had done before?

Had I stood in this same spot, climbed up that trellis and gone in that window up there before?

I shook the thought out of my head. Someplace I had read about twins, how there was thought transference. Maybe it happened to people who looked alike too. If there was anything to be remembered I didn't want to know about it. The rain muffled the curse on my lips and I swung up on the trellis.

It didn't take ten seconds to reach the window and two to open it.

The room smelled of a woman and the outlines of a bed were visible against the wall. I left the window open, eased across to the door and put my ear to it. Downstairs a radio was playing softly, but nothing else. I opened the door, looked out in the hall and stepped through.

Stairs ran down on my one side and to my left a pair of doors opened off the corridor. The one in the middle was too pinched in to be a room so I picked the last one.

I was right this time. The door was unlocked and probably hadn't been opened often in the last five years. The musty smell of disuse hung in the air and every step I took tossed back dust from the carpet. The light from the street lamp out front put a yellow glow on everything, casting long dim shadows across the floor.

There was a studio couch, a desk, a pair of filing cabinets and a safe against the walls, reminders of a man who had made this room his den. I had to be right the first time. There wouldn't be any second chance. I started across the room to the safe when the beam of light that hit me in the back threw a monstrous shadow on the wall.

I damn near screamed, swung around and stood there trembling in every muscle of my body. The light hit me in the eyes went over my face and she said, 'I knew you'd come.'

It left me with hardly enough voice to say, 'Turn that damn thing off before they see it!'

The light snicked off.

'How'd you know I was here?'

'I sensed it, young man. I have lived in this house so long listening for footsteps from this room that never came that when someone was in here I knew it. One of the benefits of old age, you might say.'

'Who's downstairs?'

'Two men.'

'F.B.I.?'

'One is. The other is a state man. They don't know you're here.'

I picked the light from her hand. 'Do you know the combination of that safe?'

'No, only Bob knew it. He never wrote the combination down and it has never been open since his death. There was never anything of any value in there. He kept all his personal papers in a safe-deposit vault.'

'What went in there?'

'Just important things he brought home from the office.'

'I'm going to open it.' I was sweating without knowing why. She said it very simply. 'Go right ahead.'

The darkness hid my grin, but she heard the shallow laugh I let out. 'You have one hell of a lot of nerve. I'm supposed to be a killer.'

'It hasn't been proven to me . . . yet.'

Some woman. Her husband would have been proud of her. I snapped the light on, shielding the beam with my hand. I walked over in front of the safe, knelt down and took a good look at it. I reached for the knob and in the soft glow of the light saw the tremble in my hand.

Everything was familiar again. Everything. I looked at the face of that damned safe and no matter where I looked every rivet, every detail of the thing was an old friend. My breath was coming in short jerks that racked my chest. There were things coming into my mind that clawed at my guts with steel nails and tried to rip them out.

I was cold. Damn, I was cold! The past was pushing by the present and I felt it ooze out where it could be seen. The dial on the safe was a face laughing at me and I knew that it wasn't just this safe I was familiar with, but a lot of them. My mind knew every one of them!

Now I was all right. I was a guy with a short memory. It was clean. For five years I had searched for that past without finding it, and when it did begin to show I didn't want to see it.

I knew she was watching me from behind. I made my hand go back to the dial and let my body follow some unnatural instinct that put extra nerves in my fingers and gave my ears some uncanny perception. I knelt there for twenty minutes patiently exploring the supposedly foolproof workings of that lock and at the end of that time I heard what I was listening for, turned the knob and opened the door.

A ten-year-old newspaper lay on the bottom shelf. A tobacco tin of Indianhead pennies was on the other. I pulled open the top drawer and there was a pink numbered ticket from Philbert's lying against the back.

My back ached from kneeling so long. I stood up, pushed the door shut and stuck the ticket in my pocket. Mrs Minnow took the light back and I saw her face. She was looking pleased.

'There was something there?'

'Yes. Do you want to see it?'

'Would it be any good to me?'

'Not now. Later, maybe, but not now.'

'Keep it,' she said, 'and good luck.'

'Thanks.'

She let out a sob as I left the room, but didn't follow me. I went back the way I came, took the same route to the car and climbed in. It was still raining and my pants were soaked from knocking up against the bushes.

But I didn't feel cold any more. Just hot. Good and damned hot.

The guy behind the counter was as white as I had left him. His mouth was dry from licking it so much and the shreds of a block of a rubber eraser were scattered all across the woodwork. He took the ticket, went in the back where I heard him pulling drawers out, then returned with a large brown envelope. Without a word he passed it across the counter, took the two bucks the tag said the job was worth and rang it up.

He was very slow in turning around. It was necessary that I wait until he turned around because I wanted him to see my face. His eyes got glassy and he nodded without anything having been said and I went out.

I drove down a block, parked under a street lamp and opened the envelope. Inside were two identical positives and the negative of a photostatted letter. It had been written in longhand and addressed to Robert Minnow.

It read:

DEAR MR MINNOW,

This letter is to inform you that in the event of my death it is entirely likely I was murdered. Somewhere among my possessions you will find positive evidence of my connection with Leonard Servo and photographic evidence of others who may be implicated in my death.

GRACIE HARLAN

That was all there was to it, but it was enough. I stuck the stuff back in the envelope, pulled up the rubber carpet on the floorboard and laid it against the boards. The carpet fell back and covered it nicely.

I drove on up the street to a bar, went in and ordered a drink and carried it back in the phone booth with me. Then I shoved in a nickel and sipped the top off my drink while I was connected with police headquarters.

A voice said, 'Sergeant Walker speaking.'

'Captain Lindsey.'

'Hang on, I'll connect you.'

A couple of clicks later Lindsey growled into the phone. I said, 'McBride, Captain. I have news for you.'

'I have news for you too.' His voice sounded raw. 'Where are you?'

'Downtown.'

'We just found your friend.'

I grabbed the phone. 'Troy?'

'No. Logan. His car was run off a cliff and smashed itself to hell in the bottom of the gully.'

The air couldn't find its way into my lungs. His words were still there in my ears and I finally got the sense out of them. 'He was . . . run off?'

'Yeah. At least that's the way I figure it. All the other experts around here think he was cockeyed drunk when it happened.'

'He was on a bat . . .' I started to say.

Lindsey cut me short. 'Yeah, we could smell it. The doctor said the same thing. There was a body in the car we couldn't identify. Smashed to pieces.'

'Damn it, what about Logan!'

His voice was very soft. Too soft. 'Logan's alive. Barely. If he lives it'll be a miracle. He's in a coma and nobody's going to get to speak to him for a long, long time.'

My breath whistled out through my teeth. 'When did it happen?'

'Evidently the other night. He's been lying there all this time.'

'The other body?'

'A man. They're working on him now. He fell out of the car on the way down and the heap landed on top of him. Not much left. What was Logan working on?'

'I wish I knew,' I said slowly. 'I wish I knew.'

'There was an envelope on the car seat beside him with your name on it.'

I finished the rest of the drink and laid the glass beside the phone. 'Yeah, now I'm beginning to get it,' I said.

'Maybe you'd like to tell me about it.'

'I'll be down to see you. I still have some time left.' I dropped the phone back in its cradle and took my glass back to the bar. Maybe Lindsey would be wondering what my news was. He shouldn't have spoken up so fast.

I started out the door.

The blonde in the booth said, 'Hello, big feller.'

She smiled and the guy she was with smiled too. A little unpleasantly. I said, 'Hello, Carol.'

'Have a drink with us?'

'No, thanks. I'm pretty busy.'

She pushed out from the booth, still smiling at her companion. 'I'll be right back, Howie. I have to talk business with this lug a second, mind?'

He shrugged and told her to go ahead.

The grin was impish and she backed me into a corner by the cigarette machine. 'You didn't come back to see me,' she said. 'I waited in every night.'

'Except tonight,' I reminded her.

She nodded. 'Pride. Besides, I got lonely. We could have had fun. I like famous people.'

'My kind of famous?'

'Especially. Will you come?'

'Maybe. I was thinking about it earlier. I wanted to ask you if anything was seen of Servo's playmate.'

The grin faded. 'I couldn't tell you that.'

'Then tell me something else.'

'What? Ask me anything else you want to.'

'Didn't that peroxide sting?'

The imp came back in her eyes and she pulled at the zipper on my jacket. 'The peroxide didn't but the ammonia did. Want me to tell you about it?'

'Maybe I'll come up and watch you do it some day.' I pushed her hands away and stepped past her.

'Do that,' she said. 'I'll let you help me.'

Pine Tree Gardens looked more dismal than before, if that was possible. I drove around it once and parked down a ways from the building. There weren't any lights in the place.

It was too close to the end of things to take any chances. I reached down beside the seat and pulled the gun out I had wedged there previously. I tried sticking it in my waistband but the handle caught me under the ribs. The pockets of my jacket held the thing as long as I let the handle stick up. I didn't like that either. If I bent over it would fall out and I wasn't in the mood to be putting a bullet in myself accidentally. There was some kind of a gimmick pocket on the leg of my new work pants that it fitted in snugly enough, so I tucked it down there, closed the flap over it and got out of the car.

The rain was slanting down, driven in my face by a stiff wind. The thunder was still upstairs, but there wasn't any sheet lightning left in the clouds. I walked back to the building and turned in the yard. There was a new sign stuck in the ground. Wind had torn the corner loose and it slapped against the backboard.

It read: For Sale. I. Hinnam, Realtors, Call 1402.

Somebody could get the place cheap, I thought. There was a curse on it now. A death curse. Maybe Lenny Servo would pick it up and make another joint out of it. The location wasn't bad. He could even have rooms for rent upstairs.

The door was locked. A skeleton key could have opened it but I didn't have a skeleton key and wasn't about to waste time picking it. I wrapped a handkerchief around my hand, punched a windowpane in, opened the catch and raised it. For a minute or so I stood there listening. The rain drummed against the windows and my breath made a soft whisper in the darkness. Nothing else. I crossed the room, stopped and listened again.

The house was the only thing that talked back to me.

A door banged at steady intervals, keeping time to the gusts outside. There was a faint creak of wood from upstairs, a rattle of windows as the foliage bent and scraped against them.

All the furniture was in the house, carelessly covered with sheets and wrapping paper. I crossed between the hulks of white, went out in the hall and found the steps. Every detail of that place was so plain in my mind it was as if I had studied a blueprint of the place beforehand. I tried to figure it out, but it didn't make sense. The last time I had just come in with Logan and breezed in. Hell, I didn't study the place at all.

Or did I?

What unconscious instinct did I follow if I did?

I could even remember the curious pattern in the newel post at the top. A door to one room had been warped. There was a worn spot in the carpet beside the wall as if a phone had hung there at one time.

My face worked itself into a grimace and I went on up. The post and the carpet was as I had expected. The door that made the steady slam was the warped one that wouldn't close all the way.

The room where the body had lain was closed off, but not locked and I went in half expecting to see it still there, the head cradled in the arms, face down.

But it wasn't the same. Not nearly.

Somebody had taken that room apart piece by piece and stacked all the bits in the middle. The bed, the dresser and the chair had been disassembled and a knife had made a tattered farce out of the mattress. Rayon satin ribbon from the blanket edgings was confetti unfurled on the floor.

The baseboard had been pried loose and jutted out awkwardly. I struck a match and looked in the closet. The cedar paper that lined it had been torn off and lay piled up on the floor. Dents in the plaster showed where something heavy had tapped around seeking out a hollow space.

It was a better job than I could have done. A much better job. So good that there wasn't any place left to look.

214

The match burned down and I lit another one.

I cursed under my breath.

At one time the answer had been here. It hadn't been too long ago. There was photographic evidence that would have pointed the finger straight at the one who counted and now it was gone.

I said, 'Damn it to hell!'

The voice standing in the doorway said, 'That's the way we felt too. Keep your hands where they are and turn around. Do it slow. Do everything slow. That is, if you wanta keep on living.'

And there was that little bastard of an Eddie Packman with a snub-nosed rod in his fist and the pimply-faced boy from the Ship'n Shore behind him backing the play with his automatic.

The pencil beam of the flash in the kid's hand ran up and down my body looking for bulges under my clothes. It passed close enough to Lenny's arm to be reflected off the cast he wore.

The kid said, 'He looks clean, Eddie.'

'Go see, you jerk,' Eddie snarled. 'You oughta know by now. Give me the light.' He took it out of the kid's hand and stuck it in the fingers that dangled out of the cast.

Trying to be casual didn't come easy to the kid. He sidled crabwise over to me, ran his hands over my pockets, patted my chest and stepped back. 'I told you he was clean,' he said sneeringly. The rod in his hand gouged into the small of my back. 'Go ahead, tough guy, start walking.'

So I walked. Eddie drew back in the doorway and let me go by. 'You can try and run for it if you like. Don't think I won't give it to you here or anyplace else.'

His beady eyes glowed at me. They were narrow and mean and almost praying I'd do something that was excuse enough to start shooting. He looked like a rat, his face drawn out in a thin-lipped snarl that showed the uneven edges of his teeth.

Like rats, all right. That's why they were so damned quiet. They must have frozen the minute I came in and stayed that way until I had walked into their hands.

The kid poked me again and said, 'We knew you'd be here. You're a sucker.'

'Shaddup, you,' Eddie spat out.

Pimples was new at being tough. He didn't like to get yelled at. 'Shut your own mouth. Who the hell you think you are?'

Eddie taught him a quick lesson with the end of his rod. I heard it hit bone and the kid let out a sob that choked off in his throat. He didn't need a second lesson. He sobbed all the way down and out to Eddie's sedan where he got in under the wheel holding a bloody handkerchief to his face.

I got the place of honour. In the back seat with Eddie's gun a cold spot under my ribs. He sat facing me with his leg under him, a laugh pulling the sneer off his face. He looked at me until the car got started then before I saw what he was going to do the cast came around and smashed against the side of my head with a sickening crack that almost churned my guts up in my mouth before I lost all feeling and dropped into a black well of unconsciousness.

My head pounded with every beat of my heart. It hung forward, limply ready to fall if my hands let go of what they were holding. But the hands weren't holding anything. They were balls of meat tied together behind the back of the chair, senseless things that dangled at the end of my arms. I opened my eyes and watched the fuzzy, distorted angles under my head take shape until they were my legs. My foot twitched spasmodically and moved an inch. I was glad they weren't tied too.

Whatever lit the room had a yellow glow to it. I made my eyes travel across the rough woodwork of the floor until they met the opposite wall, then down the side to a chair, and another chair, across again to the middle and the four legs of a table.

On the table was an old-fashioned kerosene lamp. The wick was turned too high and the smoke was making a black doughnut on the dirty cracked plaster ceiling. There was a door in the wall on the other side of the room. It was a substantial-looking door that was closed tightly against the jamb.

It was still raining outside. It made a drumming noise some-place overhead, occasionally slashing in waves against the side of the building. I sat there letting my head clear, listening to the outside trying to get in and above it all heard a faint slap-slap of water licking at something that held it back. I could smell it too. The river.

Me and the river. We were both alone.

I tried my legs, starting to stand up. The chair rose with me an inch or so but no further. The rope that tied my hands tied the chair to something too. For no reason at all I wondered what time it was. Suddenly not being able to see my watch was more important than anything else. I sat down again and strained against the ropes, and when that didn't work wiggled them enough to get the circulation started again.

That made it worse than before. They weren't senseless chunks of meat any longer. They were raw, screaming nerve-ends that pulsated with pure agony. I cursed and clamped down on my lip until the taste of blood was in my mouth. I could feel the sweat rolling down my face until it dripped off my chin. The drops made patterns between my feet.

After ten minutes or maybe thirty it passed and became a dull, throbbing ache, but at least there was some feeling in the ends of my fingers. They were wet with blood from where the ropes bit into the skin.

Every position hurt. The best I could do was lean forward like I was when I came awake and stare at the floor. I got tired of watching the floor and looked at my legs. The underside of my right thigh was pretty damn sore. I moved and it stopped hurting some.

But I moved it back where it was in case somebody came in and decided to search me again. The last time they hadn't noticed the gun in that out-of-place pocket.

Me and the rod. We would have made a good combination if my hands weren't useless lumps behind me. Great. Useless. Me, I was useless too. I walked head-on into it. I should have known as soon as I saw that room. I should have flattened myself on the floor with the rod cocked and waited for them to come in. I should have done a lot of things.

Now look.

So I sat and thought how nice they had me trapped. Now nobody would ever know. I'd know, but I'd be dead. A few other people would know, but they were the ones who wanted me dead.

Five years, a thousand miles. I had come a long way to wind up in a chair with my hands strapped together and the river close enough to smell. Soon they'd be coming in and they'd look at me and I'd look at them, but they'd be the ones to laugh. I'd just sit here until I was dead.

Maybe somebody would find my body and figure out how it happened. Unlikely. Very unlikely. I wished I could know the whole story before I died. I'd like that. I'd sure like to know how close I was.

I could see the angles now.

Before Lyncastle there was Lenny Servo and a girl named Gracie Harlan. She was a show girl until the breaks got rough, then she tied in with Lenny. They played tricks with the money boys and picked up an income with the con game. Con with sex thrown in. No matter how smart they are it always works. That is, always until somebody has sense enough to squawk.

For that she served time, but it didn't keep her from wanting to go back in business. Lenny found the heat on in the East and looked around for a spot to operate in. He was a clever character, he was. He found Lyncastle. But he was broke when he found it and didn't have the connections that could put up big money fast.

Hell, that wasn't any trouble for Lenny. He put the squeeze on a kid named Johnny McBride. He must have been pretty cute about it. Harlan sexed Johnny into a spot that would have ruined him, then Lenny came across with the suggestion that he lift some funds from the bank for the purpose of financing his operations.

The son of a bitch even had some insurance. He must have been big-time-Charlying Vera West in the meantime until she was on his side and when the bust came Johnny ran to save her neck, not his own!

218

That Bob Minnow must have been a sharp article too. With Lenny paying off the police and bribing the town into liking the whole set-up he had to be. In fact, everybody was on their toes. Harlan, she played it real cute. She found out in a hurry that when Lenny got to be top dog she was deadwood. She was the weak link that could spoil his pretty chain.

So Harlan took out some insurance too. She wrote Bob Minnow a letter and he filed it away. That was the catch. He wasn't to open it until she died, but at one point in his investigation of Lenny Servo he learned that he was connected with Harlan.

Maybe he suspected the truth. He went ahead and opened the letter anyway and found out he was right. He went out and had it photostatted in case something happened to the original. He wasn't taking any chances on his safe being cracked again.

Just thinking about it put everything right out where I could see it. The insurance wasn't any good to Harlan unless she let Lenny know what she did. That way he couldn't afford to knock her off. He had to get the letter back first. Quick, too.

It was quick. Minnow double-checked to verify his source and when the letter came in with the verification he didn't lose any time getting things started. He went down to his office, but somebody who knew where he'd be and knew damn well he'd have that letter along, passed the word up the line and there was a guy waiting for him.

Me, I said to myself. No, Johnny. Maybe he went there to spill the works to the D.A. and got panicky. Sure, a guy on the run wouldn't be thinking straight, would he? Hell, no! So he got a gun from somewhere in case somebody tried to pick him up and went up to see Minnow.

Panicky. It was hard to picture Johnny getting panicky. The guy was cold as ice no matter what he did.

Feet stamped outside. Metal rasped against metal and a voice swore softly. A door opened and shut and the feet pounded on the floor. Then the door across the room was pushed inward and Lenny Servo was there, his hat spilling water past his eyes. There was a scab on his lip and his face was still swollen.

Eddie Packman and the lad were right behind him. Eddie carried a gun. Lenny kept his hands in his pockets while he stared at me, then tossed his hat on the table and shrugged out of his raincoat.

I knew just what was going to happen and the only thing I could do was spit right in his face before Lenny's hand snapped my head back.

He said, 'You stinking bastard!' and hit me again. He kept it up until his knuckles were bloody then he kicked me in the shins with the toe of his shoe and laughed while I vomited bile on the floor.

'You shoulda wore a glove, Lenny,' Packman said. 'Now look at your mitt.'

Lenny didn't answer him. He was looking straight at me, his breath whistling in and out through his teeth. 'Where is she, damn you!'

My mouth felt like a puffball of swollen flesh. 'Who?'

'Vera! Damn it, you better start talking.'

I said two words to him and they weren't good night.

Eddie said, 'He won't talk. He's a tough guy.'

Lenny seemed to relax. He rubbed his knuckles and backed to the table. He liked that pose, perching on the corner with one leg swinging. 'That's right. Tough. I never thought he'd be so tough.'

'He got medals for it in the army,' Eddie said. I brought my head up and it was my turn to stare. I had that creepy sensation again.

Lenny's eyes were black beads of hate. He was hating me so hard he could hardly get the words between his teeth. 'Remember what I told you five years ago? I told you to get out of town and never stop running. I told you once that I'd let Eddie work you over with a knife until there was nothing left but ribbons if you came back and you came back anyway.

'You were scared then, McBride. You knew damn well I wasn't kidding. You forgot too much. Or did you wonder if I meant it? Now you can find out. Eddie's got a nasty mind. He likes to see blood run. He likes to start it going with that knife of his and stand there and watch it drip. That's why I keep Eddie around. People know what he's like and they never go too far with me.

'Except you, McBride. You had to be one of the wise ones. You and a few others. Now you'll see how stupid you were in ever coming back.'

Eddie grinned and tossed the gun on the table. It lay there beside the light while he reached in his pocket. The thing didn't show in his hand until he pressed the button, then the blade jumped out between his fingers, the carefully honed blade the only bright spot in the room.

I got smart for the last time. I said, 'You ought to be happy. Three times you tried and now you're finally going to make out.'

The two of them looked at each other and Eddie shrugged. Lenny cursed silently and lit a cigarette. His hand was still bleeding. He said, 'Show him.'

He stepped over and cut a notch out of my right ear. Then the left ear. Pimples got sick to his stomach and Eddie laughed his head off. He said, 'Now we'll have some fun,' and started to unbuckle my belt.

Everybody heard the car brake to a stop outside. The door slammed and a guy came in dripping rain all over the place. He was tall and skinny and wore a gun belt under his raincoat. He looked at the kid who was still sick and over to me. The sight didn't bother him a bit.

'I got the dame outside,' he said.

Eddie came off the table. 'Where was she?'

'Trying to hitch a ride along the highway about eight miles out. She must have been in town all this time.'

'Bring her in.' He waved his thumb at the kid. 'You go help him.'

They forgot about me. Even Bloody Eddie. The two of them stood in the doorway waiting for the others to come back. The car doors slammed again and the tall guy came in carrying a woman in a torn grey trench coat. He threw her in a chair and the bandanna came off her head.

Lenny had found Troy Avalard.

There wasn't much beautiful about her now. Her hair was a soggy mess that was plastered to the sides of her face. She had two long scratches along one cheek and her top lip was a nasty blue colour. Her eyes were a dull glaze that reflected the terror she felt, coming to life only when they saw Lenny.

He smacked her across the jaw with his open palm and knocked her right out of the chair. 'Isn't this nice? Isn't this just plain lovely?' He laughed through his words and hauled her back on the chair. 'Now we're almost finished. It's too bad Harlan had to do the Dutch or we could have made a real party out of it.'

'Lenny . . .'

'Shut up, you lousy little tart. I've been just waiting for this chance. You don't think I would have let you get away, do you? You don't think I'd let you take me for a pile then let you slip out of my fingers? You could do those things when Harlan was alive and get away with it. Not now.' His hand caught her again, this time in the mouth. The chair rocked over backwards and she lay there on the floor, her arm up in front of her face.

She tried to scream. He bent down, pulled her arm away and smashed her again. 'Lenny! Don't . . . oh, mother, . . . don't!' She cowed against the wall without being able to get away from his hand. She was screaming and sobbing, scrambling on her hands and knees, only to be tripped up by the chair.

It was Lenny who knocked her free. She rolled, her dress up to her waist, clawing at the floor as she pulled herself over to me. Her arms grabbed the legs of the chair frantically while the curses poured out of her mouth. They subsided into a long, broken sob that racked her body.

Lenny was smiling. He was happy. He walked to the table, picked up the gun and checked the chamber. His eyes met mine and the smile drew up into a sneer. 'You won't die without company, Johnny. You know why she's going to die with you?'

I knew, but I'd sooner hear him tell it.

Lenny saw the knowledge in my face. 'You have a brain, kid. Sure, she knew Harlan. They were in the same act once.

She knew why Harlan was sent up and figured the play was the same here as back East. She put the bite on me.' He leered evilly. 'Sometimes I got my money's worth back. Sometimes,' he said.

He took a short step forward, sighted the barrel of the rod at her head and his hand tightened on the trigger.

I said, 'All her dough's going to her next of kin, Servo. Your dough. It's in the bank and some aunt or uncle will get it. Maybe fifty grand.'

All the eyes were turned on me. It got so quiet I could hear Pimples trying to keep his stomach in place. A flush seeped into Lenny's face while a vein on the side of his neck bulged against his collar.

The knife blade in Eddie's hand flicked open and shut a couple of times. 'The hell with it. Let it stay there.'

'No!' He showed his teeth to me. 'I said the tough boy has a brain, Eddie. You should be so smart. Somebody will be looking for Troy one of these days. If she cleared out on her own it wouldn't be likely that she'd leave all that dough in the bank.' He half turned his head over his shoulder. 'Eddie . . . you know where the bankbooks are in the apartment. Go get them. Bring a withdrawal slip too.'

'How the hell am I gonna drive with this wing?'

'Lobin can drive.'

The tall guy grunted his assent.

Pimples said, 'I'd just as soon go too. I don't feel so good.'

'O.K., go ahead, the whole damn bunch of you. Beat it. Get back here in a half-hour.'

So we weren't too far from town. A half-hour. Fifteen minutes each way. The place was right at the edge of town on the river.

The three of them filed out. The car roared into life, spun its wheels in some gravel as it turned around, then shot off down a road.

Lenny glanced at me, the huddled figure at my feet and went through the door to the outside. I heard him slide a lock in a hasp and try it.

I had ten seconds at best. No longer. Ten lousy seconds that could kill me or keep me alive. I kicked her. I gave her a boot in the ribs and she moaned. I kicked her again, pushing her away from the chair. I got one toe under her chin and lifted her head up.

'Can you hear me? Do you understand what I'm saying? Damn it, nod or do something?'

Her eyes were blank. One was shutting fast.

'Listen. Hear what I say.' The words rushed out of my mouth in a harsh whisper. 'Under my right leg there's a gun. It's under my leg in a pocket. Look, reach your hand in and feel it. Damn it, Troy, move! Do you want to die! He'll be back any second!'

The lifeless look was still in her eyes. I let my foot down and her head dropped again just as Lenny came through the door. He shut it behind him, curled his lip up and came over.

He had to hit me again. His fist split my lips open and a grey haze clouded my mind. When my eyes opened he hit me again, but it was beyond hurting now. Just something dull that made my head move and kept my brain numb.

I was able to sit there with my head over on my shoulder and watch him work Troy over then. The devil was in his face as he punched her in the stomach and kicked at her while she lay face down on the floor. All the crazy hate he ever had in him came out until he was exhausted. He let her lie there and went back to the table. Twice, he picked up the gun and pointed it at us. Twice he put it down. The fifty grand in the bank was too much dough to waste.

So he put the gun back and pulled a chair up to the table. Troy groaned. Her mouth was making sounds like a baby, bubbling sounds that flecked her chin with red. Both hands were curved into painful talons as she pulled herself across the floor towards me in a blind direction that took her away from him.

Her hand rested on my shoe; the other clawed at my leg and she pulled herself into a sitting position. Lenny started to laugh.

'Why don't you give her a hand, McBride? Why don't you help the lady? You like to help the ladies out, don't you? Then give her a hand. She needs it bad.' He thought it was so funny that he threw back and laughed until the tears rolled down his face. He was a stinking pig sitting there, a son of a bitch of a cheap con man, not the Lenny Servo who liked fancy offices and fine clothes. He was nothing but a hood at heart and it showed on his face. He laughed and laughed and laughed.

He laughed so hard he never saw Troy flop across my lap and never saw her hand slip under my leg and pull the gun out. He was still laughing when she fell back to the floor because she was too weak to hold on any longer. I was praying under my breath when the laugh choked off.

Lenny ripped out a curse, snatched the gun from the table and swung it at her. There was a deafening blast, the sharp stench of burned cordite and Lenny stood there, a surprised expression on his face because he had a hole in his throat.

He didn't fall. He just folded up and sank to the floor cross-legged. For a couple of seconds he sat there, then bent forward and fell on his face.

'God!' I said.

She looked up at me pitifully. One hand went to her chest. The other tried to stop the blood that spilled out of her mouth. Lenny hadn't missed after all. She was dying and she knew it. She was minutes away from death and there wasn't a thing she could do about it.

The things I was thinking must have made a picture on my face. Her mouth drew back around her teeth and she pushed herself to my side with one hand. I wanted to tell her not to, but I couldn't say a word. I wanted to tell her to save every minute she could of life and not waste those minutes trying to do something she wouldn't be able to do.

Her fingers found the ropes on my hands and made a feeble effort to untie them. I could feel the torn edges of her nails rake the backs of my hands and hear her breath bubbling in her throat as she fought the knots. They were too damn tight. There wasn't one chance in a million she could get them loose and I knew it.

225

Troy knew it too. She looked up at me once, then reached out for the gun again. When I saw what she was going to do I froze in the chair. The nose of the gun went down until it lay along the knots. I spread my hands as far apart as I could to keep them out of the way of the slug. I was saying another prayer that she wouldn't get me too.

When she pulled the trigger the gun jumped out of her hand. Both my hands stung from the blast and I knew there was a furrow of raw flesh along one palm. I wasn't worried about that. I pulled at the ropes, cursed and pulled again. They gave the third time and I fell face forward on top of her, pieces of the ropes still clinging to my wrists.

Troy was smiling at me. She was almost gone, but she was smiling at me. I barely heard her say, 'Undress me.'

Sex right there at the end. I shook my head. 'Thanks, kid. You'll never know how much I'd like to thank you.'

I touched her cheek, leaned down and kissed her forehead. Her eyes closed when I did it and opened again for the last time.

'Undress me,' she said. Her eyes closed.

That was all. She was dead then. I ran my hand across her swollen mouth wishing Lenny had lived long enough for me to get my hands on him. Troy, lovely red-headed Troy who never got to wear clothes. She wanted to be naked when she died. Like cowboys and their boots. It was important to them. Maybe it was important to her too.

My fingers were too stiff to fumble with the buttons. I grabbed the cloth of her dress and tore it open down the front. Gently. I stripped it off and did the same thing with the slip.

Then I saw why it was so important that she die naked. To me it was important and she had tried to tell me that with her eyes. Fixed to her stomach with cellulose tape was a photograph. It was a picture of her without any clothes on. She was in bed.

She wasn't alone.

I sat there and laughed until I heard the car stop outside. Then I picked up the two guns and went out to the other room and stood in the dark waiting. Eddie, Pimples and the guy he had called Lobin came in, shut the door and went past me into the room where death had had such a wonderfully sweet time.

Lobin went for his gun and I shot him in the head. Pimples wasn't so lucky. He would have lived if he hadn't tried to live up to his job. He got it in the chest and died crying.

That left Eddie Packman.

I was right when I said he looked like a rat. A rat can be nasty when it thinks it has a chance, but when a rat is cornered all its ingrown instincts come out and it's a cowardly rodent with sharp yellowed teeth and eyes that dart from side to side to find a hole to crawl in.

Eddie Packman was a rat. He didn't look like himself any more. He looked smaller, the cast on his arm a huge fungus growth that weighed him down whenever he tried to move.

I said, 'Eddie . . . when I came to town I promised to do a few things before I left. I was going to kill somebody. I was going to break somebody's arms. That last one was you.'

There were two more guns on the floor. I picked them up and tossed them on the table, then laid the two I had down beside them.

Then I started walking towards Eddie.

He took his chance with the knife and had it out as he jumped me.

A chance. That was all it was. I grabbed his wrist, picked it out of his fingers and tossed it in the corner. He kicked and screamed and punched at me as I carried him to the table, screamed again when I laid his good arm across the top and fainted when I leaned on it and snapped the bone clean in two. I waited until he came out of it, broke the cast on his arm with the butt of a gun, propped it up against the table and snapped it all over again.

Eddie's eyes were staring up at the ceiling, but he wasn't seeing anything.

Lobin's gun was the best. A police positive. There were extra shells in his gun belt that I took along too. He still had his badge pinned to his jacket under the raincoat. They might think he died in the line of duty and even give him a nice military burial.

I went outside in the rain and got in the car. Eddie's sedan was parked in back of it. I turned the key, kicked the starter and pulled out on the pavement. Not far away the lights above Lyncastle threw a spectrum of colour against the low-hanging clouds.

Soon now, the lights would return to a normal shade. Someday, even, it might become a normal city.

But first somebody had to die.

CHAPTER THIRTEEN

The time was five minutes after three. I stopped in a bar where everybody was arguing at one end, covered my face with a handkerchief before going to the phone booth, and put in a call to police headquarters. Captain Lindsey wasn't there. The voice on the other end told me if it was important he could be reached at home and gave me the number.

It was that important and I reached him at home. He sounded old and tired when he said hello.

I said, 'Johnny McBride, Lindsey. You don't have to wait that week out after all.'

He sucked his breath in sharply and let it out into the receiver. 'What happened?'

'Servo's dead. One of his bunch is dead. His girl friend is dead. One of your cops is dead. Eddie Packman is minding them. He has two broken arms and he'll be minding them for a long time yet.' I sounded tired too. I didn't feel like explaining another thing. 'Stay on the main road right out to the river. There's an old house on the bank and Packman's car is in front of it. You can't miss the place.'

'Damn you, what happened?' he exploded.

'You're a cop,' I told him. 'Figure it out. Tomorrow somebody else'll be dead too and if you haven't got it figured by then I'll tell you about it.'

He ripped out a curse.

'Lindsey . . .'

'Yeah?'

'If I were you I wouldn't let your buddy Tucker out of your sight. He helped kill Bob Minnow. He left the window open for the killer to get in and arranged things so Bob would be there ready to die on schedule.'

'Johnny,' his voice quavered, 'if you don't . . .'

I cut him short again. 'You know that body of a man who was with Logan?'

'He's identified, damn it. They called me twenty minutes ago.'

'Was it a barber named Looth? Looth Tooth?'

He sounded slightly incredulous. 'That's . . . right. His wife was away and nobody notified the missing persons bureau. We got it from a laundry mark. How did you know?'

'I didn't. It just occurred to me. A couple of things just occurred to me. One is another reason for seeing that a murderer dies before morning.'

There wasn't any sound from the phone so I hung up.

I had all the answers in my pocket except one. The biggest one. But I got that one too. You know how? There was a blonde over in the corner dead drunk. Her hair was bleached almost pure white, just like Carol's. It made me think of something, then a lot of things all at once and I had all the answers, every single damned one of them. I even knew how to be absolutely sure.

But there was something I had to do first.

I reached the house just before four o'clock. I walked up to the gate and pushed the bell. This time he had on a bathrobe instead of riding breeches and he looked mad as hell. When he saw it was me he opened the gate, studied me a moment, then reached for the phone in the receptacle.

I tapped him behind the ear with the gun butt and dragged him into the gatehouse. I was very easy with him when I stretched him out on his bunk and pulled the covers up under his chin. After all, he only worked here.

Then I walked up the flagstone to the house where there was a light in the study that looked out on the drive and pushed the bell there too.

He wasn't expecting me at all. He was expecting someone else and for a fraction of a second it showed on his face. I said, 'Hello, Mr Gardiner,' stepped over the sill and kicked the door shut.

'Isn't it a bit late . . .'

Havis Gardiner licked his lips and nodded curtly. He was still a man of distinction.

When we got inside I kicked that door shut too. No, I didn't sit down. I let him sit down and I stood there leaning against the door. I never wanted to sit down again. Not in a chair.

'They're all dead, Gardiner. All but you.'

His head pivoted around as if I had pulled a string. The fingers of his hands were sunken into the upholstery of the chair. 'You?' His voice sounded strained.

I nodded. 'Me.'

He looked ghastly. The colour left his face and he slumped back in the chair. He seemed to collapse under his clothes and stay that way while he stared out the window into the night.

'You can't prove it, McBride.'

It was too bad he wasn't able to see me grin. 'No, not right now, Gardiner. It'll take a lot of work by Lindsey and whatever cops he has who still work for the city, but when they're done everybody will know what happened.

'I thought I had it a little while ago. I was ready to lay it all to Servo until I watched him go kill-crazy and beat the hell out of a woman who was half finished already. A big shot can't do that. He can't afford to mix in anything like that.

'Once Lenny was a big shot. Soon after he came to town he and Harlan got you in a fix and made you lift five hundred thousand bucks from your bank. He thought he had a nice deal and was smart enough to pay the money back to you so the temporary loan would never be noticed.

'Too bad Lenny forgot that you were a clever guy too. You saw the way he was feeding that money back and liked the way he did it. You were so damned smart you got some kind of a hold on Lenny that made you the top dog instead of him and cut yourself in for a share of the profits.

'Hell, I bet Lenny didn't even mind. He had all he needed and somebody running the show better than he could besides. A guy like Lenny isn't a smart operator in real estate like he

231

was supposed to be. Hell, no, somebody was directing every move he made.

'The catch was Harlan. What happened, Gardiner, did she want a larger cut? If she did it was a sure bet that she was sealing her own death warrant. Anybody who put the pressure on and could prove it had to go. That's why she wrote the letter to Minnow.

'Bob was catching up to you fast and that tore it. You knew he'd connect her up to Servo and through her . . . you. Bob Minnow made one mistake, I think. I'm willing to bet that you or somebody you put up to it slipped him the tailor-made idea that somebody in the bank was behind Servo. The money man. Hell, it would be logical enough if the bank's books showed the error.'

Gardiner turned his head and looked at me. The ridges of his cheekbones stood out prominently.

'The frame came when you sent Johnny handling the books he had no business using and his girl backed you up because she had a passion for your partner.

'Nice motive for murder, revenge. The public liked it, didn't they? Lindsey liked it too. It was so logical the insurance investigators and the Feds liked it too.'

'Your fingerprints . . .' he croaked.

'Were on the gun,' I finished for him. 'The gun that killed Minnow was a stolen gun that you planted under the cashier's desk until it had the prints on it. After that you switched back and kept it until you needed it for the murder.

'That was a pretty job. Well arranged. Orderly. Minnow did come to his office when he had the verification of his suspicions and he had the letter with him. Who actually shot him, Gardiner? I don't think you did. Servo is my choice. Tucker made it easy to get in and Servo did the job with your direction and approval. It would have turned out fine if Minnow hadn't photostatted the letter first. But you wouldn't have known that, would you?

'The papers would have had another murder right after that if Harlan hadn't tucked a copy of that photograph where it

232

was likely to be found. She was out of the organization now because she couldn't expose you without exposing herself to be part of a murder ring, but she could stay alive by keeping that photograph. It was a stalemate.'

I pulled a crumpled butt out of my pocket and lit it. The smoke tasted good and I kept it down in my lungs a long time before letting it go. I looked at the ceiling, then at Gardiner. He got up, tottered across the room to a portable bar and poured himself a stiff shot.

'About then was when Troy came into the picture. She recognized Harlan and cut herself in. She not only wanted money, she wanted the source, or so she thought. Lenny must have had a great time with that girl trying to keep her under wraps. If he had been real smart he would have loaded her with dough and shipped her off. He wouldn't be dead now.' I grinned at his back, 'But you don't know about that, do you? You see, it was Troy who killed Lenny.'

His hand trembled and he lost control of the glass. It slipped out of his fingers, bounced off the carpet and rolled across the floor. I waited while he poured himself another one.

'That brings it up to me. In one way, all those things that happened five years ago were simple. Until tonight you really had me going in circles. Everybody wanted me dead.

'I really must have scared the hell out of you when I walked in there that day. I made a big mistake myself in thinking I could get away with it. You must have known something was screwballed when I didn't haul off on you right away. Johnny was a key. As long as he stayed on the run the heat stayed off you. And you made sure he stayed on the run.

'I'm going to make a guess. Let's see how close I come. Johnny was yellow. Two people told me that and I saw it myself. He must have been if a guy like Eddie Packman could throw a scare into him so bad that when he came back Eddie wanted to take him on barehanded. But Johnny was in the war and he came back with lots of medals so he had a reason to be scared. Let's say he lost all his courage where it counted and he had none left to spend at home. It isn't hard to throw a scare into a mental cripple, especially if the woman he loves suddenly shows up to be a louse.'

Gardiner gave me that look again so I knew I was right.

'So after five years I come back. I get spotted and you know about it and being the kind of a guy you are you try to argue Servo into killing me right there. Servo played it cagey and wanted to wait until he saw what I was up to, but you didn't wait. You got hold of a rifle, followed me to the library, picked out a good gun platform and waited until I came out.

'That was an easy shot too. I should have known right there. You left the imprints of your elbows and knees in the gravel and I was looking for a short guy, almost like Eddie Packman. I should have been looking for a guy who knew so little about shooting he didn't know how to hold a rifle and muffed an easy target.'

He was motionless except for a slight twitching of his nostrils, staring out into the dead of night. I grinned, watching it sink in. His hand was a rigid white claw around the glass.

'Then there was that little episode outside the Ship'n Shore. That kept me guessing too. I wasn't trying to work under cover so it must have been pretty easy for you to keep check on me. Maybe somebody called you from the place, or maybe you were behind me all the way. I don't know. But I do know this.

'Before I went out that night I stopped in a barber-shop. It's the place in town where the wheels gather to talk shop over a shave. A barber named Looth Tooth who had a brilliant memory and a gift of gab thought I was going out on a date with my old girl . . . Vera West. You must have come in right after me and he mentioned it to you.'

I stopped and looked at him. The rigidity in his spine had slackened and the glass in his hand seemed to balance normally between his fingers. I cursed the bastard in my mind because I wanted to see his soul age and crawl before my eyes. I wanted to see his guts twist and fear turn his eyeballs into hard little marbles and he wasn't doing any of those things. He just stared at the night and I thought I saw him smile.

'Vera, she was another key. She was another one who could spill the beans if she wanted to take the chance of dying for her trouble. You *knew* I didn't know the score, but Vera did. You didn't shoot at me out there that night . . . you thought I had Vera in the car and were trying to get her.

'Gardiner, you should have left the guns to the pros. They're much better at it. Hell, it was you who was messing things up in your hurry to get rid of me. You sent Lenny and Eddie out to the whore house to see what I was doing with the dame in the first place. Maybe you thought she was a contact between me and Vera. Man, you just didn't know. That woman didn't have a thing to do with anything except give me an excuse to lay those two bastards out. She sure came up with some choice morsel after that though.'

He was smiling. Damn it, the son of a bitch was smiling! It wasn't on his face so much as it was in back of his eyes. He was standing there laughing at me without hardly moving a muscle. I damn near choked trying to speak when I wanted to rip him inside out instead.

'But let's not forget Logan. He was right with me on digging out the dirt. I think he had the whole story at one time there, but he was too drunk to do anything about it. He must have put a lot of things together including Looth Tooth. He was tanked up to his ears when your insurance boys met him. By some accident, or maybe careful planning, you happened to sit in on their conference. Logan had an envelope in his pocket. It had a lot of information about George Wilson.' I sucked in on the cigarette, watched him through the smoke. The bottle was half empty. He never stopped staring out the window for a minute.

'Offhand, I'd say you sneaked that stuff out of his pocket while you were in his car, hoping that he'd think he lost it while he was drunk. You called the police, disguised your voice and tipped them off. That gave Lindsey a reason for nailing me whether I was Johnny McBride or George Wilson. You didn't care what name I died under.

'Logan wasn't so drunk after all. He must have heard the news broadcast and started thinking. I wonder if he remembered that fresh haircut you had and connected things up to Looth Tooth. He sure did something, because in checking back he found out. But like everything else, Logan made a mistake too. He wanted a story. A documented story. He must have phoned you and you met him and Looth Tooth.'

Then I knew why he was smiling when he should have been praying. I remembered that look on his face when I came in. He had been expecting somebody else and somebody else was out there in the night looking back at us through the window!

'Logan isn't dead, Gardiner. He may die and he may not. Some day he'll be able to tell if you conked him with something before you steered his car over a cliff, or not. If he lives he'll tell because you won't be alive to see that he conveniently dies in the hospital. Money can do a lot of things that way.'

I leaned into the light. Deliberately. I moved a step so the light bathed me from top to bottom. I propped my shoulder against the wall and didn't move anything except my mouth while I counted the seconds it would take for a good shot with a service revolver to line up the sights on my chest, hold his breath and squeeze the trigger.

'And I'll be able to tell how I called you up just as you came home after you did the job. Your housekeeper tried to tell me you were out and I thought it was a stall, but you *were* out . . . on a murder . . . and came back in time to take the call. I'm sure we'll all be glad to tell a jury about it if we have to.'

I moved as the shot blasted the picture window into a million fragments. For a millionth of a second there was the yellow tongue of flame still licking towards me out of the blackness, a fiery yellow tongue with a red tip and the brighter white of the eye behind it. The gun in my hand bucked once. The room split open with the sound of it and died away to a brief, unholy silence.

There was no refraction now that the window was gone. The night outside was a warm, friendly thing trying to spew out the hideous face with the hole in it that seemed to stagger towards the gaping window. It staggered out and stopped and the mouth of Tucker bubbled red a moment then dropped out of sight.

Havis Gardiner hadn't moved. Not an inch. But the smile was gone and the rigidity was back in his spine and his hand was a talon around the glass again.

I grinned at his back as if nothing much had happened at all.

As if death was part of my life and always had been. As if I didn't give a damn or wonder why I was so good with a rod I could pot a guy by instinct who stood twenty feet away in the night.

Yeah, I went right on talking and this time Gardiner's soul was crawling in the mud. I dropped the gun in my pocket and spoke to his back.

'Servo must have cursed you plenty, Gardiner. Servo must have cursed the day he met you because you had him by the short hair and made him do things he knew shouldn't have happened. It would have been better if you hadn't done anything at all. I doubt if anything would have come of my little venture at all.

'No, you got so damn scared it occurred to you that Harlan might want to team up with you for a squeeze play to get even for having to take a back seat, so you found out where she was staying and sent Eddie Packman out to get her. What Eddie didn't know was that Harlan shared a room and he didn't bother to look and see who was in the bed. He just killed the girl and that was all.

'Harlan knew what happened. She knew that murder was headed her way and couldn't stop it. She knew it had to come some day and she must have lived with that fear from one hour to the next. She knew that even the photograph she had wouldn't stop it because you were quite mad by then, so she got that photo to somebody who would take care of it for her and got under cover.

'Too much whisky and too big a fear killed Harlan. She stood it as long as she could and killed herself. She didn't realize that she put Troy in a spot all the time. He figured on getting rid of Troy if and when he found it. Maybe even if he didn't find it, because if he couldn't nobody else could either. So Troy took off. One of the cops on your pay roll found her.

'Everybody made a mistake all at once. They didn't look hard enough for a gun and thought I was a sucker to boot. I was picked for a sucker all along the line when the biggest suckers of all are right here. You especially. It's done. You're left. You're the chief sucker.'

In a minute now he was going to prove it to himself. I was wondering how long it would take before he made his mind up.

He had the gun right there beside the bottle now. All the time I had been talking he was fooling around the ice well in the bar set until he had it almost under his hand.

I dropped the butt in my fingers and fished around for another one in my pocket. I took it out and wedged it between my lips and lit a match very elaborately, staring into the flame I had cupped between my hands.

Gardiner's mouth peeled back, pulling his eyes wide open so the insanity that had been there right along and so neatly covered was a naked thing, a living thing that contorted his face into a mask of madness.

He grabbed, turned and fired faster than I thought he could move and faster than I could get my hand back to my pocket. The bullet slammed into the door beside my head. The shock of the explosion staggered him and he wondered why I didn't fall.

The gun came up for a second try and I shot him in the belly a little above the belt and saw the dimple in his coat where the bullet went in. 'For Bob Minnow and Mrs Minnow,' I said.

I shot him again, a little lower. 'For Logan and Looth Tooth.'

His mouth gaped. He couldn't get his breath. The gun dropped out of his hand and his fingers ran up his body and covered the two little holes. Slowly, like a stalk bending in the breeze, he went to his knees.

I shot him in the head. 'For Johnny McBride,' I said.

There was a scream from inside. I went out the door and the housekeeper was standing there, a grotesque figure in a loose cotton robe. She was right next to the telephone stand. 'Don't bother with a doctor,' I told her. 'Call the police. Ask for Captain Lindsey and tell him he can forget about watching his buddy Tucker. He's dead too. Tell them it was self-defence.'

It was, wasn't it?

Dawn was sprinkling the sky with grey. The streets were still wet, glistening under the mist that rose from the hot surface. There were no buses in the ports, no mail trucks on the platform and nobody in the station.

The ticket window was closed.

I had to slam the door twice to break the lock.

I went over to the drawer where Nick kept my picture and opened it. I was still there. Under the pictures there were more pictures of me and more legends and they all went back a few years. I closed the door and walked back to the Ford. Now I was even sure of the very last detail.

Pontiel Road. A white house on a hill half hidden by the fog. Seven steps to the porch and a key in the flowerpot. Dark downstairs, but a shaft of light coming down the stairs. Fourteen steps to the landing and three doors. A spare bedroom on the right. A bath in the middle. A bedroom that smelled of powder and perfume on the left.

A bottle-blonde sitting in a boudoir chair nervously reading a paper. A face that wasn't hard as it was when I first saw her. A voice that exclaimed breathlessly, 'Johnny!'

'Hello, Wendy.'

She threw the paper down and ran to me. Her arms went around my neck and she buried her face against my shoulder. Her hair smelled nice. She seemed to see my face for the first time and almost got sick looking at me. Her fingers came up and touched my mouth, my eyes, then my ears. Was it terror or horror in her eyes?

She said, 'Johnny . . . what was it?'

I wasn't easy on her. I put my hands on her chest and shoved her halfway across the room. Her back slammed into the dresser and she stood there with her hands pressed to her ears not able to believe what was happening.

'They're dead, Wendy. Servo, Packman, Gardiner, Harlan, Troy. Hell, everybody's dead. It's all over.'

I think then she realized what I had come for. Her whole body trembled violently, but not having the power to move.

'I should have said, "Hello, Vera" when I came in. That's the name, isn't it? Vera West.'

Her lips got dry and she licked them. It didn't help any.

'Smart guy, Nick. He knew the score right along. He knew damn well I wasn't Johnny McBride and steered me straight to you so you could get back at Servo through me. Revenge, wasn't it? Like me.'

I took off my coat and threw it over the chair. The gun in the pocket clunked on the floor. I stripped off my belt and dangled it from my hand. 'Take off your clothes, Vera.'

It was horror I had seen in her eyes. It got bigger and brighter as she watched me swing that belt in a slow arc. 'Take off your clothes,' I repeated. 'I know I'm right but I want to make sure. See, you're getting every break.'

I saw it happen and didn't know why. The horror faded into defiance and a sob choked her up. Her fingers went to the top button of her blouse and flipped it open. Then the next, and the next until it was wide open. It slipped off one arm, then the other and fell to the carpet too softly to hear.

'There were a couple of things that never did make sense to me, Vera. They looked good, but really didn't make sense and I never gave them much thought. One was that quick way I got around to meeting you. Not many people would want a suspected killer to have the run of their house. You didn't put up much objection at all.'

The zipper at the side of her skirt hissed metallically. She let go of the hem. It fell at her feet in a circle and stayed there. Automatically her fingers worked the slip up, then her arms crossed and she lifted it over her head. The defiance came out again when she flicked it across the room and stood there in the sheerest black underwear that could be made. Tall, tanned. Calendar legs. Smooth. The curve of her thighs sweeping into her stomach and on up around the proud beauty of her breasts. The flesh rippled with her breathing across the flat of her waist and her hands came up again to the bra, very slowly.

'You live here on the edge of a wide-open town where a girl like you could rake in a pile yet never once did you go near that town. You work out on the highway under a lot of make-up and a phoney name and whenever I wanted you to see the bright lights you turned me down. That's something I should have thought about. You were afraid to go near town. Afraid somebody might recognize you. You stuck to a nice safe spot waiting for something to happen that would put you in a spot to make Lenny pay off to you and when I came along you grabbed the big chance.'

The bra had another zipper. It was right down the middle and she opened it with two fingers. Her breasts were alive and vibrant, a lighter tan than the rest of her, standing firm and proud in the excitement that coursed through her body. Her shoulders were wide and square, a sleek taper down to her waist.

My mouth felt drawn and it wasn't as easy to speak any longer. 'You dug up a lot of information on friend Tucker in a hurry. I bet you and Nick put in many a week collecting all the stuff you had in that package. Instead of looking around like I wanted you to you sat in the beauty parlour and had your hair done to waste time.'

She was almost ready to do it. My whole body started to crawl. The belt was limp in my hand.

'You had a lot of handy information about everybody. You knew about Harlan and made sure I knew it with that ad in the paper and that phone call. You knew right where to steer me for more information. You had a long time to figure out the angles and knew just what was what. All you needed was a strong arm to make the play for you. All I want to know is why, Vera. You won't die like the rest, but you'll hurt like hell for a long time and always show the marks. I'd just like to know why. Johnny was such a nice guy.'

She didn't answer me. Her forefingers ran under the elastic of the panties, then they unfolded down around her hips. She stepped out of them, held them up, then tossed them casually after the other things. She stood there like a statue,

241

naked except for her shoes, her hands leaning on the dresser behind her.

I looked at her hungrily, knowing it would be the last time I'd see her so nakedly beautiful. My head nodded and the belt swung in my hand again. 'It was a good gimmick, Vera. A lovely disguise. A natural blonde making herself an unnatural blonde right down to phoney dark roots. The hairdresser must have had a hell of a time, but it was a nice trick in case somebody looked too close and thought you were familiar. It would fool anybody.

'No wonder you didn't want me to see you in the light without any clothes on.' My mouth felt dry. There was a nasty taste behind my teeth. 'It's been a long wait, Vera. You've changed a lot since that picture Logan gave me of you was taken, but you're still beautiful. Johnny must have suffered every time he thought of you. It's been one hell of a long wait, but you're finally going to suffer a little bit like Johnny did.'

I raised the strap.

The dresser drawer opened and shut fast and she was pointing a gun at me. It was a little gun, but big enough. I had talked myself right into another trap again.

Her face was a curious mixture of emotion. She pointed the gun at the dressing-table beside me. 'Look in the top drawer.'

I was so damned mad I could hardly move. I was nearly ready to let her shoot then knock her teeth out with the barrel and if the same curious emotion that was in her face hadn't been in her voice too I would have.

I opened the top drawer. I was looking at myself again. A lot of George Wilsons. 'Nick had them too.'

'Look at the date.'

At the bottom of each one was a stamped date of delivery with notice to post. The ones on the bottom of the pile went back seven years.

She watched me until I shut the drawer. 'I've known about George Wilson ever since Johnny McBride left town. Nick has always had them. It scared me until we learned that George

Wilson was wanted long before anything ever happened to Johnny. Now look in the next drawer.'

My mind was numb. I felt cold all over. A lot of crazy things were going on in my head and I couldn't understand it. I opened that drawer and emptied an envelope out on the dresser. There was a deed there to the house on Pontiel Road made out to John McBride. There was an army discharge certificate and a letter from the War Department.

'Read it,' she said.

The letter was a full account of the war activities of John McBride. It told in detail that he had been trained for special work and operated behind the enemy lines on secret missions that included one of the successful coups of the war when he entered a German Command Headquarters building and relieved a safe of a document that listed German agents working in Allied zones.

My mind was a mad frenzy of thoughts shuttling back and forth too fast to make sense. They shrieked and hammered to be recognized and beat against my skull in despair when I couldn't sort them out.

Her voice was a soothing liquid washing away at the pain of it all. 'If George Wilson was wanted, and if a certain doubly remarkable coincidence happened . . . first meeting a man who was so like him they couldn't be told apart, and secondly having that man lose his memory in an accident . . . he certainly would take advantage of that situation, don't you think? He could change identities and no one would be the wiser. Why, he even might have planned to kill this person and let the body be identified as himself until he actually discovered that there had been a memory loss.

'After that it would even be profitable to keep him alive. If the police ever did stumble on him they would have the wrong person entirely. It was such a profitable scheme that he died to keep this person alive. When you think of it, that one wasn't a friend, but the worst enemy a man could have.'

It was too much for me. My teeth grated as I kept them together.

'That is,' she added, 'if my supposition is true. Did you ever wonder why I let you make love to me? I thought I could tell. I'm still not too sure. But like you did me, I'll give you every chance. Take off your clothes.'

I looked at her foolishly.

She meant it. The gun was still there on my stomach.

I took off my clothes.

'Johnny McBride had a scar exactly like that on his stomach,' she said.

I looked at it. Often I wondered how I had gotten it. She knew what I was thinking.

'It's described in that army medical report in the envelope,' she said.

And she was right.

The pieces came flying back together. They were all there and not making much sense, but there were enough of them so that I knew I would have it all some day. Little bits of jagged information. Things like the way I felt outside the Minnow house. Why a gun was so natural in my hand. It was too big to take all at once and I tried to put it out of my mind.

I dropped my head in my hands and pressed them against my face. Vera's voice seemed to come from a long way off. 'Now I'll tell you why I did it, Johnny. I was never part of them. Gardiner told you to check those books and I saw you with them. I actually thought you did steal that money. You had bought this house and gave me ten thousand dollars to put away for us and wouldn't say where you got it. It was a long time before I found out it represented everything you had ever saved.

'You see, Bob Minnow suspected something at the bank. He asked me privately to keep my eyes open and told me enough so that I had an idea what he was looking for. When I thought you were responsible for the theft and thought you did it to finance Servo, I went directly to Lenny to learn the truth for myself. Bob Minnow was shot in the meantime. I thought you did that too, but I still loved you. Lenny had you picked up at that vacation resort and had you hidden at your place. He gave me a choice . . . play along with him and let you get away, or turn you over to Lindsey. I didn't know then that they planned to let you get away anyway.

'I did it, Johnny. I'm not sorry for what I did. I stayed with Lenny until I realized that he was under somebody else's orders and did a little inquiring on my own. I checked on the bank and on Harlan and on Servo. During that time they found out what I was doing. I ran too.'

I saw the gun drop. It fell at her feet and landed on the skirt.

'I've been waiting, Johnny. Like you said, it's been a long wait, but I knew you'd come back some day.'

There never had been any hardness about her. There was just beauty. And love. A crazy kind of love. A wonderful kind of love. It happened to me before and it was happening to me all over again. We were there in the bedroom stark naked with two guns on the floor shaking from an excitement that was bigger than the whole night put together.

She was smiling at me.

She said, 'Johnny, empty out that envelope.'

My hand reached for it and it spilled all over the floor. It was filled with documents, but one was bigger than the rest. I could see what it said without picking it up. It was a marriage licence issued to John McBride and Vera West and the date was a month before anything had happened.

'That's how I knew about the scar,' she told me.

Her eyes were dancing.

I was hurting all over my body and inside my head. I was tired, dead tired.

But not that hurt and not that tired. We looked at the bed together. Her hand went out to the light.

I touched her. She was soft and warm. Beautiful. Mine.

'Leave the lights on,' I said.